VIGILANCE
A HEROICS NOVEL

Alex Kost

ISBN 978-1-68222-995-8
EBOOK 978-1-68222-996-5

DEDICATION

This book is dedicated to the people who helped me finish it: Allison Z., Kerri W., and Siobhan S. Never before has peer pressure been so useful.

TABLE OF CONTENTS

DRAMATIS PERSONAE

Heroics

AJ Hamil: 43; black hair; brown eyes; team medic (Anthony Sadik)

Alix Tolvaj: 26; brown hair with blonde highlights; gray eyes; "Thief"; shadow manipulation

Casey Cabot: 46; auburn hair; blue eyes; tech coordinator/boss (Robin van der Aart)

Cassidy "Cass" Hamil: 42; red hair; gray eyes; mission control (Tess Wechsler)

Jay West: 26; black hair; brown eyes; "Clash"; enhanced speed/endurance

Justin Oliver: 27; dark blond hair; brown eyes; "Archer"; enhanced accuracy

Kara Hall: 24; blonde hair; hazel eyes; "Pilot"; flight/enhanced strength

Katherine "Kate" Sullivan: 28; light brown hair; green eyes; team leader; "Targeter"; enhanced accuracy

Niall Sullivan: 29; black hair; blue eyes; tech coordinator

Ray Sampson: 26; black hair; blue eyes; "Blackout"; electricity manipulation

Security Legion

Andrew Sullivan: 33; brown hair; blue eyes; "Flare"; fire manipulation

Zachary "Zach" Carter: 45; blond hair; hazel eyes; "Kov"; metal manipulation

Other

Aubrey Hamil: 8; brown hair; green eyes
Brooke Hamil: 9; black hair; hazel eyes
Edward Caito: 44; sandy brown hair; green eyes
Finn: 18; white-blonde hair; brown eyes; enhanced reflexes
Jacob Hamil: 2; red hair; brown eyes
Logan Carter: 3; strawberry blonde hair; hazel eyes
Sarah Ajam: 34; dark brown hair; brown eyes
Warren "Tag" McTaggert: 40; blond hair; hazel eyes; volatile constructs

1

Henry and Lauren Freund knew about the number of murders that had been committed in the northern section of Caotico City in the several months before they found themselves walking along the same streets. They knew, but like so many others, they doubted that they would ever end up victims of the crimes they heard about on the news. That was why they didn't find anything suspicious about the middle-aged man with sandy brown hair who fell into step beside them on the empty street.

"Warm night, isn't it?" he said brightly.

"Yes, it is," Henry agreed. "Where we come from, the average temperature this time of year is about sixty Fahrenheit. This is downright boiling for us."

"Ah, tourists." The brown-haired man grinned. "Welcome to Caotico City. I'm sure you'll find us an interesting place."

"We're doing research for a book on cities with high levels of superhero activity," Lauren said. "You have that here, right?"

The man laughed. "Oh, absolutely. There are two different teams of superheroes acting in Caotico and Fuego Village, which is that warehouse district on the outskirts of town. There's the Security Legion, which has been around with various members for years, and

Heroics, which started out as a team of very young heroes. Of course, they're all grown up now."

"Any ideas on why they haven't stopped whoever's been committing all these murders we've been hearing about?" Lauren asked.

"Is that why you're wandering about the northern district at eleven o'clock at night, since everything near here closes at ten?"

Henry nodded. "We figured that we'd be more likely to run into a few heroes when the only people around are most likely going to be either them or criminals."

The brown-haired man grinned again. "This is the point where you're supposed to wonder why *I'm* walking around at this time of night."

Lauren and Henry exchanged an uneasy glance. "Okay, I'll bite," Henry said cautiously. "Why *are* you walking around this late?"

As if on cue, a thirty-something Middle Eastern woman and a middle-aged blond man stepped out from the alleyway in front of the three. "What the hell?" Henry asked.

The woman raised a gun and pointed it at the couple. "*Excellent* timing," she said to the brown-haired man.

"As always," the brown-haired man said with a smile. He looked at the blond man. "Do your thing."

Before Lauren and Henry Freund could even process what was happening to them, tiny balls of golden light appeared in the blond-haired man's hands. He threw them at the same time, and the lights hit each of the Freunds in the chest, right above the heart. As the couple fell to the ground, the nameless trio stood around them.

"What am I doing?" the brown-haired man said as he grinned down at the bodies. "Hunting, of course."

He looked at his two companions. "People never learn, do they? Vigilance can save your life."

2

"Tell me that this is the last escapee from Caotico Prison," Justin "Archer" Oliver sighed as he and his older sister chased after a man with long brown hair who had just attempted to blow up a ten-story parking garage.

Kate "Targeter" Sullivan laughed. "What would you do if I said that it wasn't?"

"I'd just walk away right now," Justin replied. "So if you want help with this guy, please don't test me."

"You're good at walking away," Kate joked. "How many times have you done it now?"

"Oh, shut up. How did it take us twelve years to find this guy, anyway?"

Kate dodged around a woman on a bicycle before saying, "I have no idea. We'll look into it once he's in custody."

"Which is easier said than done." Justin sped up his pace as the distance between them and the criminal widened. "How is this guy so fast? What's his power?"

"Uh, plasma generation."

"Oh, fun," Justin said sarcastically. "So once he decides to stop running, we'll get energy shot at our faces."

His sister laughed. "Just another day in Caotico."

The communications system in their sunglasses buzzed with an incoming call, and Cass Hamil's voice came through the speakers that rested in their ears. "Have you guys caught up to Plasman yet?"

"*Plasman*?" Justin repeated incredulously. "Are you kidding me, Control?"

Cass's laugh was clear in her voice as she replied, "Hey, I don't make up these names, Archer. That was this idiot's own choice."

"Idiot is right," Justin muttered.

Kate elected to ignore the side conversation and said, "Control, we're still chasing this guy. He's very fast."

"You guys must be slacking on your training routines."

"When's the last time you chased a guy for twenty blocks?" Kate snapped.

"Never. That's why I'm the voice with the internet connection."

Justin scoffed. "There's no need to sound so proud of it."

"Archer, you're fifteen years younger than me. What's your excuse again?"

"Oh, shut up."

"Gladly," Cass said. "I was just checking in on you before my shift ended."

"Who has the next shift?" Kate asked.

"I'm personally embarrassed that you don't already know the answer to that. Control out."

As Cass's voice buzzed out, Kate dodged

around a crowd of children, who all stopped to stare at the two members of Heroics as they ran past. "What's that supposed to mean?"

Her brother laughed at her and jumped over the hood of a car that almost hit him. "I'm not even that bad, sis." He nodded forward at the fleeing criminal. "I think he's slowing down. I'm not sure whether or not that's a good thing, but hey, at least the running might stop."

The chase hit its thirtieth block before the criminal turned on his heel to face them. As soon as he turned, he threw two blasts of energy in Kate and Justin's direction. He seemed to have no control over the blasts, however, as they both flew well over their targets and sizzled out before hitting anything. Before Plasman had time to try again, Kate and Justin both pulled back electrified arrows and shot them into his chest. As the criminal fell to the ground, twitching into unconsciousness, both siblings put their bows back over their shoulders.

"That seemed just a touch too easy for a last capture."

Kate groaned. "Oh, why did you say it? You *know* what happens when people say stuff like that."

As Justin shrugged at her, a new voice buzzed in over the communications system. "So, Targeter, I hear that you don't know my schedule."

Kate felt herself flush as Niall Sullivan's voice snarked in her ear. "Oh." She heard Justin snicker as she said, "Hi, honey."

"Don't 'honey' me," Niall teased. "Did you get... *Plasman* yet?"

"Yep; we just knocked him out. We're going to tie him up and leave him for the cops now."

"Good. Once you're finished, come on back to the mansion. There was another murder last night that we all need to talk about."

3

Kate and Justin walked into the conference room inside the mansion that had once been their home. The circle of team members hadn't changed much over the years. Cass was sitting next to AJ, her husband, and whispering something to him with a smirk on her face. To Cass's right was Casey Cabot, who had gained glasses only a few months earlier and was squinting as she tried to read something on her tablet without them. Jay West and Ray Sampson were next, arguing quietly. The rest of the circle— Niall Sullivan and Kara Hall —were sitting in silence, patiently waiting for the meeting to start. As Kate and Justin took their seats, Kate asked, "Where's Alix?"

"She should be here," Cass said.

"Unless she's hiding in her room again," Justin muttered.

Cass shot him a glare. The last member of their team, Alix Tolvaj, had been acting strangely recently— frequently locking herself in her room in the mansion and not coming out, at least to anyone's knowledge, for days.

Before any other suggestions as to Alix's location were put forward, the woman herself ducked into the room. "Does anyone know who this belongs to?" she asked jokingly, gesturing at the redheaded two-year-old who was sitting on her shoulders.

Cass grinned and patted AJ on the shoulder. "That would be this one."

AJ looked at her. "My turn?"

"Your turn."

"Fair enough." AJ stood and removed his son from Alix's shoulders. "I'll be back in a minute."

As he disappeared out the door, Alix took a seat across from Kate. Physically twenty-six and alive for eighteen years, Alix Tolvaj was the poster-child for why cloning was generally considered to be a bad idea. "I saw the news reports," she said. "There was another murder?"

"Jumping right into work as always, Al." Cass smiled, but Alix barely reacted. Cass's smile twitched slightly, and she hesitated before moving on with, "Yes. Actually, there was a double murder last night." She leaned back in her chair, hitting a button on the keyboard in front of her that brought up police files on the monitor in the wall at the head of the table. "Henry and Lauren Freund, from Anchorage, Alaska. Apparently, they were writing a book about superheroes and came here since, well, Caotico is a bit of a hotspot."

"It says that they were walking alone in the northern district late at night," Kate said as she read the screen. "Did no one tell them that that's not a safe place to be right now?"

Kara shrugged. "Depending on what they

were looking for, they might have done it on purpose. If they were here for info on superheroes, they probably assumed that some would be on the streets where there have been a bunch of murders."

"*Was* anyone on duty in that part of town last night?" Niall asked curiously.

Kate shook her head. "No one from our team. For the Legion, well, you'd have to ask our resident expert."

Everyone at the table turned to look at Casey, who was in the process of drinking from her coffee cup. She lowered it slowly. "... What? Why do I always have to be the one to know?"

"Gee, I don't know," Cass said sarcastically, smirking. "Maybe because—"

The door to the conference room opened and interrupted Cass's words. AJ walked back into the room, holding two children by the backs of their shirts. The black-haired girl and the brown-haired boy smiled sheepishly at the group. "These two were listening at the door," AJ said sternly. "If it was only Brooke, I would've taken her back upstairs myself, but seeing as she now has a partner in crime, I thought it best to bring everyone's attention to the problem."

Nine-year-old Brooke Hamil and seven-year-old Ciaran Sullivan looked embarrassed but excited. "Are you guys going to go after that killer?" Brooke asked eagerly.

"Remind me to hire a babysitter for the daily fifteen minute meetings," Cass muttered.

Niall frowned. "Kids, you know that you aren't supposed to be eavesdropping."

"Yeah, Daddy, but we want to know what's going on," Ciaran replied, pouting.

Cass, AJ, Niall, and Kate exchanged glances. "We'll make you a deal," Kate said. "The next time a meeting does not involve people getting hurt or people getting killed, you can sit in, but *only* if we don't catch you listening at doors anymore. Fair?"

"Yes!" Brooke and Ciaran said simultaneously.

"Then go back upstairs with the other kids. We'll be done shortly."

As both children bolted away towards the stairs, AJ shut the door behind him. "A Heroics meeting *without* violence or murder being a discussion topic? When is that going to happen?"

Kate shrugged. "Never, but by the time they realize it, they'll probably be in high school."

AJ took his seat. "Where were you?"

"We were asking Casey whether anyone from the Security Legion was in the northern district last night," Kara replied.

"And was anyone?"

Casey looked irritated. "I'll call Zach after this meeting is over."

"Good. Until we hear back from him,

we'll move on." Cass turned to Kate. "I'm assuming your criminal from this morning is in custody?"

Kate nodded. "The police were already showing up when Justin and I headed back here."

"Well, that's good, but something's funny here," Casey said. "Plasman— Colin Kilian —is a pretty useless bad guy who was once captured by police because his grand plan for escape was hiding underneath a police car. I find it hard to believe that, *by himself*, he'd be able to evade capture for twelve years."

"I did think that catching him seemed a bit too easy." Justin rubbed at his five o'clock shadow absentmindedly. "Have any of us checked with the prison?"

"I called them," Jay said. "I have an in with one of the guards; he was a friend of mine in college."

Justin scoffed. "Parvalo? Isn't that guy like the bottom of the food chain over there? Who's your next source, the canine cop that works the front gate?"

"Parvalo knows how to look up records. I told him I was doing a favor for a friend who's looking into the prisoners who have gone missing." Jay paused for a moment, taking a sip from his soda. "He told me that the records over there are apparently more of a joke than the fact that Justin ended up married."

"That's uncalled for," Justin mumbled.

Kate ignored him, saying, "What is that supposed to mean, Jay?"

Jay scoffed. "Colin Kilian disappeared from the prison at some point between yesterday and fifteen years ago."

A heavy silence fell over the table. Casey was the first to break it. "Hold on, *what*?"

"Yeah. If I'm understanding what Parvalo told me in confused whispers, at some point in 2061, a lawyer named Raylans managed to get a bunch of records of empowered people from Caotico Prison. The moment he did, all those records stopped being updated. Of those sixty-five people, twenty of them have release dates that passed without the record showing that they were released, thirty should be in prison but nobody seems to know where they are, five are dead, and ten are locked up in a secure section of the prison that no one has access to, other than the warden and his two highest-ranking guards. Colin Kilian is among the first twenty. Other than him, all the prisoners supposedly released by Alice Cage are dead or in the missing thirty."

AJ gave a sarcastic laugh. "Sixty prisoners disappear from the prison system and nobody thinks that that might be important information? Gotta love our justice system." He frowned at Cass. "What's the matter? You look pale."

"I'm a white person who is German, Irish, and English. Pale is my natural state,"

Cass retorted sarcastically.

"Honey," AJ said in a half-warning, half-tired voice.

"Raylans was a friend of my father's."

Casey snorted. "Why am I not surprised? There was never any reason to believe that Alice's fingerprints were the only ones on this."

Alix nodded. "From what I can remember, I think he had a few meetings with both Wechsler and Cage. I'm not sure if they ever met together."

Kate leaned back in her chair, spinning a pen through her fingers. "Cass, do you know what Raylans is doing now?"

"Uh, making a run for Attorney General, I think."

"Think he'd discuss possibly getting some campaign assistance from the company of an old friend?"

Cass smirked. "You mean see if he thinks I share whatever good will my father had towards him, and see where he stands on this whole thing."

"Wechsler Industries does have a lot of money," Casey said.

"More than I think even you know about, my friend," Cass replied. "I'm not sure Raylans would even consider my offer, given the fact that we're still trying to convince people that the people who facilitated that attack on Caotico all those years ago are all no longer working for the company."

"How good is this guy's standing with the people?" Ray asked.

Casey did a few searches on her tablet. "He seems very popular. Rather high in approval ratings."

Cass shrugged. "Then why don't I suggest that my offer is meant to be a way to help me get back in the public's good graces? It doesn't matter whether or not he goes for it; I'm sure as hell not giving him anything out of my well-earned bank account."

"The bank account you inherited because your father forgot to write a will cutting you out of your legally-automatic inheritance."

Justin's remark got a smirk from Cass. "I don't see you complaining about your paycheck, Oliver." There was no bitterness in her voice as she added, "Besides, I think putting up with the abuse counts as well-earned, don't you think?" Cass stood up, straightening her shirt as she did so. "I'll go call Raylans now, see if he'll bite."

As she left the room, Kate said, "So that takes care of Raylans. What should we do about the prisoners themselves?"

"What do you mean?"

Kate looked at Justin. "I want to know if this group of sixty-five people includes the people we've captured within the past several years, or if we have a terrifyingly large group of empowered criminals still unaccounted for."

"I'll get in touch with Parvalo again," Jay said. "Maybe I can convince him to slip me the list if I ask real nicely."

Justin snorted. "I doubt it. And if you even try, he'll probably try to talk you into making a deal with him. Probably try to get Kara's number from you again."

At that, Kara laughed. "I'm married and don't hit for the right team."

"You hit for *both* teams," Justin pointed out.

"I'm still married. So if he asks for my number, he's in for a rude awakening."

"Justin and I have told him that, and he seems to find it hot."

Kara rolled her eyes and groaned. "I am so glad I did not go to college with you two."

"I wish you had, if only to have seen how badly you would've beaten him up if he tried anything," Justin said with a grin.

As Justin ducked away from Kara's swing at his arm, Casey said, "Alright, children, that's enough. Does anyone have anything else to report?"

Kate let everyone else in the room shake their heads before saying, "I think we're good, Casey."

"Good. Now I need to make a phone call, and so do you, Jay." Casey stood up from the table and left the room.

"So many phone calls coming from this house at one time. We might end up on a watch list," Jay said dryly, as he too got to his feet.

AJ threw a pen at him, which Jay neatly dodged. "Don't jinx it. We have bad enough luck already," AJ said sternly.

Jay stepped out the door as Cass stepped back in. "I have a meeting with Raylans in my office tomorrow."

"Try not to get arrested for bribery."

Cass hit AJ lightly on the back of the head. "You say that like I'm some kind of criminal."

"If I respond to that, will you just hit me again?"

"Most likely."

"Then I invoke my right to remain silent."

"Smart man."

Kate got up from the table, taking her cup of tea with her. "I guess since no one has officially declared this meeting over, I will. Now if you'll excuse me, I'm going to go have a chat with my son about eavesdropping."

"Mind pulling my daughters in on that chat too?" AJ asked.

The field leader scoffed. "Yeah, because I'm going to get into a debate with those two."

"I figured it wouldn't hurt to ask."

Kate walked past AJ, patting him on the shoulder as she went. "I guess I'll give it a shot, Hamil. I'm feeling generous today."

"Christmas miracle."

"It's June, jackass."

"Christmas in July?"

Kate stopped at the door and looked back at him. "You're lucky Cass loves you; otherwise, I'd hit you."

AJ gave her a look of disbelief. "Were you paying attention thirty seconds ago? If you wanted to hit me, she'd let you."

Cass shrugged. "I'd let you."

Kate hesitated for a moment, considering this, before nodding. "Fair point. I'll hit you if I don't survive your children." She shot the Hamils a quick grin before turning and disappearing out the door.

Ray, Kara, Niall, and Justin left the room as well, leaving Cass and AJ alone with Alix, who was frowning at something on her tablet. Cass and AJ exchanged a glance. "Can you give us a minute, babe?" Cass asked him quietly.

AJ gave her half a smile and nodded. "I'll go check on Jacob."

"Good idea. Make sure the girls haven't roped him into planting listening devices in our conference rooms or something."

That got her the rest of the smile as AJ kissed her on the cheek and left. Cass walked back over to the table and silently sat down in the chair opposite Alix's. After a long moment, the younger woman looked up slowly. "What? Why are you staring at me?"

"You know damn well why I'm staring at you."

Alix set her tablet down and leaned back

in her chair. "If I did, I wouldn't have asked."

Cass felt herself get frustrated, but she pushed it aside as she said, "You've been disappearing for days. Late for meetings that you know are important. To be perfectly honest, you've been acting like a bit of an asshole, too. It's behavior that has been slowly getting more and more frequent over the past few years, but these last few months it's gotten very bad very fast. What is wrong with you?"

"I'm fine, Cass."

"You always say that, and I never believe it."

A combative look formed in Alix's metal-gray eyes. "If that's the case, why do you even bother asking anymore?"

"Gee, I don't know," Cass retorted, easily losing control of her frustration. "Maybe because I care and I want to help you."

Alix gave a sharp laugh that sounded a bit too much like the insane bark of Alice Cage. She stood up and pushed her chair in before saying, "You can't help if there's nothing wrong."

"And what if I don't believe that?" Cass challenged.

"Then you're going to have to get over it," Alix replied bitterly.

"I'm not sure I like that answer."

"And I don't care," Alix spat. She headed for the door but stopped just short of it, seemingly realizing that it was that exact attitude that had Cass worried.

"Al," Cass said softly, "what's happening to you?"

Alix looked back at her. "Nothing," she said, though her defenses seemed to have weakened slightly.

"Are you sure about that?"

"Yes. I'm absolutely positive," Alix said. "I'm okay, Cass. Honestly." She gave a small, apologetic smile before opening the door and leaving.

"Why does that not make me feel any better?" Cass whispered to the empty room.

"What kind of idiots wander around an area with an active serial killer without any sort of protection?"

The Middle Eastern woman cleaning her gun looked up at the blond-haired man who was spinning small spheres of golden light. "Tag, I thought I told you that I wanted at least, like, *five minutes* of silence."

"Silence is boring, Sarah," Warren "Tag" McTaggert whined. "I want to go out and kill people, and since I can't do that, I'm going to ponder the deaths of the people I have already killed."

Sarah Ajam rolled her eyes. "You know, remarkably, when you use words like 'ponder,' it actually makes you sound *more* like a moron."

This seemed to irritate Tag, who glared

at her and stopped the motion of the light in his palm. "You know, I could kill you quite easily," he threatened.

The woman snorted. "No, you couldn't. And besides, I wouldn't be here if I was so easily frightened by idiots with superpowers."

"She has a point, Tag," the sandy-haired man said as he stepped into the warehouse and closed the front door behind him. "I don't think you should be underestimating Sarah's abilities."

"I guess I just don't think highly of weaklings," Tag sneered.

"Permission to kill him, sir?" Sarah asked the sandy-haired man quietly.

"Denied. He's useful."

Sarah grumbled something under her breath and went back to cleaning her gun. Tag looked at the other man excitedly. "Did you come to tell us that we can go on a hunt, Caito?"

The sandy-haired man, Edward Caito, frowned. "Tag, we've talked about this. We can't kill during daylight because there are too many potential witnesses. Plus, it's scarier for the general civilian population if someone is stalking through the shadows than it is if three random people are ambushing people in broad daylight. It's psychology."

"Plus, Heroics is more likely to be out and about during the day. It's a habit of theirs," Sarah added.

Tag scoffed. "I'm not afraid of *Heroics*. If I'm not at all concerned about the Security Legion, why would I be worried about them? The first hero I see, regardless of team, is dead. One-hit kill. They wouldn't stand a chance against me."

Caito, who had been standing silently while Tag spoke, suddenly grabbed the younger man by the front of his shirt and pulled him in close. "I want you to listen very carefully," Caito growled. "Nobody goes *near* Heroics. Got that?"

"Okay, fine, geez. What's the big deal?"

"Two things," Caito said as he released Tag and took a step back. "First of all, they don't belong to us. Somebody else already has a claim on their lives, and we will respect that. Second of all, you seem to have a chronic problem with underestimating the competition. The crew that makes up Heroics has been heroing since they were small children. They might be young and they might not be as numerous as the Legion, but they are dangerous. I will not have anyone running off half-cocked in the direction of the people who took down John Wechsler and Alice Cage *and* the Alumni *and* half a city block of brainwashed heroes while only taking one loss. So we are not confronting them. If you even *attempt* to go after anyone on Heroics, I will borrow Sarah's gun, and I will shoot you between the eyes. Do you understand me?"

"Yes," Tag answered meekly, looking afraid.

"Then maybe you'll *keep* being useful. Because we all know what happens when you stop. Don't we?"

4

Zach "Kov" Carter, a tall blond vigilante who spent his free time being both the Security Legion liaison and the father of Casey's child, sat down in the office chair that was in front of Casey's desk inside the tech room of the Heroics mansion. "I'm not really used to be summoned under an official capacity by you," he said lightly, grinning.

"Why? Because you do nothing professionally?" Casey retorted.

"I'm hurt, Case. There are several things that I do to a professional level of quality."

Casey gave him an amused look. "If that was supposed to be an attempt to hit on me, it was a very bad one."

"Everyone has bad days."

"You more than most," Casey said, smirking slightly. "I didn't ask you to come here so that you could… whatever the hell it is that you're officially calling that."

"Flirting."

"Again, I'm not sure that's the proper term." She leaned back in her chair. "I wanted to know if you had any patrols going in the northern district last night."

"This is about that double murder?"

"Yeah."

Zach shrugged. "I think Raseri was on patrol around there, maybe Scarlett and Flare too. I'd have to check the records."

"That's okay. We really only wanted to know if there was someone over there. These murders are getting a bit too frequent. If we aren't careful, we'll start to take the blame."

"Ugh, the inevitable blame game." Zach grimaced. "Yeah, none of us want that." He stood and walked towards the door, stopping about a foot from it. "I'll take a look at the official records, and then ask around to see if anybody in the northern district saw something last night and forgot about it."

"Thanks. Logan should be upstairs with Jacob and Rick if you wanted to see her before your patrol starts."

Zach grinned. "I'd love to. Are we still on for tonight?"

Casey fidgeted slightly before shrugging. "Sure, I guess."

"Case, I'm not forcing you into anything, you know."

"I know. It's just be a long morning, and I didn't get much sleep last night."

"Should I be jealous?" Zach teased.

Casey groaned. "You are *terrible*, you know that?"

"Yeah, but the problem is that you like it."

In response, Casey threw a stapler at his head, which he easily caught using his metal manipulation powers. "I'll take that as me being shown the door," Zach said, still grinning.

"Oh, then I should've thrown it as soon as I got the answer I needed from you."

"Keep talking like that and I'll think you're breaking up with me."

"I've considered it many, many times."

"And yet you never do it." Zach laughed and mentally put the stapler back on her desk. "Try not to throw it at me on my way out. I might miscalculate and smash it next time."

"You'd owe me a new stapler."

"I'm not sure that's how it works."

Casey sighed and looked at him over her glasses. "Are you done? You have a patrol to get to. Go say hello to your kid."

"Y'know, with the glasses on, you kind of have a bit of a sexy librarian thing going o—"

"*Leave!*"

Laughing, Zach fled the room before she could throw any more office supplies at him. He ran into AJ in the elevator and said, "What did you put in Casey's coffee this morning?"

AJ eyed him suspiciously. "Do I want to know why you're asking me that?"

"Everyone's heads are in the gutter this morning, I tell you."

"You know, you only have like a month left on our bet," AJ said.

"Yeah, I was going to ask you about that."

AJ snorted. "Hey, you can't back out."

"Casey is incredibly stubborn and still in

denial about our relationship, AJ. She is never going to tell me that she loves me. Okay? It's never going to happen. I sleep in this mansion four nights a week, we go out to dinners, we have a *kid*, but she has insisted for so long that we have a casual relationship that I don't think she's *capable* of admitting otherwise."

"Yeah, I know that. That's why I'm getting $100 next month."

"I overestimated how irresistible I am."

"Dude, she already has you. You aren't trying to pick her up in a bar. That's why this was a fool's bet in the first place."

Zach sighed. "I should've listened to you."

"You probably should've. Unfortunately, nobody ever listens to me, which is actually only unfortunate for everybody else because I end up making a pretty decent amount of money on the deal."

"Are you sure you aren't a loan shark?"

"That would require me giving my money to other people," AJ pointed out.

"You could be. Nobody knows how much money Cass makes off of Wechsler Industries."

"If we told you, you would be mad about how much money I get off of you over stupid bets."

"You're the worst kind of person," Zach grumbled.

"I thought that was Cass?"

Zach raised an eyebrow. "Are you

allowed to say that about your own wife?"

"It's *Cass*."

"You make a good argument."

The elevator opened, and a three-year-old girl with strawberry blonde hair and hazel eyes was waiting for them. She grinned and tackled Zach around the waist. "Hi, Daddy!"

"How did you know I was here?"

Logan Carter looked up at her father, still grinning. "Kate told me. She's in Brooke's room, yelling at Ciaran and Brooke and Aubrey."

"What about?"

"... Spying?"

"Ah. That's not so bad. Let's go save them from mean old Kate then, huh?" Zach shot a mischievous grin at AJ as he picked up his daughter and headed for Brooke Hamil's bedroom.

As he heard a yelp of surprise from Kate, followed by a similar yelp of pain from Zach, AJ elected to avoid that room at all costs and went to check on his son.

Jacob Hamil was sitting on the floor of his bedroom, next to three-year-old Rick Sullivan, playing with building blocks. "Hey, boys. What are you doing?" AJ asked as he walked in.

"I'm makin' a car," Rick replied. "Jacob is... somethin'."

"I'm building the Millennium Falcon,"

Jacob replied, squinting at the terrifyingly detailed Lego model that was sitting in his tiny hands.

"Jacob, buddy, you scare me sometimes," AJ admitted.

The boy seemed to consider this for a moment before shrugging. "I'm okay with that."

AJ laughed, shaking his head. "You have way too much of your mother in you. You know that?"

"You say it a lot."

"Only because it's true."

"Bree says it a lot, too."

"That's because she spends too much time with Alix."

There was a soft knock on the door, and Kate walked in. "Rick, your father is taking you and Ciaran home."

"What about you?" Rick asked.

"Your dad's off for the rest of the day; I'm not." She helped her son to his feet and ruffled his hair. "I'll be home for dinner. I promise."

"You promised yesterday," Rick mumbled.

Kate's smile twitched slightly. "I know. But I mean it, okay? Your brother is in Brooke's room. Go on."

Rick looked annoyed, but he nodded and shuffled out of the room, grumbling under his breath. Kate swallowed, stressed. She made eye contact with AJ and said, "Can we talk for a minute?"

AJ nodded. "Jacob, why don't you go say goodbye to Ciaran and Rick?"

The boy seemed to know that something was wrong. "Okay," he said softly.

Once both boys were gone, AJ asked, "What's going on with you?"

"Nothing."

"Nothing? Casey and I sent you home in plenty of time for you to get home for dinner last night."

"I had some stuff to do," Kate said evasively.

"Kate… You need help."

"How many times do I need to tell you people that I'm fine?" she snapped.

AJ was quiet for a moment. "Okay," he said, though it was clear he didn't believe her. "What did you want to talk to me about?"

"I think it's possible that Colin Kilian only got out of prison a few weeks ago, if not a few days."

"What are you talking about?"

"He's a *really bad* fugitive. I mean like… *really bad*. And not in the threatening way, but in the 'he literally cannot sneak to save his life' way. I find it incredibly hard to believe that he would successfully be able to hide from us for as long as he did, even if he had help."

"Jay's friend did say that it was impossible to tell when he got out of prison."

"Yeah, which means that it could've been very recently."

"Okay, but who let him out, then? Isn't this the same group of people that Alice let out?"

"Yeah, and we got that list from Clarice."

AJ hesitated. "I'm not sure I like where this is going."

"Don't worry, AJ. I'm not going to do anything stupid. I just wanted to run the thought by you to make sure it sounded sane before I ran it by Cass."

"Why would you need to know that before you talked to Cass?"

Kate raised an eyebrow. "Because you're less sarcastic towards stupid ideas?"

"Fair point. I think you can talk to her. I don't think your idea is too crazy."

"*Too* crazy, huh?"

"I can't pretend that it isn't just a little crazy."

Kate shrugged and started to head out of the room. "Around here, almost everything is just a little crazy."

Cass was back in the control room when Kate went down to the basement headquarters of the Heroics team. Turning as Kate walked in, she said, "You aren't going to see Clarice."

"AJ told you *already*? What, are the two of you telepathic?"

"It's called an intercom, which you would

know if you paid any attention when Casey goes over tech upgrades."

"You can be such a pain in the ass sometimes, you know that?"

Cass smirked. "Yeah, but at least I'm not a *stupid* pain in the ass."

"I'm recalling a certain surrender deal that was particularly—"

"Anymore," Cass interrupted irritably. "I'm not a stupid pain in the ass *anymore*."

Kate grinned. "I'm still going to question that, but not right now. Why can't I go talk to Clarice? We need to know whether she was telling the truth about those freed prisoners."

Cass leaned back in her chair and gave Kate a measured look. "Kate, the last time you spoke to Clarice Wagner, you put an arrow in her and came very close to murdering her."

"In fairness to me, I was having a very bad week. Lots of trauma and fighting and the fact that my sister died because of her didn't exactly make it any easier."

"True, but that doesn't make me any more comfortable with the idea of you talking to her, especially since you're already going to be bringing up the past."

"I can handle it, Cass."

"Can you?" the older woman challenged mildly.

Kate's jaw twitched. "What are you suggesting?"

"About you? Nothing. About Clarice?"

Cass shrugged. "How about I go talk to her? I'm one of the people who knew her the least. She might have kidnapped me, but I didn't know her all that well before then, so I have less history behind my dislike of the woman. I'll ask her about the prisoners. If I'm lucky, maybe I'll get some answers. I'm pretty good at getting answers."

Kate snorted. "Usually you do that by letting people repeatedly punch you in the face while they taunt you with their plans."

"Hey, if it works."

"You really don't want me to go?"

Cass shook her head. "I really don't think it would be a good idea." Her voice lowered slightly. "You aren't right yet, Kate. I'm not going to ask you why, and I'm not going to get into an argument with you over whether it's true. But you aren't right. The last thing you need to do right now is talk to one of the people responsible for Lori's death."

"You're probably right about that," Kate admitted after a moment.

"Then let me go talk to her. I'll do it tomorrow after my meeting with Raylans. We'll have more information then, anyway."

"Okay. But if you have any reason to punch her, do it for me?"

Cass smiled slightly. "Absolutely."

A few minutes after Kate left, AJ joined Cass in the control room. "How did your conversation go?"

"Not bad. I'm going to go talk to Clarice. I don't think we'll get anything useful from her, but it'll appease Kate and keep her away from Clarice so I think it's a good idea."

"Somehow I knew you were going to end up going. Try to be careful."

"I'm always careful," Cass replied with a grin.

"Uh, no. No, you are not."

Cass laughed as AJ sat down in one of the other chairs, but the laugh died quickly when she saw the uneasy look on his face. "What's wrong?"

"Jacob's getting worse."

For a moment Cass just stared at AJ. "What is it now?"

"He's building a scarily detailed to-scale model of the Millennium Falcon. With no instructions. From memory."

"When's the last time he saw the movie?"

"At least two months ago."

Cass closed her eyes briefly. "That is worse."

"I haven't noticed the girls getting any worse recently. Have you?"

"No. Brooke somehow reprogrammed the television in her room to get access to every channel, whether we have it on the cable plan or not, but that's not remotely close to the scariest thing she's been able to do in her almost-ten very short years on this planet, so I won't consider it an upgrade in ability."

"Maybe they're starting to plateau? Like maybe once they hit a certain age, their intelligence starts growing at a more natural pace?"

"I have no idea. I don't even know how this happened." Cass rested her head on one of her hands and sighed. "Have you checked the kids out recently? Made sure they're still... okay?"

"Cass, they're fine. They're just..."

"Terrifyingly smart?"

"Yeah. Sometimes that happens."

"AJ. Honey. Our two-year-old can build exact replicas from memory after two months without seeing the object he's duplicating. Our eight-year-old can do calculus. Our nine-year-old can build complex computer programs from scratch. Neither of us taught them how to do these things. Something isn't right, AJ. They have *powers*. And they shouldn't, because I don't have a power, and you don't have a power— and not that this was ever a question, but they're *our kids*. And powers don't just show up in people."

"I'm aware of that," AJ said patiently. "Trust me, Cass. I'm aware of that. But until something shows up that makes me think otherwise, they're just normal kids, other than the fact that they're smarter than the two of us put together."

"It just makes me nervous. And,

honestly, scared."

"Me too." AJ stood up and rested his hands on her shoulders. "But it'll be okay. They'll be okay. I promise."

Cass laughed weakly. "Why are you always so calm with stuff like this?"

"One of us has to be, and it wasn't going to be you."

"Are you saying I'm not calm?" she asked, pretending to be offended.

"Given the whole 'fiery redhead' thing you sometimes have going on, I'm going to have to say that no, you are not a very calm person."

"Oh, shut up."

AJ kissed her. "Never have; never will."

"Don't I know it. What I wouldn't give for some peace and quiet."

"You're the one who wanted to get married."

Cass lightly punched him in the chest. "*You* asked *me*, asshole."

"Worst decision of my life, honestly." AJ grinned. "Do you need anything before I leave? Niall called and said he wanted to talk to me about ways to keep the kids from interrupting our meetings, since they apparently won't just listen to reason."

"I don't need anything. But good luck figuring that one out."

"I'm thinking that we duct tape them to their desk chairs while we're in meetings."

"Remember the conversation we just had about them being scary smart?"

"Good point; they'd probably figure some way out of it."

"Almost immediately."

"Hm. This might take some serious plotting."

"Like I said. Good luck."

"Thanks," AJ said dryly.

As he left, Alix walked in. Cass gave a quick laugh. "It's like a revolving door in here today." When Alix just gave her a blank look, Cass waved her hand. "Nothing. What's up?"

"Am I supposed to patrol with Kate tomorrow?"

"Yes."

"Why?"

Cass raised an eyebrow. "Uh… because that's what we do here? Go on patrols? Y'know, stop bad guys?"

"I know that, but it just suddenly showed up on the schedule."

"Oh, right. I need Kate out of the way tomorrow so that she doesn't do something stupid."

"And you can't send one of the others with her?" Alix sounded more nervous than annoyed, but Cass just rolled her eyes.

"You both need to get some air, Al. And besides, no matter what your problem is, you're still a member of this team, aren't you?"

"Yes, I am," Alix said, irritation now

seeping into her voice.

"Then unless there's something you need to tell me, I see no reason why you can't keep her out of trouble for a few hours."

Alix glared at her for a long moment before she paled and looked away. "Fine. Whatever." She started impatiently tapping a closed fist against her leg, suddenly looking ill.

"Are you okay?" Cass asked, concerned by the sudden shift.

"I'm fine," Alix replied tensely.

"Alix, seriously, you're starting to freak me out."

"I'm *fine*, Cass."

"Fine never actually means fine. Not in this team, at least."

"Cass, just leave it alone, okay?"

"I'm getting tired of the brush off every time I show concern for your well-being, Al," Cass said in a quiet voice.

"Then maybe you should stop being so concerned," Alix retorted before disappearing into shadows.

Alix stepped out of the shadows and into her room. She stumbled just slightly before sitting down heavily in her desk chair. Shadowy discs appeared and disappeared around her slowly as she stared down at her shaking hands.

"Stop it," she whispered.

A disc mockingly formed in front of her

face.

"*Stop it!*" Alix yelled in a snarl.

The disc that had mocked her flew to the other side of the room, knocking over a pile of boxes before disappearing along with its fellows.

Alix groaned softly, putting her head in her hands. She raised it again almost immediately with a noise of irritation, reaching over to grab a tissue to stop her now-bleeding nose.

"Son of a bitch," Alix mumbled, tossing the tissue into a trashcan that was almost full of identical ones. She stood, quickly straightened the fallen boxes, and walked over to the whiteboard that made up an entire wall of her room. It was covered in equations and chemical compositions that had no logical connection to each other. Alix stared at the board for a full minute before simply sitting down on the floor and putting her head back in her hands.

5

Elliott Raylans felt uncomfortable as he stepped into the main office building of Wechsler Industries. He hadn't been in the place for over a decade and a half— which, in retrospect, had probably saved his career after the mess John Wechsler and Alice Cage had caused. He wasn't too thrilled with the idea of being seen there even years later, but the call from John's daughter had intrigued him.

He remembered her, somewhat. Tess Wechsler had walked into meetings between Elliott and her father a few times when she was a child, and she had struck him as a bright, if very quiet and haunted, girl. Elliott had had some suspicions about her treatment at her father's hands, but John's support was, at the time, too important to lose over private family matters.

When he walked up to the front desk in Wechsler Industries, the young woman behind it looked at him. "Can I help you?" she asked brightly.

"I have a meeting with Tess Wechsler."

"Oh," the secretary said shortly. She seemed to lose her pleasantness instantly as she narrowed her eyes at him, and Elliott got the distinct impression that the woman, for some reason, did not like him. "What is your name, sir?"

"Elliott Raylans."

The woman glanced down at her computer. "Right. Mr. Raylans. Your meeting with… *Ms. Wechsler* is scheduled for fifteen minutes from now. You can take the second elevator on your right and head up to the fortieth floor. The secretary upstairs will direct you to the proper office at your scheduled time."

Elliott nodded and began to walk away, but paused when his desire to be liked by everyone got the better of him. "Before I go, may I ask you something, miss?"

"I suppose."

"You seemed perfectly nice until I told you what I was here for. Why?"

The secretary paused a moment. "You referred to our CEO as 'Tess Wechsler.' Around here, the only people who do that are people who used to be acquainted with *John* Wechsler. And for the people who work in this building, that is not a good thing. Similarly, using our boss's birth name is treated as an insult to her. And if there's one thing almost everyone in this building can agree upon, it's that no one gets to insult that woman after everything she has done for us." She idly straightened a pile of papers on her desk, as if punctuating her little speech. "You can head up now, sir. Have a nice day."

Deciding not to push the issue, Elliott simply nodded and headed for the elevator.

When Elliott was let into the office of the woman who was, but wasn't, Tess Wechsler, he was struck by how small and simple it was. It looked like any other office in any other office building, though perhaps with half a foot of extra space all around. Elliott took the time to look around, curious, before his gaze finally fell on the woman behind the desk.

The woman who was, but wasn't, Tess Wechsler didn't look too much like her father, though she did share his red hair. The look in her eyes— serious, stubborn, and hinting at the kind of contained anger at the world that could erupt in seconds or boil for years —was also identical to how he remembered John, and that similarity scared him more than if she had had a gun.

"Mr. Raylans," the woman said politely, standing and holding out her hand. "Thank you for meeting with me."

"It's no trouble," Elliott replied, shaking her hand. "I'm not sure what to call you, however. Your secretary downstairs advised me that you no longer go by your birth name."

"Not anymore. I distanced myself from my father a long time ago, and then I got married. A few name changes later, and I now go by Cass Hamil."

"Mrs. Hamil, then. May I sit?"

"Of course," Cass said, gesturing at the chair in front of her desk.

Elliott sat down and leaned back in it. "I'll be honest, Mrs. Hamil, I was surprised and a bit intrigued by your call. I haven't spoken to anyone in your family in a very long time."

Cass smiled faintly. "Neither have I."

"Right. Ah, what is it exactly that you're looking for?"

"Well, Mr. Raylans, I'll be blunt. Wechsler Industries needs some good PR. It's been a very long time since our company was involved in anything illegal, but it's still a bit difficult for the public to trust us."

"I don't mean to sound rude, but keeping the name probably isn't helping."

"This is true. When I originally took over WI, I was going to change the name. But it's a catch-22. If I were to change the name, I would lose brand recognition, and the subsequent quality recognition. Without changing the name, I have to deal with all of the negative opinions caused by my father's... hobbies. Ultimately, I thought that it would be quicker to repair the negative image than it would be to build a new customer base."

Elliott gave a slight smile. "How is that working out for you?"

"I think you know. Although, I'm not sure the other option would have been faster. Tobaggon Securities went through something similar fifty years ago, and they took option one. Became Squarel Incorporated."

"What's Squarel Incorporated?"

"Exactly."

Elliott studied Cass for a moment. He could tell that she was playing at something, but he found her engaging enough that, for the time being, he would play along. "So, you picked the faster route. It just isn't working very fast."

"Curse of inheriting a poisoned company." Cass slowly spun from side to side in her desk chair. "Let's cut through the bullshit, Mr. Raylans. Why don't you ask what you want to know?"

A smirk flicked onto Elliott's face. The woman in front of him might not have possessed a very good poker face, but she was very good at seeing through one. "What is it that you want me to do for you, Mrs. Hamil?"

"It's more what I can do for you." Cass paused, as if unsure of how to continue, and then said, "Part of my company's plan to win back the community is a series of public service projects and other programs for citizens of this city. Another is to make donations to areas with high popularity among the population. Such as to very popular men running for Attorney General."

Elliott raised an eyebrow. "I'm listening."

"Of course you are. You are, in fact, at the top of our list for where our money can go; however, we do have some slight reservations. I can't authorize a donation without an explanation for something that my employees found while going through old WI files."

For some reason, a feeling of dread washed over Elliott. "And what would that be?"

"Several years ago— I'm talking over a decade here —you requested files on some prisoners from Caotico Prison. Those files vanished, and the prisoners essentially did as well. Some ended up back on the streets in a time frame that doesn't seem to match when they should have been released."

Elliott swallowed, years of deals flashing through his head. "What exactly are you accusing me of, Mrs. Hamil?"

"I'm not accusing you of anything, Mr. Raylans. I'm simply curious as to what your response to that bizarre coincidence is."

For a moment, Elliott just stared at the woman seated in front of him. His jaw tensed, but he gave her a small smile. "There are a lot of bizarre coincidences that happen with Wechsler Industries, Mrs. Hamil. I'm sure you're aware of that."

"True. I'd just like to know which coincidences are actually that and which ones are, shall we say, not very coincidental."

Cass's voice was calm, but Elliott could hear the danger in it. "Mrs. Hamil, I know damn well when someone is threatening me, no matter how nicely it's being said."

"Mr. Raylans, I'm not threatening you. I want to know what the hell you and my father did before someone else finds out about it and tries to pin the blame on me."

"And let me guess. The knowledge will be traded for a campaign donation."

"That would be illegal, Mr. Raylans." Cass folded her hands in front of her on her desk. "However, honesty would certain make me more likely to support your endeavors."

"You talk like a politician, Mrs. Hamil."

"Truthfully, Mr. Raylans, I talk like someone who had to be very careful not to piss off a psychopath as a child. Now are you going to give me what I want, or no?"

Elliott leaned back in his chair, studying her for a moment and noting that the contained anger in her eyes had increased in fire. In that moment, he decided that he would rather be on the woman's good side than anywhere else. "I believe I can help you find what you're looking for."

Once Elliott Raylans had left her office, Cass checked her watch. She had just enough time to go down to the prison and talk to Clarice, though it wasn't a conversation she was looking forward to. Cass stood up but paused, leaning against her desk and staring down at the pattern of scars that circled her left wrist. The damage— done by a few dozen needles and a mind control device —was a fairly constant reminder not to do anything stupid. Letting Kate talk to Clarice Wagner qualified as something stupid, so whether she liked it or not, Cass was going to have that conversation. If she could do anything about it, she wasn't going to let Kate get any more broken than she already was.

Clarice Wagner's hair had once been pink, but now, at her age of thirty-eight, it was a mousy brown color. Her green eyes— duller than Cass remembered —watched the older woman as she stepped into the former hero's tailor-made cell.

"Tess Wechsler," Clarice said, her voice hoarse. "Not really the Heroic I was expecting."

"Heroic, huh? That's a new one. Run out of actual insults over the years?"

"You aren't worth the effort," Clarice muttered. She put her feet up on the metal bench she was sitting on and pushed her back up against the wall of the cell, hugging her knees to her chest and smirking slightly at Cass. "What do you want, Wechsler?"

"It's Hamil, actually."

Clarice's smirk widened. "Ah. What, did AJ get you pregnant or something?"

Cass laughed loudly. "That's more the attitude I was expecting from you."

Clarice seemed bothered by the lack of a real reaction from Cass. She put her feet back on the floor and leaned forward, her eyes narrowing and her old fire replacing the dull look. "Did you actually want something, *Hamil*, or are you just here to be a pain in the ass?"

"I see prison hasn't cured you of your attitude at all. I'm going to go out on a limb here and guess that you pretend that it has around the guards, though."

The former hero chuckled. "I've become a better actor than I was the last time I saw any of you Heroics jackasses."

"I'm sure." Cass leaned back against the cell door and folded her arms across her chest. "We arrested Colin Kilian yesterday."

"Am I supposed to know who that is?"

"Plasman. He's on your list of empowered people freed from this prison by you and Alice Cage."

Clarice bit her lip, thinking. After a moment, she said, "Right, the really useless guy." When Cass just raised an eyebrow at her, Clarice smirked again. "Useless enough that you're doubting his ability to be a fugitive."

"Yes."

"I don't see how I could've given you his name if I didn't have it," Clarice said innocently, putting her feet back up on her bench.

Cass mirrored her smirk. "You gave us those names slowly over eight years, Clarice. Do you expect me to believe that it's impossible that you didn't get more information during that time?"

For a long moment, the two women just

stared at each other. Clarice's expression was unreadable. She began to slowly drum her fingers on her knee, and her eyes narrowed again. "If I say anything to you, I want something in return."

"I'm shocked."

"Drop your sarcasm, Hamil. I'm offering you a lot here."

Cass checked her watch as if bored. "If I were to entertain this deal of yours, what is it that you'd want?"

Clarice smiled slowly. "You know, if the ethical guardians of our society had any idea of how empowered people are imprisoned, they'd be furious." She fidgeted with the metal device around her ankle that directed constant and varying amounts of pain into her to prevent her from teleporting.

"Given the fact that you tried to murder all of them and would undoubtedly try again if you ever got out of here, I think they'd get over it."

"That's where you're wrong, Hamil," Clarice said. "I didn't try to kill the mortals. I was trying to kill people like us."

"Yeah, and you never did explain why," Cass replied quietly.

"Send Targeter in here someday and maybe I will."

Cass tensed. "That's never going to happen."

"Then I guess you'll never know." Clarice

stood up and wandered towards the back of her cell. "If I tell you the truth about Colin Kilian, you have to have me moved to general population— and have this thing removed from my ankle. I know you have the pull to do it, given the company your father built."

Cass's hands tightened into fists. She could practically feel her circle of scars prickling into her wrist, but she said, "Fine. You have a deal."

Clarice seemed surprised. "You must be desperate."

"It's going to take some time before I can get that kind of transfer through. But I'll do it."

"You actually will, too," Clarice murmured, still looking stunned. "You have too much stupid honor not to."

Cass moved her left hand around uncomfortably. "I don't have all day, Clarice."

Clarice slowly sat back down and gave a small sigh. "Colin Kilian was one of the last names I gave you, correct?"

"Yes. I checked. He was in the last round of names."

"I figured he might have been," Clarice muttered. "A week before I gave you that last list, I got a visitor. I'm not sure how she got in. It was after visiting hours. She gave me most of the names that were on the last list. Said that it wouldn't matter if I gave them to you because you wouldn't find them for at least a few years anyway."

"What's that supposed to mean?"

"I honestly don't know, Cass," Clarice said, and for once she actually seemed to be telling the truth."

"Who was she?"

"A kid. Fifteen at most. Pale blonde hair and brown eyes. She mocked me for getting arrested and I threw a punch at her and she dodged faster than anyone I'd ever seen that didn't have superspeed like Jay. I have no idea who she was, but she knew every name that I had already given you, and a few of the ones that I had left."

Cass frowned slightly, adjusting her watch. "But if she was fifteen, she could've only been… what, six or seven when Alice Cage died and you were arrested?"

"I know that it seems improbable, but I'm telling you, Hamil. That kid knew exactly what she was doing."

"You really don't know who this girl was?"

Clarice shook her head. "I really don't. I would tell you if I did, Hamil. To tell you the truth?" The woman looked at Cass, her green eyes serious. "That kid scared the hell out of me. If I didn't know exactly what a young Alice Cage clone looked like, I would've thought she was one. I don't know who that girl was— or is —working with, Hamil, but I have a feeling that if you've captured the last guy on your list, you'll be finding out pretty soon. And when that happens, I'll be glad to be right where I am."

"You are an absolute *fool*," Sarah was snarling as she dragged Tag back into their base. She threw him in the direction of the table, and he diverted his fall clumsily towards the couch at the last moment.

Caito, studying a newspaper article about the Caotico City killings, looked up at them slowly. "What's going on?"

"This— This *imbecile* almost took a shot at Niall Sullivan while we were patrolling!"

"Who cares?" Tag whined.

"Not only is it *daylight*," Sarah hissed, "but he's a member of *Heroics*, you *moron*."

"I thought," Caito said slowly, "that I made it *explicitly clear* that they were not to be touched."

"How was I supposed to know the guy was in Heroics? He was just some skinny, nerdy-looking guy. I know you said that daylight kills wouldn't be useful, but I thought that maybe one would be—"

"You never think," Caito spat. "As for how you were supposed to know…" He took a deep breath to calm himself. "Do you remember that binder I gave you that detailed information on the Heroics team?"

"Yeah."

"*That's how, you complete jackass.*" Caito

looked at Sarah, actually shaking with rage. "Sarah, give him a rundown on the Heroics team members before I wring his neck."

Sarah looked disappointed, but she nodded. "Of course, sir." She put her hands in her pockets and began, "There are two sections of Heroics: a field team and a base team. The field team is led by Katherine Sullivan, codename Targeter. Twenty-eight, brown hair, green eyes, enhanced accuracy, married to Niall Sullivan, two sons. Her biological brother is Justin Oliver, codename Archer. Twenty-seven, blond hair, brown eyes, enhanced accuracy, married to Erin Oliver, one daughter. Next is Jay West, codename Clash. Twenty-six, black hair, brown eyes, enhanced speed, ex-wife Abigail Quinn. Then Ray Sampson, codename Blackout. Twenty-six, black hair, blue eyes, electricity manipulation, married to Olivia Sampson, one son. Kara Hall, codename Pilot. Twenty-four, blonde hair, hazel eyes, flight and enhanced strength, married to Claire Tyson, one stepson. The last field team member is Alix Tolvaj, codename Thief. Her age is a bit complicated but from what I understand she's twenty-six, brown hair with blonde highlights, gray eyes, shadow manipulation, no family.

"The base team is led by Casey Cabot, forty-six, auburn hair, blue eyes, one daughter with Legion hero Zachary Carter, codename Kov. She's helped by Cassidy Hamil, forty-two, red hair, gray eyes, two daughters and one son with her husband AJ Hamil, forty-three, black hair, brown eyes. The only remaining base member is Niall Sullivan, twenty-nine, black hair, blue eyes, family status as previously mentioned when I spoke of Katherine Sullivan."

Sarah finished neatly and took her hands back out of her pockets. Tag looked like he had a headache. "Why are there so many of them?" he asked weakly.

"Maybe because this is a large city and there are a lot of criminals here." Sarah shrugged. "Maybe because most of them are people experimented on by John Wechsler and Alice Cage, and they were the kind of people who wanted to commit mass murder."

Tag shook his head as if trying to clear it. "Why can't we just kill them, Caito?"

"I've told you before," Caito growled. "They aren't ours to kill." As he walked towards his office, he added, "Do your research, Tag. If you make one more mistake, it'll be your last."

6

"I don't need a babysitter," Kate grumbled as she jumped from one rooftop to another in the northern district of Caotico City.

As Alix followed her, she said, "Yeah, I know. I thought you were babysitting me."

"Don't patronize me, Thief," Kate snarled.

"I... wasn't," Alix said, confused.

Kate didn't seem to hear her. "You've been just as distant and screwed up as I've been."

Alix gave a sarcastic laugh, her eyes darkening. "You're right. I have been. But I don't have kids to bring down with me when I implode."

Kate pulled an arrow out of the quiver on her back, raised her bow, and aimed directly at Alix's chest. "Don't start with me. I'm not in the mood."

"You really think I am?" Alix waved her hand, and Kate's bow and arrow both vanished into shadows. "Need I remind you that your powers are a bit useless against someone like me?"

"I don't need that reminder, thanks," Kate retorted bitterly. "Give me my weapons back, Thief."

"So you can try to put an arrow through

my ribcage? I think not. I'll return them when you aren't being a whiny jackass."

As Alix tried to walk past Kate, the other woman grabbed her shoulder. "I'm the field leader," Kate growled. "I'm your boss. You need to do what I tell you to do."

"Get back to me when you start acting like you're my leader," Alix replied quietly.

Kate recoiled as if she had been physically struck. "You know what, Thief? If you think you know so much better than I do, patrol by yourself. I have better places to be." She turned as if to leave, then spun back around and took a swing at Alix's head. Alix disappeared into shadows, reappearing behind Kate and kicking her feet out from under her.

As Kate tumbled onto the rooftop, Alix's eyes began to lighten in color. "You need to cool off, Targeter."

"Yeah," Kate said hoarsely, her voice trembling. "Yeah, I think I do."

"Come on. Let's just get this patrol over with."

Alix held out her hand, but Kate didn't take it. She stayed where she was for a moment, before stumbling to her feet and sprinting off back the way they had come. Alix watched her go, her eyes now fully back to their normal color. She gave a quiet, regretful sigh and reached for the communications system in her sunglasses.

It was oddly quiet in the base of operations for the serial killer group. Tag had run off to sulk, leaving the area in peace and free from the loud roar of Tag's *Generic War Video Game #23843* matches that usually assaulted the ears of anyone coming through the door. The noise made Sarah almost consider volunteering to be one of the next murder victims. At the very least, it made her wish she could volunteer Tag for the role.

"He almost blew everything by being an impulsive little prick. You're *furious* with him. And yet, I still can't kill him."

Caito, who was sitting across from Sarah and still reading the newspaper, didn't look up. "You really do hate him, don't you, Sarah?"

"He's everything wrong with straight white men," Sarah grumbled. "No offense."

"None taken. I agree with you."

"*Why* do we need him?" Sarah asked.

"His power is useful."

Sarah scoffed. "Guns are useful too, and they're much easier to housetrain."

Caito smiled slowly. "We need to make sure that it's clear that empowered people are the ones committing these murders. If we use a gun, the plan won't work."

After a brief pause, Sarah asked, "Once we're done with the plan..."

"Can you kill Tag?"

"You said it, not me."

"Yes, you can kill Tag. However you

wish."

Sarah smirked. "Then I will continue to do things your way, happily."

"Good." Caito turned his tablet off. "I'm going to go to a Legion meeting tonight."

"A-Are you sure that's wise, sir?" Sarah asked, startled.

"I can blend in well. I'll sit in the back and remain quiet. All I want to do is see what kind of information they have on what we're doing. Those fools won't even notice I'm there. And if they do, I'll simply kill everyone there." He stood up. "Go find Tag. Make the useless idiot kill some of the *right* people while I'm gone. And in case this isn't clear enough, you're in charge."

"I figured as much. I'm not the one who thought putting a television and a gaming system in a serial killer base was a good idea. I don't trust his judgment at all."

"I only let him keep it because it keeps him busy while we do actually important things." Caito walked over to the coat rack and picked up a black leather Legion jacket with pale violet embroidering. "Who knows? If you do well, maybe I'll bring you back a hero to murder."

Niall walked through a row of tombstones that had become far too familiar to him over the years. He always knew exactly where to find Kate if she was missing but not on patrol, and when he got further into the cemetery he saw that nothing had changed.

Kate was still in her purple Heroics uniform, but she had removed her sunglasses. Her eyes, watery and red from tears, were staring down at the stone on the ground in front of her.

"I thought I'd find you here," Niall said quietly as he approached her. "Alix called me."

"Alix should mind her own business if she doesn't want me butting in on hers."

"That's not fair, Kate." Niall stopped next to her, joining her in looking down at Lori Marquez's tombstone. "Alix wasn't exactly tactful with you, but you know that something's wrong with her. You've been suffering too. And you know that sometimes you say things you don't mean because of that suffering." Niall gave her a sideways glance. "You also know that if you were on a patrol and *she* ran off, you'd worry too."

"Maybe I won't from now on."

Niall was silent for a long moment. "I can't do this anymore, Kate."

Kate's voice wavered just slightly as she said, "What can't you do?"

"Pretend that we're okay in front of the others."

She bowed her head. "I think AJ already knows."

"What makes you think that?"

"I… Rick made a comment at me in front

of him. About me not coming home for dinner."

"In fairness to Rick, you haven't been home at dinnertime for a month. You haven't been home at all in a week." Niall reached out and put a hand on her shoulder. "Kate… you can't blame yourself for everything. You can't still be blaming yourself for Lori's death; you know that. And you have to stop blaming yourself—"

"How can I?" Kate interrupted bitterly. "Julian—"

"Entered a confrontation he couldn't win," Niall finished. "You were pinned down, babe. There was nothing you could have done to save him."

"That doesn't make me feel any better. I'm the leader, Niall. I'm not supposed to let things happen. I'm not supposed to get pinned down."

"You're *human*. Humans aren't perfect, no matter how much power they have. You need to understand that."

Kate's eyes flicked over to the grave next to Lori's, which only had a small temporary plaque on it until the five-month post-funeral process for getting a stone put in place was complete. "I shouldn't have to. I shouldn't be letting people die. I thought we were done with that after Lori, but…"

Niall sighed, putting his hands in his pockets. "Take some advice, Kate. You need help. You need to talk to someone. Because we both know you aren't actually talking to me. I don't care who you talk to, whether it's me, or Justin, or AJ, or Casey, or *anyone*, but please. You need to fully tell someone what you're feeling."

"Alix doesn't tell anyone anything, and I don't see anyone 'advising' *her*."

"Don't bring Alix into this. It isn't the same."

"Why not?" Kate challenged.

"Because Alix is the genetically compromised clone of the psychopath who tortured her and her best friend. She has good reason to be distant and unwilling to discuss her problems."

"I'm an orphaned superhero raised by a sociopath forced to lead my adopted siblings into what is apparently certain death every day. What do I have?"

Her husband gave her a faint smile. "A reason to *talk to someone*."

Kate hesitated, looking a mixture of surprised and confused. "I'm still not pleased with you, but I will admit that I walked right into that."

"Yeah, you did. Because, like it or not, you know I'm right."

They stood in silence for a long moment. Kate crouched down and rested her hand on Lori's tombstone. "You know what the hardest thing about Lori's death was?"

"What?"

"In the days leading up to it, I barely spoke to her. I was so caught up in everything— in Justin and Alix and the whole Wechsler and Cage debacle —that I barely interacted with her. She was closer to me than my own blood brother, and I spent most of her last week talking to her like we were just coworkers." Kate gave a long, slow sigh. "And as for Julian, I... He had just gotten up the nerve to challenge me, Niall."

"What do you mean?"

"He could tell that I was slipping again, ever since the anniversary of Lori's death, and he flat-out told me that if I couldn't handle being the leader I should stop doing it."

Niall gave a soft whistle. "That doesn't sound like something Julian would do."

"It wasn't. But that day I was second-guessing myself so badly that Kara almost got hurt, and he saw. He noticed. And he called me out." Kate closed her eyes, her voice shaking. "And apparently he was right."

"You aren't a bad leader, Kate," Niall said gently, crouching next to her. "Julian knew that. Lori knew that. The rest of us *know* that. You just have trouble accepting that with this job, people are going to die."

Kate swallowed. "How am I supposed to accept that?"

"I don't know, sweetheart," Niall admitted. "That's something you might need to figure out for yourself."

"And if I can't?"

Niall leaned forward and kissed her on the side of the head. "Well," he murmured, "let's cross that bridge when we get to it, okay?"

"Okay," Kate whispered.

"Come on." Niall stood up, gently pulling her up with him. "Let the ghosts have some rest. They'll still be here when you want to come back to them."

Kate's eyes were dark as she let him lead her out of the cemetery. "They always are."

Alix stopped at the edge of a rooftop that allowed her to look out onto the center of town. It had been completely rebuilt since the battle against Wechsler and Cage's controlled empowered people in 2063, but the area still unnerved her. She was about to head back to the Heroics mansion, when she spotted a young police officer sprinting after two college-aged boys who looked like typical spoiled rich kids. They were carrying a 24-pack of beer each and laughing to each other as they ran down the dead-end alleyway directly below her. Alix rolled her eyes and waited patiently for the cop to catch up.

As soon as the police officer rounded the corner, however, the typical stupid crime turned ugly. The taller man, a blond-haired kid in a red polo shirt, pulled a gun out of the back of his khakis and aimed it directly at the officer. Alix made a noise of irritation and disappeared into shadows.

She reappeared in between the officer, who hadn't even had time to react to the gun, and the red polo man, just as the gun was fired. The bullet disappeared into shadows about a foot from Alix's face.

"Oh, shit," the second man, a blond in a green polo, stammered.

"What the hell was your plan here, guys?" Alix demanded as the cop behind her took out his gun.

The green man didn't seem to know, glancing at his cohort nervously. The red man just fired two more shots, which also disappeared. Alix raised an eyebrow. "I see that the plan is to keep wasting perfectly good ammunition. Good. I see that running down a dead-end street wasn't intentional and was instead because you are incredibly stupid."

"Let us out of this alley," the man in the red polo snarled.

Alix glanced back at the cop, who seemed just as incredulous as she felt. "No."

Another bullet fired and disappeared.

"I-I can't go to prison, man, my dads will kill me," the man in green polo whimpered. "We were just supposed to swipe some beer; what did you bring a gun for?"

"Hey, green shirt, I think we can work out a deal for you if you surrender right now. What do you say, Officer?" Alix glanced back at the cop again, who paused briefly before nodding.

The green man immediately dropped onto the ground with his hands out in front of him. The red man swore, calling his friend every imaginable curse word. While he was distracted, the gun disappeared into shadows. The red man looked down at his empty hand, startled. "What the fu—"

"*Get down on the ground, right now!*" the cop yelled, storming forward with his gun aimed at the red man.

Once both men were searched and cuffed, the officer walked back over to Alix. "I owe you one. You're Thief, aren't you?"

"I didn't think anybody knew my name."

The cop scoffed. "Please; you're the badass one as far as Heroics is concerned. Your powers are awesome."

Alix hesitated. "Yeah. Pretty awesome." She waved her hand, and the gun and associated bullets appeared on the ground at the cop's feet. "I figure you'll need that."

"I will; thanks." The cop frowned. "Hey, are you okay?"

"Hm?"

"You're bleeding."

Alix put a gloved hand up to her face and lowered it, seeing that it was covered in blood. Her nose was bleeding again. She mumbled a curse under her breath. "Yeah; I'm fine. I have to get back to what I was doing, though. Try not to get yourself shot at so easily next time."

"I won't. Thanks again."

Alix disappeared into the shadows, reappearing in an alleyway near the Heroics mansion. She fell onto her hands and knees, coughing up blood and shivering. The uncontrolled disks of shadows formed around her again, mocking her by zooming in close to her face at random. Kate's bow and arrow clattered to the concrete behind her. Alix tried to get to her feet, but she had barely begun to rise when she collapsed to the ground, unconscious.

7

Casey smiled softly when she walked into the mansion conference room and saw Zach in a chair with Logan sitting on the table in front of him, playing with a chunk of metal that he was manipulating into various animals. The girl was trying to mimic his motions to move the metal herself, Casey realized, and for the first time in a long time she thought about the very real possibility that her daughter could have Zach's power. She had known that from the start, of course, but rarely did it hit her as hard as it did in that moment.

Zach looked up at her and grinned the stupid handsome grin that he had used on her in her bar two weeks before he had become the Heroics/Legion liaison. "Nice of you to show up, Cabot. Without the glasses, though. I'm disappointed."

"Your *daughter* is *right there*," Casey grumbled as she walked over to take her seat.

"Yes, and I'm sure she agrees with me." Zach looked at Logan. "Doesn't your mom look nice in glasses?"

Logan considered the question for a moment. "Yes."

"See? Kid agrees with me."

Casey gave Zach a tired look. "She'd agree with you about anything."

"Untrue. Logan, isn't the rabbit the best

common forest animal?"

Logan looked disgusted. "No."

"What is?"

"The squirrel," Logan and Casey said simultaneously.

Zach smiled. "See?"

"She always says squirrel. That's cheating." Casey leaned back in her chair. "Logan, honey, can you go upstairs? We need to have a meeting."

"Sure, Mommy." Logan got down off of the table with some help from Zach and calmly walked out of the room.

Cass raised an eyebrow at Casey. "How do you get one to actually listen when you tell them things?"

"Good genes," Casey joked.

AJ scoffed. "No, seriously, because there's no way anything good you put in counterbalanced Zach's half."

"This coming from the two of you," Zach said.

"What's wrong with us?" Cass demanded.

Casey smirked. "A lot of things. I mean, for starters, the two of you make out in your car because it's the only place your children never think to look for you."

Cass glared at her. "That was *one time*."

"Once is enough."

"Oh, okay. If once is enough, then let's talk about the time you snuck Zach out of your room at three in the morning so that no one would see him since you had sworn to me and AJ five hours earlier that you could totally go two days without seeing the guy."

Zach grinned at Casey. "Wait, really?"

Casey stared at Cass, pale. "How the hell do you know about that?"

"I have my ways," Cass replied smugly.

"Alix," Casey muttered, in the way one would say a curse word.

"She's very useful."

"She won't be when I kill her."

The rest of the Heroics team filed into the room. Niall was following Kate, a worried expression on his face. The field team leader looked tired and like she had been crying, but she shot a weak smile at Niall as she sat down. Once everyone was seated, Cass looked around quickly and sighed. "Has anyone seen Alix?"

"She didn't check in after her patrol," Casey replied.

"Do you think she's okay?" Kara asked, concerned.

Casey's eyes were cloudy, but she said, "She's missed check-ins and meetings before. It wouldn't be anything new. She's probably fine." She paused. "But if you wanted to check around town after the meeting, I wouldn't stop you."

Kara nodded. "Of course. I'm not expected at home for another hour or so anyway."

"Good. So. Cass, what's going on?"

"First of all, I talked to Clarice. I got a bit of pushback that I'm dealing with, but the important thing is that Colin Kilian's name didn't come from her. It came from a teenage girl who showed up right before our last meeting with Clarice. Clarice said she didn't know her, and I believe her."

"Somebody who used to work for Alice?" Ray asked.

"I thought about that, but if Clarice's guess on age is right, this kid couldn't have been more than six or seven years old when Alice died."

"Yeah, but you could say the same thing about Alix," Kara said somberly. She slowly spun her wedding ring around on her finger, an anxious habit she had picked up over the past two years. "What should we do?"

"At the moment, there's probably nothing we *can* do," Justin pointed out. "It was four years ago; we don't have much hope of finding out who that girl was, especially if the records at the prison are as bad as Jay says they are."

"Yeah, apparently they're quite bad. Oh, and Parvalo couldn't give me any more information or records."

"Speaking of records," AJ said, turning to Cass, "did you meet with Raylans?"

Cass chuckled quietly. "Oh, yes. He is exactly the kind of lawyer politician my father would've tried to be buddies with."

Casey snorted. "Homicidal and insane?"

"No. My father never sought out people who were just like him. Then they might try to take over his plans. I guarantee that the only reason he ever worked with Alice Cage is because he'd known her for a while and she helped him build his plans from the start." Cass leaned back in her chair, quietly drumming her fingers on the table. "Elliott Raylans is easily manipulated, yet still smart. The perfect person for my father to try to get his claws into."

"Did he admit anything?" Niall asked.

"In a roundabout way, yes. Extrapolating from his politician speak, apparently my father paid him to get all of those records from the prison. He gave him a specific list of which ones, and they were all empowered people. Raylans got paid so much money for each record that he never asked any questions and he never asked why. Afterwards, he started putting distance between himself and my father so that no one would get suspicious."

"Ended up being a smart move on his part," Casey muttered.

"This is all great, but we're back where we started," Kate said, sounding frustrated. "All of our information has led us to people who are dead or to someone that we have no hope of finding."

"We'll figure it out, Kate," AJ replied gently. "We always do."

"Sure we do." Kate stood up. "Are we done, then? Because I have a patrol to finish." Without waiting for an answer, she turned and walked out of the room.

AJ shot a glance at Niall, who was staring at his hands. "I think we're done here," AJ said, his voice quiet.

Justin nodded once and hurried after his sister. Kara followed him out the door soon after. Zach reached out and softly tapped Casey on the hand. "I have a Legion meeting tonight. Do you need to go to your bar?"

"Yeah, I do. Cass, can you make sure Logan goes to bed?"

Cass gave a thin smile. "She's probably already there, but sure."

"Thanks."

Casey and Zach both stood up and left the room. Soon the table was empty except for AJ and Niall.

"AJ, I..." Niall trailed off with a frown, a troubled expression on his face.

"Let me guess. Kate?" AJ shifted in his chair so that he was facing Niall. "How many times in the past month has she come home at night?" he asked sympathetically.

"... None. Maybe once, but I don't think so." Niall swallowed. "She gets lost out there, AJ. Distracting herself with hunting down bad guys and roughing up idiot kids so that she doesn't have to deal with her own pain. I don't know what to do. She's barely home anymore, and I know she's not doing any of it maliciously, but... the boys are confused. They don't understand why it's so hard for them to talk to their own mother. I found her in the cemetery today. I find her there a lot, when I work up the energy to go looking for her. I-I'm losing her, AJ." Niall looked at the older man, stress clear on his face. "I don't know what to do."

AJ paused for a long moment before sighing. "Kate's biggest flaw is that she's too hard on herself and too stubborn to listen when anyone tells her not to be. I don't know how to fix that, Niall. I really don't. Unfortunately, I don't have all of the answers. And I can tell that you're frustrated and tired. I don't know how to fix that, either. I can try to talk to her if you want."

Niall gave a humorless smile. "Think that would actually do anything?"

"Probably not. But I can try."

"It's okay. She won't listen to you and we both know it." Niall paused. "I love her, AJ, but I don't know how to help her."

"Sometimes we can't," AJ replied softly. "Sometimes we just need to give space."

"How much more space do I need to give her?" Niall asked exasperatedly.

"I don't know. But from what I've seen, Niall? You won't need to wait long."

"What do you mean?"

AJ sighed. "Kate is on the brink of an

explosion. It happened once or twice when she was little. She'd get upset and frustrated and bottle it all up until she lost it and picked a fight with one of the other kids. It wasn't healthy, and she grew out of it, but her behavior right now is that exact same thing. And once she explodes, she's going to need someone to help her. The question is: Are you willing to wait for that?"

Niall ran a hand through his hair. "I'd wait forever if she needed me to."

"Then that's all you can do."

As Niall left, Cass reentered the room. "The kids are all in bed. Brooke and Aubrey are going to stay up reading for another hour or so."

"Good."

Cass stood behind AJ and put her arms on his shoulders, resting her chin on the top of his head. "You okay?"

"Yeah," he murmured. "Worried about Kate. And Alix."

"Well, you might have one other thing to worry about," Cass sighed.

AJ turned his head to look up at her. "What did you do?"

"Why is it always something *I've* done?" When he just raised an eyebrow at her, Cass sighed again. "Clarice wouldn't give me information until I made a deal with her to move her to general population in the prison."

"Oh, Cassidy, tell me you didn't," AJ

groaned.

"I did. I'm working on figuring out exactly what I'm going to do."

"Given your honor system, you're going to follow through on it. Hopefully just with a bit more sense than some of your other plans."

Cass laughed and ran her fingers through his hair. "You're awfully calm about this."

AJ shrugged as he leaned back against her. "I learned a long time ago that you make terrible choices."

Cass grinned. "What, like marrying you?"

"No, that was *my* terrible choice."

"I dunno," Cass said teasingly. "I think I could've done better."

AJ scoffed. "Please. I'm the best you were ever going to do."

Cass kissed him on the cheek. "Luckily for me, my best was pretty damn good."

Casey reached down and took Zach's hand as they walked through the southern district of Caotico City. "Are you okay?" she asked quietly.

"Why wouldn't I be?"

"You seem tense."

Zach gave an irritated sigh. "The meeting the Legion is having tonight is about the murders. I know somebody is going to start giving me a hard time about it."

"Why would they give you a hard time?"

"Because Chuva made me in charge of the

northern district last month."

Casey stopped dead in her tracks, and her grip on his hand forced him to stop as well. "Are you serious?"

"Yeah."

"Why didn't you *tell* me?"

Zach pulled his hand away from hers and ran it through his hair. "Because it's bullshit, Casey. It's Chuva throwing me to the wolves. Nobody has any idea of how to stop these murders, so anybody in charge of that district is going to be more and more screwed the longer it goes on. And to make matters worse, I'm *awful* at it, Case. I could barely tell you who was on patrol. People are dying, I'm getting thrown under the bus because of it, and I can't do a damn thing to stop any of it."

"Then don't try to do it by yourself," Casey said, her voice soft.

"I have to. I can't ask for your help. It's my job."

Casey's eyes narrowed. "Zach, the things that involve you involve me, too."

Zach tensed and avoided eye contact with her. "Oh they do, do they?" he asked, an edge of bitterness to his voice.

"What's your issue?" Casey asked, startled by the sudden burst of irritation.

"My *issue*, Casey, is that you won't make up your freaking mind. You're involved in things that involve me now? Because yesterday you wouldn't have said that, and the day before you might've, and the pattern just keeps going. You have me in your bed half the week, you won't see anyone else, and we both know that you'd be upset if I started dating anyone other than you. Not that I'd even want to. I'm yours, Casey. But I don't have any real clue as to whether I'll ever get you to settle for me, because one day you act like it and the next day you don't. I'm not going anywhere unless you tell me to, but I still want you to make up your mind already."

Casey stared at him for a long moment, stunned to see that he looked almost like he wanted to cry. "I-I don't know how to say whether I love you, if that's what you want," she admitted quietly. "Otherwise?" She put her arms on his shoulders, linking her fingers behind his neck. "I had your kid, Zach. And it might have been an accident, but it wasn't a mistake. I'm not going anywhere, and I don't want you to go anywhere, either. I'm right here, and that's not going to change no matter how bad I am at saying things the way you'd like me to say them."

Zach took a deep breath, calming down. "You don't need to say them, Casey. I just can't keep feeling like I matter one day and then like I don't the next."

"I know that. And I'm sorry. There's a lot that you don't understand, that I've never told you, and you don't deserve that. There's no time tonight, but I promise you, I'll explain. I owe you that."

"You don't owe me anything," Zach said quickly.

Casey just smiled. "Come on, Carter. We have work to get to." She took his hand again and pulled him as she continued down the street.

Kara owned a car and used it, but on clear nights when she was only going to the mansion she didn't waste the gas. As she floated through the air, high enough up that few would notice her but she could still see what was going on below, she put her sunglasses on and hit a few buttons on her white bracelet. After a moment, a voice popped into her ear.

"*Hello?*"

"Hey, it's me," Kara said.

"*Hey, honey. You on your way home?*"

"In a roundabout way."

A pause. "*What's wrong?*"

Kara cursed silently. How Claire could know something was up within four words never ceased to amaze— and, admittedly, aggravate —her. "It's Alix. I just have a bad feeling. I'm checking to see if I can find her in the city."

"*She can take care of herself, you know,*" Claire said calmly.

"I know. I just worry."

"*You're going to get worry lines at*

twenty-four."

"Oh, shut up."

Claire laughed. *"Just be careful, okay?"*

"I'm always careful."

"Are you using 'always' as a synonym for 'never'?"

"Har har. I'll be home soon."

"Good. James probably won't go to bed until you're here."

Kara grinned. "Maybe I'll stay out a bit longer, then."

"I hate you."

"You don't."

"Sadly true."

"I— shit!"

"Kara?"

Kara stared down at the ground in shock, no longer even hearing Claire's voice.

"Kara? Kara!"

"A-Alix," Kara whispered.

"What?"

"I'm okay. I have to go. I'll explain later." Kara disconnected from her call and dropped into an alleyway. She hurried over to Alix, who was lying face down on the ground, and turned her over onto her back. The woman was unconscious and covered in blood. "Alix? Can you hear me?"

Alix groaned quietly and opened her eyes. "Son of a bitch," she mumbled.

Kara helped her into a sitting position. "What happened to you?"

"Nothing."

"Bullshit."

"I'm fine," Alix said grumpily.

"Also bullshit."

Alix pushed herself to her feet and stumbled, but Kara caught her by putting a hand on her shoulder. "It's not a big deal. I'm fine."

"Alix, you're covered in blood. It is a big deal."

"I'm just going to go home."

"No, you aren't." Kara's grip on Alix's shoulder tightened. "You don't look like you're in any condition to use your powers, so what's the plan? Just walk into the mansion covered in blood? Where Cass and AJ and Casey and the kids are? You really think you aren't going to get interrogated?"

Alix looked down, and Kara could tell that everything she had said had been effective. She shifted and put her arm around Alix's shoulders. "Come on, Al. You're coming home with me."

The other woman gave a soft chuckle. "Like I won't get interrogated at your house."

"True. But the only kid there is one that doesn't ask questions."

Alix hesitated then nodded. "Fine, Kara," she said.

Kara smiled, trying to keep the fear out of her eyes. Alix had given in far too quickly for her comfort. "Good. Come on, then."

Claire Tyson looked up quickly when Kara and Alix entered the house. "Oh, hell," Claire murmured. She hurried over and took Alix's face in her hands. "What did you do, run your face into a brick wall?"

"Actually, my nose just decided to start bleeding on its own accord," Alix replied.

"For some reason, I actually believe that." Claire pulled Alix into the kitchen and sat her in one of the chairs while Kara got a towel.

"I found her in an alley," Kara said as she handed the towel to Alix. "I'm still not convinced that she didn't get her ass kicked and she just doesn't want to admit it."

"You're the one who does that," Alix muttered as she wiped blood off of her face.

Kara's hands tightened into fists. "Care to tell me what happened now?"

"The answer's still no."

"Look, jackass, you—"

"Mommy? Mom?"

Everyone looked over at the doorway into the kitchen, where Claire's son James was standing. "I wanna go to bed," the four-year-old mumbled.

"Sure, buddy. I'll be there in a second," Claire said gently.

"I want Mom."

There was an awkward pause before Claire looked at Kara. "I can take care of Alix.

Go."

Kara shot a glare at Alix, as if telling her that the conversation wasn't over. She walked over to James, picked him up, and disappeared down the hallway towards the bedrooms.

Once they were gone, Alix muttered, "Your wife is a pain in the ass."

"You said you *didn't* get hit in the head or anything?"

Alix looked confused. "No."

"Good." Claire smacked Alix in the back of the head.

"*Ow*! What the hell?"

"I don't know what's wrong with you right now, Al, but for some reason it's making you completely ignorant of what's going on with other people," Claire said angrily. "You realize that Kara is terrified, right? She lost Lori, she lost Julian, she knows she's losing Kate, and she's painfully aware of the fact that she could lose anybody at any time because of the job you guys do. She went looking for you tonight, Alix. She went looking for you because she had a bad feeling and she was worried. So, can you set aside your stubbornness for five minutes? Please? She's not going to stop worrying if you don't tell her what's going on. You're covered in blood, for hell's sake."

Alix gave a thin smile. "You know, when Kara started dating you, I was a bit confused. A quiet banker and a loudmouth superhero? How the hell was that going to work? But you're just as stubborn and passionate as she is."

Claire mirrored Alix's smile. "It took four years for you to figure out whether we worked?"

"No. But I'm not used to seeing you show it as strongly as you did just now."

That got a grin out of Claire. "Don't get used to it, Thief. Yelling at you is Kara's job."

"Oh? What's yours?"

"Looking disapproving or disappointed while Kara yells."

Alix rolled her eyes. "Why am I not surprised?"

Kara walked back into the room and stood beside Claire, her arms folded across her chest. "So. Are you going to tell me what's wrong with you? Because people don't get covered in blood for no damn reason."

"I'm..." Alix hesitated and bowed her head. Her hands tightened into fists. "I'm sick," she whispered hoarsely.

Claire and Kara exchanged a confused glance. "What do you mean?" Claire prompted.

Alix's hands began to shake. "I'm sick. My powers are killing me."

"Al," Kara murmured, crouching down in front of her.

"Every time I use my powers, I get worse, and if I use them too long, I get nosebleeds. But more recently, it's been getting even worse. That's what happened today. The blood was all mine, and it was because I used my powers too much."

"Oh my god, Alix." Claire sat down in one of the kitchen chairs. She glanced at Kara, who was pale. "Why haven't you told anyone?"

"Because I'm trying to fix it," Alix replied, looking up at her with pale gray eyes. "I think I know what caused it, and I think I can make it stop. I just need the time." Her gaze shifted to Kara. "Can you give me the time? Before we tell the others?"

Kara met her gaze shakily. "You really think you can fix it? So that you don't die?"

"I-I do."

"Okay." Kara took in a deep breath. "I'll give you some time. But if it gets worse, Alix, you have to tell the others. Please."

"I will." Alix stood up slowly. "Thanks for the towel. I think I can head back to the mansion now."

"Should you use your powers?"

Alix gave Kara a thin smile. "I can't just stop doing what I need to do, Kara. It's not how my life works." At that, she disappeared into shadows.

Claire watched Kara silently for a moment. "Are you alright?" she asked softly.

"I don't know," Kara admitted.

Claire shifted so that she was kneeling down next to her. "It's going to be okay."

"I'm not so sure about that, Claire."

"You're supposed to be the optimistic one."

"Sometimes being the optimistic one is exhausting."

"I know it is." Claire pulled her into a tight hug. "I know it is. Luckily for you, your superpower is strength."

Kara gave a quiet laugh. "That was quite a line, Tyson."

"Yeah, it was. But I think it might have worked."

"I think you might be right."

8

Zach was one of the last to walk into the Security Legion meeting, five minutes before it was scheduled to start. He pointedly ignored the glare from Davi "Chuva" Esteves and sat down between Wade "Raseri" Toracid and Andrew "Flare" Sullivan.

Andrew leaned over and whispered, "I think Chuva was hoping you wouldn't show, Kov. What did you do to piss him off, anyway?"

"Hell if I know," Zach muttered. "Want to ask him for me?"

"Absolutely not."

Zach stifled a laugh. "Brave one, aren't you?"

"Don't see you asking."

"I never said I was brave."

"If all of the chatter is done," Davi said stiffly as he got to his feet, "I'd like to get this meeting started." He paused to wait for the gathered group to finish talking. "Now, as you all know, there have been multiple murders in Caotico these past few months. We haven't been able to stop a single one of these killings. This is bad for business, folks."

"We aren't a business, Chuva," Rob "Cryo" Munroe said quietly.

"I don't remember asking you, Cryo," Davi snapped.

Rob just smiled. "You didn't. But I'm not

sure what you want us to do."

"*You* are in charge of the eastern district. *You* don't have to do anything other than what you have been doing, aside from that unfortunate incident where you and the other Alumni tried to kill us all." As Rob looked down at his hands, upset, Davi turned to Zach. "You, Kov, are the one who's been embarrassing us."

Zach snorted and leaned forward, resting his arms on the table. "How is that? The murders started *long* before you handed the northern district to me. You expect me to walk in and solve a problem like this within a few weeks? We're trying, Chuva."

"I doubt that," Davi said sarcastically.

Tamara "Redwood" Kingston, head of the southern district, smacked her hand down on the table, causing the wood to vibrate. "Knock it off, Chuva," she growled. "You know damn well that this isn't Kov's fault. It isn't our fault at all. It's the fault of whoever is killing these people, and we need a way to stop it."

"What should we do?" Wade asked.

Davi looked around at the dozen Legion heroes in the room, all either district leaders or top ranking members of the group. "We're the best of the best," he said in a low voice. "We need to develop a plan. We're going to have another meeting sometime soon, and one of you had *better* have some ideas the next time we're all together." With one final glare around the room, the Legion leader turned on his heel and left the room.

Niall hurried along the streets of Caotico, looking for Kate. He was still worried about her, and he didn't want her out alone, no matter how skilled she was. Skill wouldn't help her if she was too distracted by her depression to defend herself. With Ciaran and Rick sleeping over at his brother Andrew's house, Niall knew that he had more than enough time to look for Kate. He'd stay out all night if he had to.

Casey walked into the bar she owned and headed directly over to the bartender and general manager, Kaita Dragovic. "Good evening, boss," Kaita greeted brightly.

"Hey, Kaita. How is everything going?"

"Fine. There's a Legion meeting going on right now that should be breaking up in about a half hour, so those idiots should be here in about forty-five minutes." Kaita grinned. "Of course, you probably already knew that, given your boy toy."

Casey sighed. "Must you?"

"I was the first one to know about you two, so yes."

"It wasn't like I *told* you."

Kaita shrugged. "So? I fail to see how that changes the facts."

Casey gave a quick laugh and shook her

head slowly. "Jackass."

"It's a common problem around here." As Casey sat down on one of the barstools, Kaita said, "Want something, Case?"

"Yeah, sure. The usual."

Kaita poured Casey a glass of scotch and slid it across the bar to her. "How's Thief been?"

"Not good. I wish I knew what was wrong, but I don't even have much of an opportunity to ask. She usually locks herself in her room all day and doesn't answer if we knock. Honestly, given her power, I can't even tell if she's in there."

"What's she doing in her room all the time?" Kaita wondered.

"I wish I knew."

Kaita hesitated. "Casey... I don't really want to suggest this. Because Alix is an adult, and she's a friend. But..."

"But what?"

"Have you ever..." Kaita gave a slow sigh. "Have you ever looked to see just what was in her room?"

Casey took a long drink from her glass. "That's an interesting idea."

"Please don't do anything stupid."

"Who do you think I am?"

"Casey Cabot," Kaita deadpanned.

Casey finished her scotch, then said, "You make a decent point."

"In all seriousness, Case. Please don't

hurt Alix."

"I'm pretty sure she'd be better at hurting me than I'd be at hurting her."

Kaita took Casey's glass and started to wash it. "You know, you guys don't really notice it, do you?"

"Notice what?"

"That Alix is the most scared one of all of you."

"*Alix*?" Casey scoffed. "I doubt that."

Kaita gave a thin smile. "That's exactly what worries me."

Niall turned down a thin alley and almost walked directly into Kate, who was on her way out of it. "I've been looking for you," he said.

"I know. I've been avoiding you."

"You ran out of that meeting awfully fast."

Kate sighed and headed back into the alley, Niall following behind her. "People are going to die, Niall. Because we aren't doing our jobs."

"People are going to die because somebody's out there killing them." Niall shook his head slowly. "That's not on us."

"I can't do it, Niall. I can't accept that it's not my fault when people I'm supposed to protect get killed."

"You're going to have to," Niall said firmly, grabbing her arm to stop her. "Kate, this is bad. You need to have your head on straight. I know that it's not that easy, and I know that it's going to take a while for you to be better. And I will wait for you as long as I need to. But your job isn't going to wait for you, Kate."

She was silent for a long moment. "You'd wait for me to get better?"

"Of course."

"You shouldn't."

Niall blinked, surprised. "What do you mean?"

"You know what I mean, Niall. I'm not an idiot. You're worried about the effect I'm having on the boys."

"Of course I am, but that doesn't mean—"

"It does, and we both know that."

Niall took in a deep breath. "Yeah. I do know that."

Kate nodded, a grim smile on her face. "Just… let me know when you hit that point, okay? Don't be afraid to tell me."

"You won't get to that point," Niall insisted. "There's nothing wrong with you, Kate. You're just a little bruised right now, is all."

"It's not just a bruise, honey. You know that, too." Kate rested a hand on his cheek. "It's okay. It will get to that point, probably soon, but it's okay."

"I don't want to lose you, Kate."

"I don't want to lose you, either." Kate

lowered her hand and turned. "I just think it's a bit too late for it to be prevented." Her voice hitched on the last word as if she was about to cry. She tightened her grip on her bow, squared her shoulders, and walked away from Niall.

Once the morning meeting dismissed, Casey made her way up to Alix's bedroom. She knew that the younger woman had been talked onto a patrol with Kara, so the room would be empty. Casey paused in front of Alix's door, her hand resting on the doorknob. A large part of her knew that she shouldn't do what she was about to do, but she knew that if she didn't at least look, she would be furious with herself if something happened to Alix. After taking a deep breath, Casey opened the door to Alix's room and stepped inside.

"Holy hell," Casey murmured to herself. The room was a mess. The whiteboard that made up the side wall was covered in mathematical equations and scientific formulas that made no sense to her and weren't organized at all. Alix's bed was being used as a bookshelf for books on mental illness, organic chemistry, biology, anatomy… almost everything connected to science and health. There were boxes all over the place, with various labels on them. Some of the labels were familiar to Casey: John Wechsler, Austin Sadik, Giada Sadik, Brooke Cassidy Wechsler,

One box in particular caught Casey's attention. Shoved into a corner, as if hidden, was a box labeled 'Diana van der Aart.' Casey made her was over to it cautiously. She gripped the lid and hesitated, realizing that her hands were actually trembling. After a moment, she lifted off the lid. The box was full of papers. Casey started flipping through them curiously, her hands still not functioning all that properly.

Most of the papers seemed to be scientific things— notes and diagrams and charts. Among the pages were her mother's college diploma and her real birth certificate. "Son of a bitch," Casey mumbled. "You were like five years younger than you told me you were. Why would you hide that?"

Saving that question for later, Casey continued rifling through the box. In the very back was a thick leather-bound book. Casey pulled it out and flipped through it. It was a diary that looked to have been written while her mother was at college. As Casey glanced through the book, a folded-up piece of paper fell out of it. She picked it up and unfolded it.

Casey actually felt herself go pale as she stared down at the piece of paper. "Oh my god," she whispered.

9

When Cass walked into the living room of the mansion, she found Casey sitting in one of the chairs, her feet up on the ottoman and a half-filled glass of scotch in her hand.

"It's barely the afternoon. I hope that whole thing didn't start off full," Cass said quietly.

The other woman continued to stare at the lit fireplace. "It was."

"That's not like you," Cass commented as she sat in the chair next to Casey's.

"I have my reasons," Casey murmured.

"Feel like sharing?"

Casey sighed. "I'm not sure you want to know."

"Try me. Maybe I can help fix whatever it is that's got you like this."

Casey gave a soft laugh. "I like you, Cass. But this isn't something that can be fixed."

Cass shifted in her seat. "Okay, now you're starting to scare me."

"I went into Alix's room. She has boxes from the Vigilance Initiative all over the place. I found my mother's diary from college, when the VI was first formed."

"I bet that's an interesting read."

"I only read one page. The diary isn't what..." Casey cleared her throat uncomfortably and handed Cass a piece of paper. "This was inside the book."

"Paper was in a book? No way." When Casey didn't even slightly smile, Cass unfolded the paper. "Your birth certifi— oh."

"Yeah," Casey whispered. "I checked it's accuracy in the diary already."

Cass stared down at her father's name on Casey's birth certificate. "Oh, hell, Casey, I'm so sorry."

"Don't apologize to me," Casey whispered. "That'll make it worse."

"How?"

"Because John Wechsler was your *father*, Cass. You had to live with the guy, you were *tortured* by him, and here I'm..." Casey took a large gulp from her glass of scotch. "God, this is so pathetic."

"It's really not," Cass said quietly. "Case, I hate being his child, and I wasn't even lied to. You have no reason to be anything other than upset about this."

"I don't know what I'm going to say to the others. I don't know if I *can* say anything to the others."

"That's your call. I do think that you can and should talk to Zach about it. But you don't need to talk to anyone if you don't want to."

"I'll see." Casey set her glass down on the table between their chairs. "I guess that the scotch won't help much."

"That depends on your perspective, really," Cass replied with a grin.

Casey laughed weakly. "Well, at least I get a decent half-sister out of this."

Cass took Casey's glass and finished it. "Let's be real, Case. I've been your sister for a while. The fact that John Wechsler was your father too just makes it true by blood."

Ray stood at the edge of a rooftop in the western district of Caotico, scanning the various banks in the area for any signs of trouble.

Jay skidded to a stop next to him. "There doesn't seem to be anything going on over by the train station."

"There usually isn't," Ray commented quietly. "The police do a good job of keeping that area under control."

"If only they could keep the rest of the city under control," Justin joked as he jumped from one roof over to the one Ray and Jay were on.

"What exactly are you implying about our police force, Archer?" Ray asked, a teasingly dangerous edge to his voice. His wife, Olivia, had moved from her home country of Mexico at seventeen to become a police officer in Caotico.

"I wouldn't dream about implying anything, Blackout," Justin replied, grinning cheekily.

Before Ray could respond, Kara dropped down onto the roof. Her lip was bleeding. "Son of a bitch," she mumbled.

"Are you okay?" Ray asked, concerned.

"Yeah, I'm fine." Kara wiped a line of blood off of her chin. "Get this, though. I stopped two muggers in the park, and as I was tying them up for the cops, the victim sucker punched me."

"What the hell for?" Justin demanded.

"Apparently, his sister was one of the people killed in the northern district last month, and he figured that if I could stop two muggers, I should've been able to stop those murders a long time ago." Kara moved her jaw around a bit experimentally. "I don't blame him for being upset, but punching me isn't going to solve anything."

"Caotico's civilians are getting restless," Jay said quietly. "They're pissed about these killings, and pretty soon a lot more people are going to start blaming us."

"It's not like we're the ones killing anybody," Justin growled.

"That's not going to matter soon, and you know it." Ray took in a deep breath and looked out towards the northern district. "The people are angry. And if we aren't careful, they'll take us apart, whether we're at fault or not."

Alix walked into the library and saw Aubrey Hamil sitting on the floor, a textbook and a notebook opened in front of her. "Hey, kid. What are you up to?"

"Summer math work," Aubrey replied. She put her pencil between her teeth and pulled her brown hair into a neat ponytail. "Cn y hlp m?"

"Care to try that again?"

Aubrey sheepishly took the pencil out of her mouth. "Can you help me?"

As Alix sat down next to the girl, she said, "The eight-year-old math genius needs help with her math homework? What did they give you, advanced calculus?"

"No." Aubrey bowed her head. "I don't really need help; I just want to spend time with you. You've been hiding in your room so much I barely see you."

Alix rested a hand on Aubrey's shoulder. "I'm sorry about that, kid. I'm just taking care of some stuff. You're still my favorite, though."

Aubrey grinned brightly. "Promise?"

"Promise. Now let me look at this math. You don't get to ask me for help and then deny me the chance." Alix pulled Aubrey's notebook towards her and studied it. "Ah, algebra. I love algebra."

"So do I. It's kind of relaxing."

Alix laughed. "Don't say that in school or the other kids will call you a nerd."

Aubrey laughed and watched as Alix read the assignment. "I thought you liked science more than math."

"Who, me? No way. I like math a whole

heck of a lot more."

"Why?"

Alix hesitated. "Science… changes. You can wake up tomorrow and everything you know about it can be proven wrong. The Earth isn't flat. Velociraptors had feathers. Something that you thought would help you live is actually killing you. Math is a lot more predictable. Two plus two is four. If a plus b equals c, c minus b equals a. It evolves, it grows, but it's not going to turn on me." Alix looked down at her hands as they started to tremble slightly. "If— When I wake up tomorrow, math will still be math," she murmured.

"What's wrong? Are you okay?" Aubrey asked.

"I'm fine, kid," Alix said lightly, not sounding entirely convinced.

Aubrey didn't seem to notice the hesitation, saying, "Math's my favorite, too. It makes sense to me, and in my life a lot of things don't make sense."

"You're too young to say things like that and sound like you mean it," Alix said gently.

Aubrey shrugged, avoiding eye contact. She began spinning her bracelet around her wrist in slow sets of three rotations. "Promise me that you're okay."

"I don't know if I can promise you that, Aub."

The girl finished a set of rotations and

shakily put her hands down in her lap. "I don't want to lose you," she whispered.

Alix hugged her. "It's going to be alright. I know what I'm doing, Aubrey." After a moment, she stood and pulled Aubrey to her feet. "Come on, kid. Take a break from the homework for a bit. Let's go get some lunch."

"Okay," Aubrey said, her voice still quiet.

"Hey." Alix crouched down in front of the girl. "You aren't going to lose me." Her voice faltered a bit. "I promise." She took Aubrey's hand, and they both disappeared into shadows.

AJ leaned back in his chair as he looked up at the various screens in the mansion's control room. Everyone was on patrol except for Alix, who had taken Aubrey out. Niall was with his boys and Jacob and Logan were with Zach, leaving AJ alone in the building. *Almost alone, of course*, AJ thought as he heard the door quietly open behind him. He smirked and spun his chair around slowly, catching Brooke as she attempted to sneak up behind him. She immediately straightened out of her stalking pose, looking at him innocently.

"Good afternoon," AJ greeted, folding his arms across his chest.

"... Afternoon." Brooke continued staring at him, fidgeting slightly.

He raised an eyebrow curiously. "Did you need something, kiddo, or were you just practicing your ninja skills?"

Brooke took in a breath, seeming to struggle with whatever she was trying to say. After another moment, she started, "Daddy, can—"

"Oh no." AJ sighed as he stood up and pushed the chair back under the desk.

His daughter blinked. "What?"

"Any question that you preface with 'Daddy' usually means that either I'm in trouble or you're about to be."

"It's nothing bad. Can I take the bus into the city? There's an engineering event at the college and I want to see it."

"You want to go alone?"

The girl shrugged. "Yeah."

"Brooke, you're *nine*."

"So?" Brooke asked rebelliously. "I don't *act* nine."

"It's still a terrible idea. Why not just ask one of us to go?"

Brooke made a face. "It's smart people stuff, Daddy."

"Ouch. I see I ended up with an insufferable genius child, as if having to deal with three genius children in general wasn't painful enough." AJ shook his head. "You've got no chance, kid. Don't bother asking your mother, either. I already know what she's going to say."

Brooke looked down at the ground and shuffled her feet. "She said no."

AJ patted Brooke on the head and walked

over to the filing cabinet. "Listen to your mother, Brooke."

"But that's *boring*," Brooke whined. "And Logan doesn't listen to Aunt Casey."

"First of all, she kind of does. Second of all, Logan is *three*."

"Jacob doesn't listen to Mom."

"Jacob is two. You're on your last strike. How unhelpful to your case will your next argument be?"

Brooke seemed to consider this for a long moment. "Aubrey doesn't listen to Mom either?"

"Strike three. *You* taught her that." AJ crouched down in front of Brooke, smiling slightly. "Maybe if you start listening when you're told things, one of us will take you to whatever this thing is that you want to go to." He poked Brooke in the stomach lightly, making her giggle despite how determined she was to frown irritably at him. "We *can* tolerate 'smart people stuff,' you know."

"Oh, alright," Brooke agreed grumpily.

"Just so we're clear: If you don't listen to me and try to go by yourself anyway, you'll be grounded until you're thirty."

"I would never ignore your instructions, Daddy," Brooke said.

AJ grinned. "Yeah, I'm sure. Now—"

Another voice cut him off. "I love what you've done with the place."

There was a horrified moment of silence

as AJ paled and stood back up. He turned to the door, pushing Brooke behind him as he did so. An older woman with gray hair and metallic gray eyes was standing in the doorway.

AJ swallowed, looking terrified. "Alice Cage."

10

"You're supposed to be dead," AJ breathed, taking a step back and pulling Brooke with him.

"So are you. So is your wife. So is my clone." Alice shrugged. "The people around here are very bad at dying."

"But it's not *possible*. Alix—"

"That girl didn't stay to watch me die any more than she stayed to help me escape. I saved myself, and she never even had a clue."

"It's been… twelve years? Why would you hide that long?"

Alice smiled cryptically. "I have my reasons."

AJ snorted. "You always do."

"Be nice, Anthony." Alice shot a cold grin at Brooke. "Wouldn't want to set a bad example in front of the little one."

AJ's grip on the front of Brooke's shirt tightened, and he pushed her back further.

Brooke was staring at Alice curiously. "I know you."

Her father looked down at her quickly. "What?"

"I know her. She's Ms. Shade. She was a science teacher in my school."

"A *teacher*?" AJ turned back to Alice. "You, dealing with children? How did you even get hired?"

Alice shrugged. "I'm a scientist who is very good at lying. It wasn't very difficult." She narrowed her eyes slightly. "Since I knew I had to wait a while before I could reveal myself, I figured it would be the best place to keep an eye on your family. Just in case."

"In case it hasn't been made abundantly clear, if you come *near* my family, Cass will—"

Alice's sharp bark of a laugh interrupted him. "Anthony, please. I know what Tess is capable of. All I want to know is where I can find Alix."

It was AJ's turn to laugh. "If you think I'll tell you that, you're out of your mind."

The woman's trademark smile— the one that disguised itself as polite but told you that you were treading dangerously —formed on her face. "I'm only going to ask you one more time, Anthony. Don't make a mistake you'll regret. Where. Is. Alix. Tolvaj?"

"I already told you, I'm not—"

Alice pulled a gun from behind her back and shot him. AJ tried to support himself against the desk but failed, collapsing onto the floor in front of Brooke as a look of shock spread over his face.

Alice watched him fall impassively. "I warned you not to make a mistake," she said in a flat voice. "Finn!"

A teenage girl walked into the room. She was tall, with white-blonde hair and dark brown eyes. "Yes, ma'am?" the girl asked in a quiet, terse voice.

"Put these two in the storage room in the hall. Make sure you tie them up and barricade the door." Alice's gaze went back to AJ and Brooke, and she gave an almost gleeful smile. "Maybe if they're lucky, someone will find them before Anthony bleeds to death in front of his own child."

In Casey's empty bar, Cass and Casey sat across from each other at a table. Casey was nursing another glass of scotch, while Cass quietly read Diana van der Aart's diary.

"Why are you wasting your time with that thing, Cass?" Casey asked.

"I want to know," Cass replied simply.

"Be careful what you wish for."

Cass set the diary down on the table. "Casey, why don't you tell me what's really bothering you about this?"

"Uh, how about the fact that John Wechsler was a psychopath and also apparently my father?"

Cass gave a thin smile. "You're avoiding."

"That's your specialty, so maybe it's a family trait," Casey said sarcastically. She finished off her glass and set it down on the table slowly, sighing. "You know, I'm forty-four. I thought I was forty-six, but apparently my birthday is January 26, 2031, not January 26, 2029."

"Well, you're actually younger than Zach,

which I'm sure you can mock him about."

"That's not the point, Cass!" Casey snapped. "My mother lied to me about so much that I don't even know how old I am!" She looked down at her hands, which were clenched into fists so tightly that her knuckles were white. "The thing is, Cass, John Wechsler being my father isn't even the thing that I'm most upset about. To be honest, as soon as I found out that my mother had worked with him, I... I had my suspicions, whether I wanted to actually think about them or not. But having it *proven*? It..." Casey took off her glasses, pinched the bridge of her nose, and closed her eyes. "When my mother told us that she left you there, left you with your father, I hated her. I hated her more than I've ever hated anyone, but at least I could explain it— not excuse it, but explain it —by her reasoning that John Wechsler was your father and he could do with you as he pleased."

Casey swallowed and met Cass's gaze, her blue eyes shining as if she was close to tears. "But that's bullshit, isn't it? If that was her reasoning, *she should've left me too*."

Cass was silent for a few seconds. "You wouldn't have wanted that. *I* wouldn't have wanted that."

"I know. But we both were born to the hell that was John Wechsler, and you're the only one of us who had to suffer for it."

"Casey..." Cass whispered.

115

"I'm going to go get another drink," Casey muttered. She stood up and walked over towards the bar counter.

While she was gone, Cass sat still for a long moment. Then something dawned on her, and she pulled out her phone and checked it. She bit her lip as Casey joined her again.

"What's wrong?" Casey asked.

"I haven't heard from AJ in a while."

Casey gave a soft laugh. "It's been like three hours. If you're checking in with him that often, I'm not sure your marriage is as strong as we all thought."

"It's June 16th, Casey," Cass said quietly.

"Oh." Casey paled. "That's the only date when it's okay for him to talk to you every hour."

Cass fidgeted with her wedding ring. "And he does, every year."

"Okay, you're both idiots, and I'm never going to stop thinking that." Casey stood up and set her glass of scotch down on the table. "But I agree with you that this is weird. Come on."

The Heroics base was quieter than Cass had ever seen it. "Something's not right," she said uneasily.

"Who all was still here when we left?" Casey asked.

"AJ, Alix, Brooke, and Aubrey." Cass's hands tightened into fists and her voice went hoarse. "Case, the girls are here."

"Don't panic. Maybe they all just went out, and AJ decided to be an idiot for the first time in eleven years."

"I really hope you're right," Cass whispered.

Casey rested a hand on Cass's shoulder. "Hey. Let's just take a look around, okay?"

Cass nodded and headed towards the control room. She had barely taken a step inside when she came back out. "C-Casey?"

Casey heard the fear in Cass's voice, and she was at her side in an instant. There was small pool of blood on the control room floor. Casey gripped Cass's hand tightly and pulled her so that she wasn't looking at the blood. She put her free hand on Cass's shoulder. "Don't lose focus, Cassidy." She was relieved to see that despite the way Cass was shaking, her gray eyes were solid metal.

"I'm not going to lose focus. But I have a really bad feeling about this, and I'm going to figure out what the hell is going on."

"We both are," Casey said with a smile.

As they walked through the base, Cass pulled a handgun out from a holster at the small of her back. Casey gave her an incredulous look. "Are you serious?"

"What? Are you really that surprised?"

"I shouldn't be, but I honestly am a bit. How long have you been keeping that there?"

Cass shrugged. "Ever since the murders

117

started up. I figured it would be a good idea."

"You can beat the crap out of almost anybody."

"Ah, yes, but that is only helpful if they come close enough for me to be able to."

Casey paused. "Fair enough."

As they came up to the storage closet, they saw that a chair was in front of the door. Cass frowned. "What the hell?"

There was a loud banging sound on the door. Casey and Cass exchanged a glance. "What do you think?" Casey asked.

"I don't know."

A small voice came from behind the door. "M-Mom? Aunt Casey?"

"*Brooke*?" Cass quickly put her gun back in its holster as Casey, looking stunned, opened the door.

Brooke immediately burst out of the room and practically tackled Cass, hugging her tightly around the waist and sobbing. "Daddy's hurt," she managed, her voice muffled by Cass's shirt.

Cass felt herself go pale. "What?"

Casey walked into the storage room, but Cass forced herself to stay where she was. She gently pulled Brooke away and knelt down in front of her. "Are you okay, baby?"

Brooke opened her mouth to speak, but no sound came out. She put her arms around Cass's neck and hugged her again, still crying.

Inside the storage room, Casey found AJ

sitting on the floor, his hands zip-tied to one of the shelving units. He had a blood-soaked towel duct-taped to his left shoulder. He was conscious and staring up at her with a scared and furious look in his eyes.

"Is Brooke okay?" he asked, his voice low and hoarse.

"I don't know. She's with Cass." Casey crouched down next to AJ and pulled a pocketknife out of her boot. As she cut the zip-ties off of his wrists, she said, "Are *you* okay?"

"Not really." AJ got to his feet shakily.

Casey grabbed his good shoulder. "Whoa, AJ. Wait a minute. Slow down." Since he ignored her, she helped him out of the room.

When Cass saw him, whatever color was left in her face drained. "What happened to you?" she demanded.

AJ leaned against the wall and sat down, looking exhausted. "I got shot."

Brooke, her face still buried in Cass's shirt, whimpered. Cass's grip on her tightened. "Who shot you?"

There was a pause as AJ put pressure on the towel taped to his shirt. "Alice Cage."

Casey and Cass exchanged a glance.

"I know it sounds crazy, but I swear to you, it was her."

"Why don't we get you stitched up, and then we'll talk about what happened, okay?" Casey held out a hand to help AJ back onto his feet. "Also, where are Alix and Aubrey?"

"They went out," AJ said with a grunt of pain as he stood up again.

Casey nodded. "I'll call them."

Alix grinned as she watched Aubrey struggle to get the last possible drops out of her milkshake. "I think you're done there, kid."

"I'm not done until I give up," Aubrey retorted.

"Oo, boy, if that ain't the Hamil family motto."

Aubrey stirred her straw around her glass. "You're worried about me, aren't you?"

Alix took a slow sip of her soda before responding. "I don't know what you mean."

The girl gave an irritated sigh, and despite the difference in hair color, she suddenly looked strikingly like her mother before her eyes had changed to gray. "You *do* know, Al."

"Yeah, I do." Alix reached across the table and gently flicked a strand of hair out of Aubrey's face. "It's my job to worry about you. You're a kid."

Aubrey paused. "If you can worry about me, can I worry about you?"

Alix's own words echoed in her head. *I don't have kids to bring down with me when I implode.* "I can't stop you, but try not to, okay, Aubrey? You shouldn't have to worry about me. You shouldn't have to worry about things a whole heck of a lot older than you are."

"Knowing us, I don't think I'll have a choice," Aubrey said ominously.

As if on cue, Alix's phone rang. She looked down at the caller ID and then looked up at Aubrey suspiciously. "Are we sure you don't have powers?"

Aubrey shrugged and took a drink from the dregs of her milkshake as if it was alcohol. "Mom said I'm too much Dad's kid for that to be true. I don't know what that means, though."

Alix gave a small laugh. "All you need to know is that it's true." She answered the phone. "What's up, Casey?"

Alix listened in stunned horror as Casey detailed what had happened. "I'll be home as soon as I can," she said.

As she hung up, Aubrey asked, "What's going on?"

"I'm not completely sure. I need to go back to the mansion, but just in case, I'm going to drop you off at Zach's, where your brother is. Okay?"

Aubrey looked nervous, but she nodded. "Whatever you need."

"Good girl. Let's go."

Cass stood still in the middle of the medical bay with her arms folded across her chest, as AJ delicately maneuvered his navy blue Heroics t-shirt on without moving his damaged shoulder. "We figured that at least one of us would end up getting injured on one of our wedding anniversaries," he joked. His wife didn't seem to see the humor, as she just stood there in silence for a moment before turning on her heel and heading for the door. "Where do you think you're going?" AJ called after her.

"I'm going to kill Alice Cage."

"Don't even *think* about charging off out there half-cocked. We need to talk about this."

"I'm not very good at talking," Cass replied briskly as she turned back towards him. Her expression softened when she noticed Brooke, curled up in Alix's lap and staring up at her mother with wide, scared eyes. Cass swallowed. "Brooke, could you go upstairs for a few minutes, please?"

"I think she should stay," Alix said, before Brooke could get up.

"Why?"

Alix held Cass's gaze steadily. "You think better when you have to be an example."

"Please," Cass whispered.

She and Alix stared at each other for a long moment before Alix looked down at Brooke. "Your dad hid the cookies in the cereal cabinet behind the boring fiber cereal. Why don't you go get a few?"

Brooke nodded and left the room. Alix glanced at Cass. "The fact that she's not talking is concerning to me."

"That's why I wanted her to leave. I don't

feel like traumatizing her any more today."

"And getting yourself killed won't traumatize her? You know what happened the last time you got reckless, Cass."

Cass rubbed her wrist absentmindedly. "Yeah, Al, I know that, but I vote we take Cage out before we have to deal with whatever the hell she's planning."

"Do I get some say in this, seeing as I'm the one who took a bullet?" AJ asked.

Cass's jaw twitched, but she nodded at him. He stood up carefully. "I'm not saying that we should sit around and wait for her to kill us all. I'm saying that we have absolutely no idea where she is, we don't even know why she's still alive, and we need to take this slow or we'll be getting nowhere fast."

"I know that."

Alix scoffed. "I should hope so, or you'd look like a damn idiot."

"I'm not an idiot," Cass grumbled.

"A case could be made. You did marry AJ."

Cass narrowed her eyes. "If I can't kill Alice, can I at least punch Alix?"

"No," AJ said, smilingly slightly. He kissed Cass on the cheek. "I'm okay. Isn't that the important thing for right now?"

"Yeah." Cass hugged him lightly, avoiding his injured arm. As she helped him put his left arm in a sling, she said, "You scared the hell out of me. And to make it worse, I knew the girls were here, and—"

"Everyone is alright," AJ interrupted gently. "The bullet just went through muscle and didn't hit anything that won't heal fairly quickly. Brooke wasn't hurt. Aubrey wasn't even here. We're okay."

Cass nodded and let him go. She sat down next to Alix shakily, still looking pale. "When Casey gets back, we'll need to know exactly what happened."

"Luckily, Casey is back," Casey said as she walked into the room. "I filled the others in. Zach is on his way over here with the kids. Aubrey knew something was wrong, and you know how persuasive she and Jacob can be if properly motivated. Kate and Niall are going to check on all of the other Heroics families to make sure Alice didn't make any more house calls. The others are going to finish up their regular patrol and then do a sweep through the whole city to see if they find any traces of mad scientist."

"Good." AJ sat down on the exam table again. "I'm honestly not sure what happened. I was talking to Brooke in the control room, and Alice just showed up out of nowhere. I thought I was imagining things. She postured a bit, bragged about not being dead, made her usual threats. She was looking for you, Alix."

Alix made a derisive sound. "Probably so that she can put a bullet in my head, although that would probably be too quick for her."

"I told her that I didn't know where you were— which was true, in fairness to me —and she apparently didn't like that answer because she shot me. Then she had some minion of hers tie me up and put me in the storage closet."

"What minion?" Casey asked curiously.

AJ shrugged, winced, and said, "Some girl. Alice called her Finn."

Cass's eyes widened. "Teenager? Pale blond hair? Brown eyes?"

"Yes. How did you...?"

"That's the girl who gave the names to Clarice."

AJ gave a low whistle. "Well, I think some of these dots are starting to connect, then. The girl was odd, though."

Alix frowned. "What about her was odd?"

"Alice basically told her to tie me and Brooke both up and leave me to bleed to death in the storage room, but she's the one who put that towel on my wound, and she refused to put those zip-ties on Brooke." AJ's brow furrowed. "She seemed almost... *apologetic* when she locked us in. That seems a bit strange for someone working for Alice Cage. No offense, Alix."

"None taken," Alix replied. "I agree. Especially if she's been isolated and working for Cage for a few years. By now, the sense of humanity should've been tortured out of her."

"Who she is and whether she has a conscience isn't important right now," Casey said. "What *is* important is that we find out why Alice wants Alix and why she decided to show up now."

"What's more important for *me*," AJ said as he stood up again, "is making sure my daughter is okay."

"Of course."

Zach walked into the room, looking worried. "You still in one piece, brother?"

AJ chuckled as Zach gave him a quick hug. "For the most part."

"I keep telling you that base work is more dangerous than field work. Especially if your shirt says 'Heroics' on it. You guys need hazard pay."

"Hold on; let me check with my payroll."

Before AJ's gaze had even shifted to Cass, she said, "Not a chance in hell."

AJ smiled slightly. "Where are Aubrey and Jacob?" he asked Zach.

"They found Brooke in the kitchen, and they all went up to her room."

"Good. I should talk to all of them together. Do Aubrey and Jacob know what happened?"

Zach nodded. "Aubrey pried it out of me. That kid is terrifying sometimes."

"I know. She's great, isn't she?" Alix sounded almost proud.

"Al, what are you teaching my children?" Cass asked in an accusing tone.

"Honestly, if anything they teach *me*

things."

Cass sighed. "Come on, AJ."

Once she and AJ had left the room, Alix said, "What do you need me to do, Casey?"

Casey seemed to be avoiding looking at Alix. "I don't know, Alix. Just try to stay away from your creator, if you can handle that."

Confused by the jab, Alix frowned. "Y-Yeah, I can."

"Good." Casey turned and walked out of the room.

"What was that about?" Zach asked.

"I-I don't know," Alix admitted.

Zach put a hand on Alix's shoulder. "I wouldn't take it personally. She's stressed out right now."

An odd shiver ran through Alix's body. "Gee," she said dryly. "I wonder why."

"Do you want to tell me what that was about?" Zach asked as he caught up to Casey.

"Where's Logan?"

"She's taking a nap in her room. You're avoiding my question."

Casey walked into the control room, stepping over the pool of AJ's blood that hadn't been cleaned up yet. "I didn't hear your question."

"I asked if you wanted to tell me why you were being so short with Alix."

"I don't know what you're talking about."

Zach scoffed. "I find that hard to

believe."

"What do you want from me, Zach?" Casey demanded, turning on her heel to glare at him.

"I... just want to make sure you're alright. You seem stressed."

Casey gave a loud, almost crazed laugh. "Oh, I do? I haven't the faintest clue why I'd be stressed right now."

"Hey." Zach put his hands on her shoulders. "What's going on with you?"

"I don't have time to explain it to you." Casey pulled away from him roughly and sat down at the keyboard. "I'm going to check in with the others. Why don't you try being useful and actually go out and do your damn job, Kov?"

Zach stared at her for a moment. "Alright. I will." His voice lowered. "But you can talk to me about anything, Casey. I hope you know that." He turned and left the room.

Once he had been gone for a few minutes, the weight of the day caught up to Casey. She took in a shaky breath, put her head in her hands, and started to cry.

In the elevator up to the third floor, AJ glanced at Cass, who was rubbing her left wrist. "I'm okay, you know," he said quietly.

"Yeah, well, you'll have to convince your children of that," she retorted.

"I will. But I want to make sure you're

okay."

"Oh, I'm great. I'm perfect."

AJ turned to her and put a hand on her cheek. "Cass, I'm okay." He kissed her lightly. "I'm okay."

She stared at him, her eyes watery. "How many times are you going to say that?"

"As many times as it takes for you to believe it."

Cass put her arms around his neck. "You're really okay?"

"I'm okay."

"Alright. And if you say okay again, I'm going to kill you."

AJ grinned. "Okay."

Cass rolled her eyes and kissed him before resting her forehead against his. "Don't do that to me again, AJ. I don't know how to raise our kids without you. I don't know how to…" She paused, swallowing. "You saved my life, AJ. I don't know what would happen if I lost you."

"I didn't save your life, Cass," AJ murmured. "You saved your own life. All I did was help you believe that you could." He lifted his head to look at her. "And don't worry. You won't be losing me that easily. I'm not going anywhere. Okay?"

Cass chuckled quietly. "I'm going to kill you."

"That would be counterproductive, now wouldn't it?"

She kissed him again. "Don't try to logic me out of it, Hamil. It's already too late for you."

AJ laughed. "Cass, it was too late for me the day I met you. Just hadn't quite figured it out yet."

As they stepped out of the elevator, AJ said, "Would you mind if I had a few minutes to talk to them myself?"

"Go ahead. I understand. Just don't say anything stupid."

"*I'm* talking to them, not you."

Cass gave an irritated sigh. "Eleven years. I've put up with eleven years of this."

"I'm pretty sure I'm worse off than you are."

"True." Cass kissed him on the cheek. "I'm going to wait out here."

"Alright." AJ took in a deep breath and walked into Brooke's room.

Brooke and Jacob were both seated on her bed. Aubrey had taken the desk chair.

"Can I talk to all three of you for a minute?" AJ asked quietly.

Aubrey glanced at Brooke, who wouldn't make eye contact. "Yeah, Daddy," she said, when her older sister didn't speak. "Sure."

"Okay." He smiled slightly, as if laughing at an inside joke, and then sat down between Jacob and Brooke.

The girl shifted away from him a bit, still

not looking at him. Jacob looked at Aubrey, confused, but she simply looked at their father and said, "What do you want to talk about, Daddy?"

AJ took in a deep breath. "I want you three to understand that I'm alright. I've been hurt before, but I'm still here. I'm still going to be here. I know that I scared you." He looked at Brooke. "I know that it was a terrible thing to have to see. But I'm alright."

"Why did that lady hurt you, Daddy?" Jacob asked.

AJ turned to him, sighing. "That woman's name is Alice Cage. She's... She's an evil person. She worked with your grandparents and your Aunt Casey's mom, and she's not my biggest fan. Alice Cage enjoys hurting people, so when I didn't give her what she wanted, she used it as an excuse to hurt me."

Aubrey swallowed. "What did she want?"

"Alix," Brooke whispered, speaking for the first time. "She wanted Alix."

"Why?" Aubrey wondered, her voice hoarse.

AJ hesitated. "Alice is Alix's mom. Since she's not a good person, Alix no longer associates with her, but sometimes Alice can't accept that. It's not Alix's fault, but that's why Alice was here."

"And that's why you got hurt," Brooke murmured.

AJ put a hand on her shoulder. "I got

hurt because Alice Cage shot me. She shot me because she's a psychopath. That's it, Brooke. It's nothing more than that."

Brooke looked up at him. "It *is* more than that. You got hurt and I couldn't do anything."

"Honey, there wasn't anything you could've done." AJ carefully pulled her into his lap. "Alright? You're a kid. You're *my* kid. It's my job to make sure you don't get hurt, not the other way around."

Brooke swallowed, tears in her eyes. "You promise you're okay?"

"I promise."

She hugged him around the neck. AJ hugged her back, glancing over at his other two children. He noticed Aubrey raise an eyebrow at Jacob, who nodded and grinned mischievously.

"Don't you dare," AJ said quickly.

"Don't dare what?" Brooke asked, confused.

"Not you. Your—"

AJ was cut off as Aubrey and Jacob tackled him and Brooke on his right side, knocking him flat on his back on Brooke's bed. As he struggled under the weight of three children, he said, "Ow! You know I did still get shot!"

"Sorry, Daddy," Aubrey said, still grinning.

"This is what I get for having children with your mother," AJ groaned.

"What on Earth is going on in here?" Cass asked as she opened the door and stepped into the bedroom. She just stood there for a moment before folding her arms across her chest. "Kids, please get off your father."

Jacob was the first one off the bed. He made his was over to Cass and stood next to her, mimicking how she was standing. "Yeah, get off Daddy!"

"Momma's boy," Aubrey muttered as she too got off the bed.

Cass gave a sharp laugh and ruffled the boy's hair. "Don't think I missed you being just as involved as the girls, J."

"Darn."

"They didn't hurt you, did they?" Cass asked, walking over to AJ.

"No; I'm fine. They kept it to my right side, thankfully."

"That was *stupid*, Aubrey!" Brooke yelled. She started towards her sister, but Cass smoothly grabbed her around the waist and pulled her back up onto the bed.

"Calm down, Brooke. Nobody got hurt, and nobody is going to try it again."

"Dad *could* have gotten hurt! He already got hurt, and Aubrey and Jacob could have hurt him *again*!" Brooke struggled against Cass's grip. "They shouldn't have done that! They shouldn't have! They..." She broke down into tears in Cass's lap.

Cass gently ran her hand up and down

Brooke's arm soothingly. "Shh. It's okay. It's alright." She shot a helpless glance at AJ over her daughter's head, but he looked to be at a loss for what to do as well.

Aubrey and Jacob, stunned, made their way back over and got onto the bed next to their father. And for a long time they all just sat there in silence, only interrupted by Brooke's sobs.

11

Over the next four days, the Heroics team attempted to get itself back to a routine, with the added task of looking for Alice Cage. While most of the team, including Kate, did their best to keep everything as normal as possible, two members seemed to have broken completely.

Alix had locked herself in her room since AJ's shooting. Whether she had slipped out using her powers was unknown, but since any time someone knocked on her door she threw something at it, the assumption was that she hadn't.

Casey had been staying in the apartment she kept over her bar. Since she, Cass, AJ, and Zach basically shared responsibilities for all four children living in the mansion, it hadn't caused any particular problems with Logan, but that fact didn't make anyone feel better. Everyone seemed to have figured out that Cass knew exactly what was going on with Casey, but she refused to tell them anything.

An hour before the bar opened, Casey sat across from Kaita at the counter, finishing a glass of scotch.

"How many of those have you had today?" Kaita asked quietly.

"Does it matter?" Casey asked, her voice low and bitter.

Kaita finished stacking glasses and leaned on the bar. "Yeah, Casey, it does."

"I'm not a drunk, Kaita," Casey grumbled.

"No, I've seen drunks. You're not a drunk. You're a bar owner with issues who is trying to hide them and using your job as a way to do it. Having quick access to a lot of alcohol definitely makes drinking your problems away easier, but you shouldn't be taking advantage of that. I don't know what your issues are, Casey, but take it from someone who knows. This isn't the way to hide from them."

Casey stared silently at her empty glass for several seconds. "Do you know who John Wechsler was?"

"The psycho who wanted to murder all the heroes?"

"Yeah," Casey said shortly, flinching.

"What about him?"

"I just found out that he was my father."

Kaita stared at her for a long moment before taking her glass and refilling it. "I still don't approve of your methods," she said softly, "but I'll give you this one."

Justin opened his bedroom door quietly. His patrol had gone long, and he knew that his wife, Erin, a teacher and soccer coach at the local high school, would be taking advantage of the summer vacation and would already be in bed.

As he fumbled through the room in an attempt to get changed, he heard Erin ask, "Is everything okay?"

Justin jerked in surprised, smacking his knee into the dresser. He mumbled a curse and then whispered, "I thought you were asleep."

Erin turned on the light on the nightstand and sat up. She was in pajamas but didn't look like she had been sleeping, as her glasses were on and her blonde hair was still neatly in a ponytail. "It's hard to sleep when you don't come home and don't call."

"I'm sorry." Justin sat down on the edge of the bed and rubbed the back of his neck tiredly. "I should've called."

"Yeah, you should've, but I'm not all that surprised that you didn't." Erin shifted forward and rubbed the spot on his neck that he had been touching. "You've been distracted recently."

"There's just so much going on, and this past week has added so much more on top of it." Justin sighed. "Kate's working with us, but she's not all there. I think Casey's developing a drinking problem and I don't know why. Alix has lost her goddamn mind. AJ went and got himself shot." He shook his head slowly. "This whole team is going to hell."

"You've survived worse."

"We have, but I'm not sure that will be true by the time Alice is done with us."

Erin kissed his cheek. "You beat her

once. You can beat her again."

"At what cost, Er? We have families now. We have people she can use against us. What if..." Justin swallowed. "What if she goes after you and Riley? I don't know what I'd do if something happened to either of you."

"Nothing's going to happen to us, Justin." Erin lightly slapped him on the back of the head. "And do you really think I'd let her do anything to Riley?"

Justin didn't smile. "I know that you wouldn't, Erin, but this woman is dangerous."

"I'm aware of that." Erin ran her fingers up and down Justin's spine. "I'm running out of ways to make you feel better, though."

He laughed. "I appreciate the effort, babe."

"You had better," Erin teased.

Justin turned so that he was facing her and kissed her. "Can you promise me something? Can you promise me that if anything happens, you'll take Riley and run like hell?"

Erin rested a hand on his cheek. "I promise." She pulled him towards her to kiss him again. "Just as long as you promise to keep coming back," she whispered.

"Getting shot hurts a hell of a lot more than I'm pretending it does," AJ murmured as he lay in bed next to Cass.

She gave a soft laugh. "Trust me; I

know."

AJ traced a finger over the bullet scar on her chest that she had obtained years ago courtesy of John Wechsler. "I'll never understand why he did that to you."

"He was a complicated man," Cass said quietly.

"I know that, but…" AJ lowered his hand so that he could interlace his fingers with hers. "I don't know how someone could point a gun at their own child at all, let alone pull the trigger. The thought of doing that to one of the kids just—" His voice cracked slightly. "It makes me feel honestly sick."

"That's because you are a much, *much* better father to our children than John Wechsler ever was to… to me." Cass stared up at the ceiling for a long moment. "AJ, I need to tell you something. I shouldn't, but I can't keep things from you. I just can't do it."

"What is it?"

Cass hesitated. "My father was Casey's father, too."

AJ looked at her quickly, startled. "*What*?"

"Casey found her birth certificate and her mother's old diary in a box in Alix's room. John Wechsler was her father."

AJ was silent for a few seconds. "Well, that explains a lot."

Cass elbowed him gently in the side. "It's not funny, AJ."

"I'm not saying it is. But it explains why you two look a bit similar. It explains why you act similar. It explains why Casey hasn't left her bar in... what is it, five days now?"

"She's scared," Cass admitted. "I don't know if she even realizes it, but she's scared."

"Why? You proved that someone with Wechsler's blood could be a good person and could live a good life."

"Yes, but while my mother was far from the greatest person in the world, she loved me. She loved me, and she died trying to protect me. Casey's not all that sure she can say the same about her mother, especially not after everything she did." Cass gave a small, sad sigh. "I think she's afraid that she isn't strong enough to fight all of the bad blood that's building up in her."

"Casey's one of the strongest people we know," AJ commented.

"Stubbornness isn't strength," Cass pointed out. She rested her head on AJ's good shoulder and closed her eyes. "And trust me when I say that just because you have that strength, it doesn't mean you believe it can save you."

"What are you going to do?"

"Today? Try to drag Alix out of her room, literally if necessary. And I'm going to call Zach and tell him to stop being a coward and go drag Casey out of her bar."

"Offensive approach. I like it."

"Good. Because while I'm hitting Alix upside the head, you get to be in charge of all four children."

AJ's hand went to his neck as if to adjust a tie he wasn't wearing. "Oh. Wonderful." He sighed. "At least Logan won't be a problem."

"Logan is never a problem."

"I doubt that will last, though. Her parents are both sarcastic jackasses, as are at least two of her cousins and both of us. There's not much hope for her."

Cass shrugged. "Then you should appreciate her good behavior while you can."

"I will." AJ kissed her on the top of the head. "And you make sure that you aren't too harsh on Alix. You know that Alice being back isn't going to help whatever is going on with her."

"I know. I'll be as nice as I can."

AJ scoffed. "Poor Alix."

Cass elbowed him again. "You should watch your mouth."

"You won't hurt me. I was shot."

"Don't remind me," Cass said. She kissed him on the cheek before getting up and heading towards the bathroom to shower.

AJ watched her go and then rested his head back down on the pillow. "I don't like to," he said quietly to the empty room.

Cass did end up almost literally dragging Alix out of her bedroom. The confrontation involved ten minutes of Cass banging on Alix's door, lots of yelling, and an intervention from Kara to prevent Cass from getting teleported to the next state. After about a half hour of arguing, Kara took Alix on a patrol to get her out of the mansion and away from Cass, while Cass went to the gun range to vent her frustration.

"Cass is just worried about you, Al," Kara said as she and Alix jumped from one rooftop to another.

"I'm fine," Alix replied grumpily.

"We both know that's not true."

Alix tightened a trembling hand into a fist. "I'm so close, Kara. I'm so close to figuring out how to fix this."

"I really hope you are, Alix. You're a pain in the ass, but you're *our* pain in the ass, and we aren't going to lose you without a damn good fight first."

"Trust me, I'm not going to let that happen."

Kara lightly slapped Alix on the back. "You had better not, Thief. You had better not."

"Caito, can I ask you a question?"

Caito looked at Tag, a sigh clear in his eyes. "What do you want, Tag?"

"Why are we only killing normal people? Why not kill a few empowered people? I know why we aren't killing anyone from Legion, but there are other empowereds out there. Fine, you have some pathological fear of killing the Heroics idiots, whatever. But give me a challenge! Normal people don't stand a chance against me."

"Oh, really? You honestly believe you could survive a fight against Sarah Ajam?"

Tag's confident expression twitched slightly. "I-I *know* I can."

"Clearly, given the way you're stammering like a fool right now." Caito set his paper down. "Mind your place, Warren. Don't question my plans."

"My, my," a female voice said from the doorway. "Losing control of your underlings, Edward?"

Caito and Tag looked over at the gray hair who had walked into their base of operations. Spheres of light immediately formed in Tag's hand. "Who the hell are you?" he demanded.

The woman looked bored. "Edward, please tell your dog to heel."

"Back off, Tag," Caito said dangerously.

Tag turned to his boss. "But—"

"*Back. Off.*"

Tag immediately extinguished the constructs in his hand. "Y-Yes, sir."

Caito stood and smiled at the woman. "Alice Cage. It's been a long time."

"Indeed it has." Alice glanced at Tag. "I see your choice in muscle hasn't improved."

"He has his advantages."

"Hm. Not many, I'd imagine."

Tag hadn't even heard the insult. He was too busy staring stupidly at the woman. "You're *Alice Cage*?"

Alice raised an eyebrow. "Takes him a while to catch up, huh?"

"I thought you got blown up," Tag said.

She gave an irritated sigh. "No. I didn't."

"Alice is the one who has a claim on Heroics," Caito said. "She's had a claim on them for years, so I figured that she has a right to continue it."

Tag seemed to regain himself, as he scoffed, "She didn't do a very good job of killing them before. What makes her think she can kill them now?"

Alice gave a cold smile. "I only failed before because my clones turned on me. One of them paid with her life. The other will pay the same price soon enough."

"It doesn't bother you at all to kill someone who is your exact duplicate?" Tag asked curiously.

"If it did, I wouldn't have already killed so many of them." Alice made a shooing motion with her hand. "Can I excuse you now?"

"Go away, Tag."

Tag gave Caito an incredulous look. "Are you serious?"

"I am."

"... Fine." Tag stormed out of the room.

"I'm surprised you haven't killed him yet, Edward," Alice commented, giving Caito a sideways glance.

Caito shrugged and took a sip from his coffee mug. "I told Sarah she could, once he was no longer needed."

"Good. She'll enjoy that."

"What do you want, Alice?"

Alice folded her arms across her chest. "I wanted to ensure that our deal regarding Heroics and the Security Legion was still in effect."

"Of course. Have they found out that you're alive yet?"

"Yes. It was enjoyable. I shot one of the Heroics base members a few days ago. I didn't kill him because that wasn't the point of the exercise— fear was —but it was enjoyable nonetheless."

"Good." Caito drummed his fingers against his mug. "Let me know if I can do anything for you, Alice. You've been quite helpful to me, so I'd like to continue returning the favor."

"Trust me, Edward. If I need anything from you, I'll expect you to provide it." Alice gave him the same cold smile she had given Tag and left the base.

When Zach walked into Casey's bar, Kaita made eye contact with him immediately and nodded toward the door that led to

Casey's apartment. Zach nodded back at her and headed upstairs. Casey was sitting on the couch, idly swirling scotch around in a glass.

"From what I hear, you've had a lot of that."

"It works," Casey said simply.

"You don't seem drunk, so you can apparently handle it very well."

"I've been spreading it out."

"Good. You always could hold your liquor, though, so I guess I shouldn't be surprised even if you hadn't been."

Casey gave a small sigh. "If you don't get to the point, Zach, I'm going to lose my hold on this particular glass of liquor and send it directly at your head."

"I don't think you'd waste a perfectly good piece of glassware on my skull."

"Don't test me," Casey muttered as she took a sip of her scotch.

Zach sat down on the couch and took the glass from her. He took a moment to finish off what was left, before saying, "Do you want to give me that explanation now?"

To his surprise, she didn't react to his taking her drink. "I don't think you want the explanation, Zach. For any of it."

"You're wrong about that." Zach set the glass down on a nearby table. "Casey, I love you. Whatever the problem is, whatever's wrong, whatever you're going through, it's not going to change that."

"I'm not so sure," Casey whispered.

"Casey, please."

For a long moment, she just sat in silence, staring down at her hands. Then, in a voice that was almost inaudible, she said, "John Wechsler was my..." She cleared her throat. "John Wechsler was my biological father."

A thousand questions ran through Zach's head, but when he saw that she was shaking, he decided not to ask any of them. "It's going to be okay, Case," he said gently.

"How? How can it possibly be okay? For hell's sake, Zach! It was bad enough that Diana van der Aart was my mother, but now I have John Wechsler's blood, too? At least Cass's mother gave a damn about *somebody*. I have nothing. All I get are sociopaths and psychopaths." Casey rested her head in her hands. "God, Zach, I'm so sorry. Half of your kid's DNA is that of sociopaths and psychopaths."

"No," Zach said firmly. "Half of my kid's DNA is that of a brilliant, strong-willed woman who is far better than either of her parents ever were."

Casey lowered her hands slowly. "How can you be okay with this?"

"Because it doesn't change you," Zach replied. "It doesn't change who you are as a person, as a member of Heroics, as a mother, as the woman I'm in love with. You get to choose whether you want to follow your blood, Casey, and you never have. So don't doubt yourself now."

There was a pause. "You know, Zach, you aren't half bad at pep talks," Casey finally admitted with a quiet chuckle.

Zach grinned. "I try my best."

Casey closed her eyes for a brief moment. When she opened them again, she said, "I need one more night away from the mansion. I just... I just need one more night."

"That's okay."

Casey gave him a sideways glance. "Would you... stay with me?"

"Yeah," Zach said softly. "Yeah, I'll stay with you."

"I think we can head back to the mansion," Kara said as she finished tying up a woman that she and Alix had caught picking pockets in the center of the city.

"Sounds good to me," Alix replied.

They started to walk towards Fuego Village, ignoring the glances and glares from the people around them.

"I see that everyone is still pissed at us for something that isn't our fault," Alix muttered as she adjusted her navy blue sunglasses.

Kara fidgeted with the collar of her maroon vest. "I don't think that's going to change until people stop dying."

Alix gave a dry laugh. "This is Caotico. What are the odds of that happening?"

"Fairly decent, if you ask the right person, I'd say, Thief."

Kara and Alix turned to look down an alley that they were walking past. A young blonde-haired woman in a black combat outfit was leaning against a building.

"Who are you?" Kara demanded.

"My name is Finn," the girl replied. "My employer sent me for Alix Tolvaj." Her gaze flicked to Alix. "And I'd appreciate it if you'd come with me."

"You work for Alice," Alix said.

"Yes."

Kara's hands tightened into fists. "Why the hell would Alix go with you?"

"I have no interest in fighting you, Pilot. Ms. Cage only wishes to speak with Ms. Tolvaj."

"Oh, of course," Kara said sarcastically. "I totally believe that."

Alix narrowed her eyes, studying Finn in silence for a moment. "It's okay, Kara."

"Are you out of your goddamn mind? You aren't seriously thinking about *going with her*."

"Look, we need all of the information we can get," Alix said in a quiet voice. "It's not ideal, Kara, but it's a plan."

"What if she decides to just shoot you?"

Alix smiled thinly. "My powers might

weaken me, but they aren't weakening. I'll be fine."

Kara took in a deep breath. "I don't like it, Al."

"I know. You don't have to."

Kara shot a glare at Finn. "If Alix isn't back in an hour, I'm going to hunt you down and make you take me to Alice Cage yourself. And you aren't going to enjoy the trip. Got that?"

It was impossible to read the blank look in Finn's eyes. "I understand."

Instead of meeting with Alice Cage in her territory, Alix moved her with shadows to neutral ground on a rooftop in the northern district of Caotico. When Alice reformed, she irritably straightened her shirt.

"That was hardly necessary, girl," she growled.

"I'll be the judge of that," Alix said coldly. "Give me one good reason why I shouldn't haul you to the nearest police station."

Alice put a hand over her heart as if she was hurt. "Why, I've done nothing wrong."

Alix laughed. "I'm pretty sure all the evidence of the crimes you and John Wechsler committed prove otherwise."

"Ah. But you see, Alix, there's a tiny flaw in your plan. According to all databases in Caotico City, I'm not the person who committed those crimes. According to all databases in Caotico City, I'm Ada Shade, schoolteacher." Alice smiled. "You can't prove that I'm Alice Cage."

"Fine then," Alix snarled. "If I can't touch you, why don't you tell me what you want from me? Besides the obvious death part."

Alice put her hands in her pockets and began to pace slowly. "I'd like to offer my assistance in catching this horrible murderer."

"No thanks," Alix said immediately.

"I think I can help you quite a bit, Alix."

"Why would you want to?"

Alice gave a dramatic sigh. "Well, Alix, this killer is targeting the innocent citizens of Caotico City. As a fellow innocent citizen of this city, I feel that it is my duty to do the best I can to bring this menace to justice."

Alix snorted. "You're far from an innocent citizen, Alice. And I didn't see you caring much for innocent citizens when you set those empowered people on the city."

"Those actions were performed by John Wechsler and his Alumni band. Not me."

"I'm sure." Alix took a small step towards Alice. "I wouldn't take your help if I was moments away from dying. And if you think I'd ever buy the idea that you've done nothing wrong, you're a fool. You tortured me. You tortured my best friend. I know you've done much, much more than that." Alix moved forward quickly and punched Alice in the face, knocking her down. "That's for shooting AJ in front of Brooke. You're nothing but an evil old woman, Alice. I don't know what game you're playing. I don't really care. But if you come near my friends… if you come near my *family* again, I won't have any problems doing to you exactly what you did to every clone that came before me. And that's a promise." Her entire body was trembling as she turned around and disappeared into shadows.

"Are you okay, ma'am?" Finn asked, not moving from her post a few feet to the side.

"I am, no thanks to you," Alice spat as she got to her feet. "You really are *useless*, aren't you, girl?"

"I'm only as useful as you trained me to be," Finn replied.

Alice gave a sharp bark of a laugh. "That's the only thing I like about you, Finn."

"What's that, ma'am?" Finn asked curiously.

"You're a lot braver than any other underling I've ever had."

"I try, ma'am."

Alice pulled a cellphone out of her pocket and hit one of the speed dials. "Hello? This is Alice. Meet me at the warehouse tomorrow at 2100." Alice gave a thin smile. "The girl didn't take the bait, which doesn't surprise me, but that's okay. There are plenty of other ways to get what we need from Heroics."

Alix walked into the Heroics kitchen, where she found Kara pacing and Cass sitting at the table looking anxious.

"*Are you out of your goddamn mind?*" Cass demanded, on her feet in an instant.

"I'm fine, Mom," Alix replied sarcastically. Her eyes lightened and her gaze softened simultaneously when she noticed Cass rubbing her left wrist. "Cass, I'm okay. I knew what I was doing. I was prepared to get the hell out of there the entire time."

Cass grabbed her by the front of her navy vest. "Don't you *ever* do something that stupid again, do you understand me?"

"I understand."

Kara stopped pacing, diverting the nervous energy to her fingers, which began drumming against her legs. "What did Alice want?"

"Get this: She wanted to *help us* catch the serial killer."

Cass and Kara both laughed. "Did she hit her head when Allison lit that building on fire around her?" Kara asked.

"I have no idea what her deal is. I'm sure she's up to something. We'll have to watch our backs, even more so than we have been."

Aubrey wandered into the kitchen. Her face lit up when she saw Alix. "Hi there, recluse!"

"Hi there, smartass," Alix replied with a

smirk.

"Alix," Cass groaned.

"Please, as if you've never called her that before."

"I haven't!" Cass paused and looked down sheepishly. "I've called *Brooke* that..."

Alix laughed and shook her head. "Hypocrite."

Cass glanced at the clock and rested a hand on Aubrey's head. "Go to bed, kiddo."

The girl looked up at Cass and pouted. "Kara and Alix are still up."

"Do you know what Kara and Alix have in common?"

Aubrey paused. "Sexualities that make them invisible to society?"

Kara burst into loud laughter. "She has a point, Cass." She pointed at herself. "Bisexual." She pointed at Alix. "Asexual. We could have a sitcom. Hey, Al, what do you want to do with our invisibility superpowers?"

Alix raised an eyebrow at her. "Hide from all of you?"

"See? The dialogue is already written; all we need is a camera."

Cass sighed. "Aubrey, what Kara and Alix have in common is that they are both adults that don't have bedtimes."

"We probably should," Kara said.

"We *definitely* should," Alix snarked. She picked Aubrey up and put her over her shoulder. "You're getting heavy, kid."

"That's probably because I'm eight," Aubrey grumbled. "Come on, Al, you never take Mom's side."

"Yeah, and she usually looks at me like she wants to kill me. Say goodnight."

Aubrey sighed. "Okay. Goodnight, Mom and Kara."

"'Night, kid," Kara said.

"Goodnight, Aubrey." Once Alix and Aubrey were gone, Cass gave a frustrated sigh. "Why does she listen to Alix and not me?"

Kara scoffed. "You can't be serious."

Cass gave her a confused look. "What do you mean?"

Kara patted Cass on the shoulder. "Alix is the cool aunt. She could get those kids to do anything for her. You never stood a chance."

12

When Casey stepped back into the Heroics mansion, she felt a wave of anxiety rush through her. She wasn't prepared to deal with anyone else asking her what was wrong, and she had no interest in explaining it yet again.

Logan seemed to have heard the door, as she came down the stairs two at a time. Casey winced. "Log, you're going to give me a heart attack."

"What's a heart attack?"

"It's… never mind."

Logan hugged her. "Are you okay now, Mommy?"

Casey crouched down in front of her. "What do you mean?"

"Uncle AJ said you were gone so long because you were hurt and you needed some time to get better."

So Cass had finally broken and let AJ in on the secret. Casey rested a hand on Logan's cheek. "I'm not fully better, but I'm getting there."

"Good."

Zach walked into the mansion. "I hate parking my car here."

"There's an underground parking garage and a driveway that's a quarter mile long, Zach. It can't be that hard to park."

"I know. There are too many choices."

Casey rolled her eyes. "Logan, can you stay with your dad for a bit?"

"Sure, Mommy."

Zach looked wary. "What are you going to do?"

"I just need to have a conversation with a friend."

Casey opened Alix's door without knocking and found the younger woman engrossed in an equation on her whiteboard, headphones in her ears and the faint sounds of indie rock audible all the way over where Casey was standing.

"Alix. Alix! *Alix!*" Casey picked up a paperback book from a nearby table and threw it, hitting Alix in the back.

"Ow! What—" Alix turned and pulled her earbuds out, looking confused. As soon as she saw Casey, her expression went flat, and she put her marker down. "I figured you'd come to me eventually."

Casey shut the door behind her. "How long did you know? From the time you had that box, or the entire time you've known me?"

Alix leaned against an empty spot on her whiteboard. "What do you want me to say, Casey?" she asked quietly.

"I want you to tell me the truth! You've known me for over a decade! How long have you known who my father was?"

"I knew the day I met you, sort of."

"What does that even mean?"

Alix sighed. "As you know, a few of the clones whose memories are in my head were around when you, Cass, and AJ were children. The fact that you were also John's child wasn't exactly a secret. You knew that Cass was your little sister. So the knowledge was in my head, but I tried my best to ignore it."

Casey leaned back against the door. "Why?"

"You didn't want to know, Casey."

"Maybe not. But I deserved to know, didn't I?"

Alix gave a sharp bark of a laugh. "I don't know, Casey. You don't seem very capable of handling the knowledge. You did turn into an alcoholic."

"I'm not..." Casey gritted her teeth and tightened her hands into fists. "What are these boxes even from, huh? Where the hell did you even get them?"

"I saved them from the building Allison set on fire when she tried to kill me and Alice. I grabbed quite a few things from there before I left. I hid them away before I came back to the fight. But I wanted to see exactly was in these boxes before I let anyone else see anything. I knew that none of you were ready for some of the things you don't remember."

Casey gave a sarcastic laugh. "Why? It's not like anything can be worse than what we already know."

Alix's eyes darkened, and she took a few steps towards Casey. "Are you sure about that? Are you really, truly sure?"

In a resigned voice, Casey asked, "What could possibly be worse?"

"You really want to know? I'll give you a small sample. One time when Cass was eight, she politely asked John not to experiment on her. Just once. Just one break. He got so angry about the 'lack of respect' that he specifically made that day's torture more painful than necessary and forced her to suffer for an entire day before he let finally let her pass out."

Casey shivered and looked down, but Alix continued. "You were there. He made you watch, to see what happens when people disobey him. But you fought back anyway. You tried to get him to leave Cass alone. His response was to beat the hell out of you, because a deal he made with Diana prevented him from experimenting on you, but it didn't protect you from three broken ribs and the fracture that made your jaw crooked like it is."

Alix took another few steps forward, and Casey whispered, "You can stop now, Alix. I don't want to know anything more."

"I didn't think you did," Alix growled. She turned to walk away, but then paused and turned back. Her eyes were so dark they were almost black. "You came in here looking for the truth. Here it is: You're a lot like your father. You're hard-headed and arrogant. You're incapable of loving other people. Hell, you can't even tell your own *kid* that you love her. If it came down to science or your daughter, you'd pick science." Alix gave a soft chuckle. "If you're afraid of being your father, Casey, you should be terrified. Because you're a genius— and, unfortunately for you, so was your dad. And look what he did with his talent." Alix walked back over to her whiteboard. "Now get out of my room, before I throw you out."

For a moment Casey just stood there, pale and close to tears. "Alix isn't even in there anymore, is she?" she asked hoarsely. "Whatever you are, you aren't Alix Tolvaj."

"I guess I'm not," Alix replied, staring at the equation in front of her.

Casey swallowed. "Unless you find her, we're done." Shaking so badly that she could barely grip the doorknob, Casey opened the door and hurried out of the room.

Once she was gone, random shadows began to appear around Alix. She sat down on the floor, bowed her head, and didn't even try to stop them.

Kate sprinted across the rooftops of the eastern district of Caotico. She wasn't on patrol, but recent events had put her on edge and given her a buildup of nervous energy, so she was attempting to vent it by practicing her speed. After she made a particularly difficult jump from a building to one three feet taller, she found herself face-to-face to a young woman in a black combat uniform.

"Let me guess," Kate said as she caught her breath. "You're this 'Finn' everybody's talking about."

"Yes."

"What do you want?"

Finn paused, staring at her curiously. "Why do you do what you do?"

Kate blinked. "Huh?"

"Why do you do what you do? Your vigilante work, I mean."

"I-I dunno. It's what I was born to do."

"That's not a very good reason."

Kate tightened her hands into fists. "What's *your* reason for what *you* do, then?"

Finn thought for a moment. "I don't want to end up like the others."

An odd shiver ran through Kate. There was a disturbingly distant look in Finn's eyes. "What does that mean?"

"I think I'll let you figure it out."

"Then I'll let you figure out why I'm still fighting." Kate took an arrow out of the quiver on her back and aimed it at Finn. To her surprise, the girl neither moved nor looked the least bit concerned.

"Your arrows won't help you, Targeter," Finn said calmly.

"We'll see." Kate released her arrow, and it flew directly at Finn's chest.

Normally, the point of the arrow would have made contact and collapsed instantly, converting into what was basically a taser and sending an electrical shock into Finn's body. This time, however, the arrow never had a chance to make contact. Finn caught it in midair.

"What the hell?" Kate breathed.

Finn broke the arrow over her knee. "I told you, Targeter. Arrows won't help you."

Kate sent three more arrows at Finn, with the exact same result. Frustrated, Kate tossed her bow aside and took her quiver off of her back. "If you want a real fight, Finn, bring it."

"That's not going to help much, either," Finn said mildly.

Kate barely heard her, as she moved forward and threw a punch at Finn's head. Finn dodged easily, grabbed Kate's wrist, twisted her arm behind her back, kicked Kate's knees out from under her, and pulled out a knife. As quickly as the confrontation had started, it was over— with Kate on the ground, her arm painfully tight in Finn's grip, and a knife resting against her throat.

"You're right," Finn murmured. "I figured out why you fight."

"And why is that?" Kate asked through gritted teeth.

"Because you don't think you have anything else to live for." Finn put the knife away and released Kate, shoving her down onto the rooftop.

Kate pushed herself up onto her knees, massaging her shoulder. "If you work for Alice Cage, why didn't you just kill me?"

"I don't see the point," Finn said softly. "You're going to get yourself killed one of these days anyway. Why waste my conscience?"

"One of Cage's minions has a conscience?" Kate gave a sharp laugh. "I doubt that."

"You seem to forget that Alix Tolvaj was once a minion of Alice Cage as well."

"Alix was a completely different story. She had no choice."

Finn smiled thinly. "What makes you think I do?"

Before Kate could reply, Finn walked towards the ladder off of the roof, and she was gone.

13

At nine o'clock, Alice was standing in the center of an empty warehouse in the northern district. One minute after the hour, the door into the space opened, and Sarah walked in.

"You're late."

Sarah laughed. "Are you always this strict with timetables, Cage?"

"One minute can be the difference between a success and an explosion in a science experiment," Alice replied grumpily.

"Ah. Well, I'm sorry." Sarah started wandering around the warehouse, looking around. "So what's the plan, Cage? Since your clone didn't exactly jump to get help from you."

"I didn't expect her to. I just wanted to gauge her reaction to me. She was surprisingly steady, if a bit angry."

"Gee, I wonder why."

Alice smiled thinly. "True. Anyway, the plan is for you and your boss to continue killing citizens, making it as obvious as possible that the deaths are being committed by empowered people."

"That might be a bit difficult for me."

"Use your imagination. We need the public to turn on the heroes."

Sarah came to a stop a few feet in front of Alice. "May I ask why exactly the plan is to get the public to turn on the heroes? Why not just kill them all?"

"If we kill monsters that the public respects, the public will never truly see them as monsters. They'll act like we're in the wrong. The only way to destroy the empowereds for good is to ensure that no one in this city still respects them."

"Makes sense."

The door to the warehouse opened again, and Finn entered.

"What took you so long?" Alice asked irritably.

"It's a big city," Finn replied in a calm voice. "It wasn't easy to find Targeter."

"Well?"

"You have an advantage over the Heroics field team," Finn reported. "Targeter is shattered. She could barely put up a fight against me. She has almost no spark to her battle, and she gives into anger far more quickly than any leader should."

Alice nodded thoughtfully. "I thought she might have broken by now. She was always the weak one, even as a child. I was stunned when I realized she was the leader. I have no idea why Heroics has been successful for so long with her in charge." She turned to Sarah. "Make sure Caito keeps doing what he's doing. If Heroics is fracturing, now is an even better time than previously thought."

Sarah gave a short nod. "It will be done."

"Good." Alice turned back to Finn. "As for you, I have a task that you might find odd."

Finn frowned. "Oh?"

"Do you know who Casey Cabot is?"

"Yes."

Alice smirked slightly. "I need you to get some of her blood."

"If you don't let go, you're never going to get anywhere."

Erin laughed and lowered the bow and arrow she was holding, without using them. "How about I just take the arrow by itself and stab you with it?"

"You wouldn't." Justin took a small step away from her anyway and glanced at Riley, who was sound asleep in a car seat next to them. "At least, you wouldn't in front of Riley."

"She's asleep. She'd never know."

Justin rubbed the back of his neck nervously. "I love you?"

"You mostly love me because I was the only one who would put up with you." Erin aimed the arrow at the target at the other side of the room and released, sending the arrow flying into the target an inch from the center.

"Not bad." Justin pulled another arrow from the quiver sitting on a nearby table and said, "Also, not true. You utterly refused to put up with me. You were about the only girl at our college who wouldn't."

"Not the only girl at our college, just the

only girl on the soccer team." Erin paused. "Okay, maybe the only male-interested girl in the entire athletic department." She frowned thoughtfully. "You slept around a *lot* when we were in school, didn't you?"

"Only one mattered, babe."

"Ugh, that was *awful*. Why did I marry you again? It certainly wasn't for your sense of humor."

Justin handed the arrow he was holding to her. "Must've been my good looks."

"Mm. That helps." Erin took a step forward and kissed him. "I guess you're also a fairly nice guy."

"Don't tell anybody else; it'll ruin my reputation."

Erin rolled her eyes and aimed her second arrow. "You're a jackass, Justin."

"There; that's exactly what you should tell everyone else."

"Oh, don't worry. I will."

As Erin released the arrow in her hand, Justin walked over to check on Riley. "She's so quiet right now," he murmured.

"Don't jinx it. If you wake her up, I'm leaving you both here."

"I'd like to see you explain that to Casey, Cass, and AJ."

Erin laughed. "Cass and AJ have *three* kids. I think they'd understand."

"Point." Justin walked over to the target and pulled the two arrows out of it. "I'm going to put the quiver and the bow back in the armory and then we can go home."

"Alright."

As Justin headed towards the armory, he got the strange feeling that something was wrong. He paused, his grip on his bow tightening. "Is somebody there?"

"I have just as much of a right to be here as you do," Jay said lightly, exiting the exercise room.

"Sorry, Jay. I had a bad feeling."

Jay raised an eyebrow. "Justin Oliver apologizing. Sign of the apocalypse right there."

"I've apologized to you before," Justin retorted.

"Yeah, but you were usually drunk." Jay's brow furrowed, and he turned towards the armory. "Did you hear that?"

"I did," Justin replied warily.

Kate stepped out of the armory, her quiver strapped to her back and her bow in her hand. Jay relaxed. "Oh, hey, Kate. I didn't know you were here."

"Justin, I need you to fight me," Kate said, her voice hoarse.

Justin frowned. "What? Why the hell would I do that?"

"Just fight me."

"Not unless you tell me why."

"I don't need to explain anything to you! Just fight me!" Kate had a wild look in her eyes, and her entire body was shaking.

"Okay, now I am *absolutely* not going to fight you. What is wrong with you?"

Kate didn't answer. "You're going to fight me, Justin. You won't have a choice." At that, she pulled an arrow from her quiver and shot it at him.

"I'll be home in about fifteen minutes. Love you. Bye." As Kara hung up her cellphone, she noticed Ray laughing at her. "What's so funny?"

"Nothing. It's just still weird picturing you as being married."

Kara frowned. "It's been nearly two years now."

"Yeah, but in my head, you're still my twelve-year-old sister."

"That's okay; I still can't believe my fourteen-year-old brother has a four-year-old son."

Ray cringed. "It is really uncomfortable when you say it like that."

Kara smirked at him. "Yeah, it is, isn't it?"

"... Well played."

Jay supersped up to them. "We have a problem."

"Of course we do," Kara muttered.

Ray shot her a look before saying, "What's wrong, Jay?"

"Kate and Justin are downstairs

fighting."

Neither Kara nor Ray had much of a reaction. "Isn't that a fight we all saw coming?" Kara asked.

Jay gritted his teeth, frustrated. "You don't understand! Kate *attacked* Justin! She. Is. Using. *Arrows.*"

Kara and Ray exchanged an alarmed glance.

"Okay, yeah, let's go put a stop to this," Ray said quickly.

"Definitely for the best," Kara agreed, following him towards the elevator.

"That's what I was saying," Jay mumbled as he headed after them.

When they got downstairs, they found that their assistance wasn't necessary. Kate was on her back on the floor, and Justin was standing over her with a taser arrow aimed at her chest. Erin, hovering off to the side, was watching them with a worried look on her face.

"Enough, Kate," Justin was saying as the others arrived. "That's enough. You've lost."

"No," Kate whispered. "I can't have. I can't. I can't have."

"Kate," Justin murmured, his voice surprisingly gentle. "Please, Kate. Stop this."

"I can't." Kate tried to reach for her bow, which was lying on the floor about a foot away from her.

Justin released the arrow in his hand and

let it hit Kate directly in the chest. She went ridged for a moment and then collapsed, unconscious.

"*Justin!*" Erin yelled.

"It's okay," Justin said as he crouched down next to his sister and removed the arrow from her. "It was enough to knock her out, but not enough to do any lasting damage." He carefully brushed some of Kate's hair off of her forehead. "An explosion like this has been a long time coming. It was safer for her, and for everyone around her, to knock her out."

"I-I don't think she's slept in weeks," Ray whispered. "I've been trying to pick up any slack I've seen so that none of you noticed anything, but..."

"It'll be okay." Justin unclipped Kate's quiver and slid it out from under her. "She'll be okay." His voice dropping so that it was almost inaudible, he said, "She has to be."

Kate didn't wake up until two days later, when the sheer exhaustion she had been suffering from finally wore off. When she opened her eyes, she found herself strapped down by the wrists to a bed in the medical bay.

"I'm sorry about that," AJ said gently as he walked over to her. "I wanted to wait to see what kind of mindset you were in when you woke up."

"Mostly a tired one," Kate murmured.

"I'm not all that surprised. But I need to

make sure you aren't a danger to yourself or anyone else." AJ sat down in a chair next to her bed. "I did some asking around. Everyone's pretty sure you haven't actually slept in at least two weeks. Is that true?"

Kate was silent for a few seconds. "It's probably closer to three."

AJ adjusted the strap of his sling. "What's going on, Kate? Because I've known you for a long time, and you've struggled with things, but not like this."

For a moment, it didn't seem like Kate was going to say anything. Then, quietly, she said, "None of it ever got better. I pretended that it did. I pretended that I was stronger, but I wasn't. It wasn't swallowing up my life, but it was always weighing me down. And then Julian died and everything got bad again and I couldn't get away from it. It was just constantly there, and it just kept getting worse and worse." Kate's gaze was distant. "I just wanted it to stop."

AJ swallowed, his brown eyes dark. "Kate... were you hoping you could force Justin to kill you?"

"It doesn't get better, AJ," she whispered. "So what's the point?"

"That's not an answer," AJ said.

Kate gave a dry laugh. "We both know that it is."

AJ smiled humorlessly. "Get some more rest, okay? You need it."

"Is it my fault that Lori and Julian died?" Kate asked suddenly.

AJ studied her briefly. "Were you the one who killed them?"

"... No."

"Then it's not your fault that Lori and Julian died." AJ reached over and squeezed her hand. "Katherine, just because you're the leader doesn't mean you need to carry the weight of everything that ever happens to your team. Sometimes things happen that you can't control. That's the job. You don't need to get used to it. You don't need to be okay with it. But you can't let it crush you, either."

"I don't know to stop it, AJ," Kate admitted, her voice cracking.

AJ smiled, his grip on her hand tightening. "By not trying to do it all by yourself."

Sarah glanced up as Caito walked into their base. "Where have you been?" she asked mildly.

"Committing murder," Caito replied, his voice casual.

"Out of curiosity, do you do anything *else* with your time?"

"Do you?"

"I have hobbies," Sarah grumbled.

"Like whatever it is you do for Alice Cage?"

Sarah paused. "I don't know what you

mean."

Caito smiled slightly. "Do you think I don't know that you work for her and not me?"

"I have no idea what you're talking about."

"Of course not." Caito walked past Sarah, heading for his office. "Make sure Cage understands that I'm not a man who will be used. This isn't her city anymore. It's *mine*."

Once he was out of earshot, Sarah murmured, "If you believe that, you're even more of a fool than I thought you were."

Kate opened her eyes slowly and saw that Niall was sitting in the chair next to her bed. His eyes were red, and he looked like he hadn't shaved in a few days. "Hey," she mumbled.

"Hi."

"You look like hell."

"You don't look much better," Niall replied softly. He cleared his throat. "We need to talk. I... I can't..." He trailed off, looking down at his hands, which were fidgeting in his lap.

Kate took in a deep breath. "It's okay, Niall. We both know what you have to do."

"I don't want to."

"I know." Kate smiled weakly. "But I attacked my own brother. I'm a danger to myself and to other people. I'm a train wreck, and I'll take everyone I care about down with me. And you need to do what's best for the boys."

"Yeah; I do." Niall rubbed at his eyes and sighed. "I love you. Always will."

"I love you, too." Kate swallowed. "But you need to do it. And I need you to say it out loud. Please. Do that for me."

Niall kissed her on the forehead. His voice dropped to an almost inaudible whisper. "I need you to move out of the house."

"I *cannot* believe that you let that guy get away," Ray said as he ran up to Jay, panting.

Jay glared at him. "I didn't *let* him."

"You can run at the speed of sound and yet you didn't catch the criminal. If you didn't let him get away, you really, really suck at your job."

"Shut up, man."

Ray chuckled quietly and clapped Jay on the shoulder. "I—"

"Hey! Assholes!"

Jay and Ray turned towards the new voice and found a group of twenty-somethings standing behind them. The person at the front, a man in a green sweatshirt, spoke again. "You have time to joke around with each other but you don't have time to stop people from getting killed?"

Ray raised his hands defensively. "We're doing the best we can, sir. We're not detectives. We try to find and stop criminals when we can, but we aren't magic. There are some criminals that just aren't that easy to catch."

The man sneered at him. "Well, then what's the point of all of you? Huh? My older sister is dead because you people didn't stop this maniac months ago. *People are dying*! Aren't you supposed to stop that?"

"Sir, I told you, we don't know—"

Ray was interrupted by an unopened soda can smacking into the side of his face. He let out a colorful stream of curses and took a few steps backwards, his hand pressed to his bleeding nose.

"*Blackout*!" Jay hurried to Ray's side and put a hand on his shoulder. "Are you okay?"

"What the hell was that for?" Ray demanded, glaring at the crowd in front of him.

"Because you don't seem to get it, *hero*," the leader said derisively. "We don't believe what you say anymore."

The woman next to him elbowed him in the side. "Hyeon, something occurred to me."

"What's that?"

"What if the reason the vigilantes haven't caught this killer is because it's one of them and they're too embarrassed to do anything about it?"

Jay and Ray exchanged a nervous glance. "That's ridiculous," Jay said, keeping his voice steady.

The leader, Hyeon, raised an eyebrow. "Is it?"

"Yeh, i' is." Ray spat blood onto the ground. "S'absurb."

"Absurd, huh?" Hyeon smirked as the group of people with him began to form a circle around Jay and Ray. "As absurd as a serial killer going unchecked for months?"

"We need to get out of here," Jay whispered to Ray.

"No, boys, stay a while." Hyeon picked a stray pipe up off of the ground. "We insist."

14

"Still drinking, I see," Kaita said dryly as she leaned on the bar counter across from Casey and Casey's glass of scotch.

"This is my first one in, like, a day," Casey replied grumpily.

"I'm so proud of you."

"You are the worst kind of friend."

Kaita raised an eyebrow. "Because I said I was proud of you?"

"It's the tone, Dragovic."

"My apologies." Kaita frowned slightly, her gaze focusing on someone behind Casey. "Hey, kid, aren't you a little young to be hanging out here?"

"I'll only be here for a few minutes," the girl behind Casey replied.

Casey turned around and came face-to-face with a teenage girl. She realized who the girl was almost immediately. Casey swallowed, but she kept her voice even. "You must be Finn."

The girl smiled. "So you've heard of me."

"Yes. You seem to be a hurricane through my family's life at the moment."

"Not without reason."

"Right. Alice Cage."

"She's good at motivation," Finn replied in a quiet voice.

"I'm sure she is." Casey took a large gulp

from her glass of scotch. "Let me guess. She beats the crap out of you whenever you don't come to her with blood on your hands?"

"Casey," Kaita murmured, a warning tone in her voice.

Finn put a hand on the counter and leaned in towards Casey. "You have absolutely no idea."

"Yeah; whatever. What do you want, lap dog?"

"It's not exactly what *I* want." Finn bowed her head for a moment. "I'm sorry about this, Ms. Cabot."

Casey glanced at Kaita before setting her glass down. "What are you sorry about?"

"This." Finn grabbed Casey by the back of her head and slammed her face down on the bar counter.

"*Case*!" Kaita yelled as Finn tossed Casey onto the floor. She vaulted the bar and knelt down next to her boss.

Finn calmly picked up a towel and wiped Casey's blood off of the countertop. "Ms. Cage would like you all to know that no matter what you do, none of you are safe."

"No kiddin'," Casey muttered through the blood in her mouth as she tried to sit up.

"Case, hush," Kaita whispered as she gently held her down.

Finn casually stuck the towel in her back pocket and crouched down in front of Casey. "I am legitimately sorry, Ms. Cabot."

Kaita pulled the knife out of Casey's boot and leveled it at Finn. "Back off, lap dog. I may not be a vigilante, but I am fully capable of stabbing you in the chest."

"Capable, yes. Able, no." Finn easily twisted the knife out of Kaita hand and stabbed it into the floor directly next to the bartender's foot. She stood up slowly, staring around at the other bar patrons, who were stunned into silence. The teen calmly finished off a shot that was sitting on the counter and walked out of the bar.

"Are you okay?" Kaita asked urgently as Casey cautiously sat up.

"Feel like m'head hit solid wood," Casey mumbled. She frowned, a confused look on her face. "Everythin's bright and spinnin'."

"Oh, good, the concussion symptoms have fully taken hold." Kaita gently dragged Casey to her feet. "Come on, Cabot. Let's get you upstairs. I'll call the others. Especially AJ." She paused. "And probably Zach."

Zach was the first to get there, bursting into the apartment only five minutes after Kaita's call. "Casey..." he whispered when he saw the woman's blood-stained face. "Good god, what happened to you?"

"We got a visit from the friendly neighborhood pawn of Alice Cage," Kaita replied. She handed Casey a damp washcloth and walked over to Zach. "She's still kind of confused. I think she has a concussion." A look of realization crossed Kaita's face, and she winced. "Oh, hell. What's going on downstairs?"

"Nobody's there. There was a pile of money on the bar that I put on the shelf below before I came up here, since the door was unlocked."

"They didn't drink and dash. I'm impressed. I knew we had loyal patrons, but that's above and beyond." Kaita sighed. "I'd better go secure everything. I'll bring AJ up when he gets here."

Once she was gone, Zach sat down across from Casey and rested his hands on her knees. "Are you okay?"

"Not sure," Casey replied. There was dried blood under her nose and mouth, and a thick bruise was beginning to form around her left eye.

Zach gently took the washcloth from her and began to clean some of the blood off of her face. "I wish I had been here."

"Happened so fast. Wouldn' have stopped anythin'."

"That doesn't change how I feel."

Casey smiled slightly. "M'alright, Zach." She squeezed his hand comfortingly.

Kaita returned with AJ and Cass. "I need to start charging based on the hour," AJ joked, covering up the worry in his eyes. "It's two a.m., Casey. Can't you get hurt at a reasonable time?"

"Do better next time," Casey replied with a weak grin.

"Congratulations, you got your head bashed in," Cass said brightly, patting Casey on the shoulder. "Now you're a true Wechsler."

"Did our dad ge' his head bashed in?"

Cass grinned. "I made sure of it."

Casey gave a short laugh. "Knew I liked you."

AJ swapped places with Zach and took Casey's face in his hands. "What the hell did she hit you with?"

"Don' remember."

When AJ glanced at her, Kaita said, "Finn slammed Casey's face into the bar counter."

"Bitch!" Zach and Cass muttered simultaneously.

"Why would she do that? What did she want?" AJ asked as he shined a flashlight in Casey's eyes.

Kaita shrugged. "All she said was that none of you guys were safe."

"No shit," Cass grumbled. "My husband has the bullet wound to prove it."

There was a pause, as something seemed to dawn on Kaita. "Oh, hell. I didn't even remember it until now, because I was focusing on Casey."

"What is it?" Zach prompted.

"She wiped Casey's blood off of the counter with a towel and then pocketed it."

"So she has Casey's blood," Cass said slowly.

"Swear t'god, if she clones me..."

"I doubt she would. She's only ever cloned herself. Some narcissistic thing." Cass put her hands in her pockets. "I'm more worried about her trend of not killing us, but drawing blood. How do we know she didn't take any of AJ's blood, too?"

"But what would she do with it?" Zach wondered.

"It's Vigilance blood," AJ pointed out. "Casey and I are all that's left, DNA-wise, of three of the Vigilance Initiative members— my parents, Casey's parents, Cass's parents, Alice. Maybe that's what she needs."

"Four."

AJ turned to look at Casey. "What?"

"Four of the Vigilance Initiative members," Cass answered. "Though, if that's what she's after, she'll need my blood, too. For Brooke and maybe John, if she doesn't know about Casey."

An alarmed look formed in Zach's eyes. "Where are the kids?"

Everyone stared at him. "What?" AJ asked.

"The kids. Logan, Brooke, Aubrey, and Jacob."

AJ shrugged. "Alix is watching them. They're asleep. Why?"

Cass caught on first. "Because if Alice

183

can't get to me, she can get to one of my children."

"Oh, hell," Kaita murmured. "What are you going to do?"

"None of them can be in the house until we know what she needs Casey's blood for," AJ replied. "If she's collecting Vigilance blood, they might be targets. If it's something else, they're at risk. If, god forbid, she *is* going to clone Casey, we can't take the chance that the clone would be able to get close enough to the kids to hurt them."

"I know what we can do," Cass said, her voice hard. "I know who to call."

Casey gave her a curious look. "Who?"

Before Cass could respond, the door to the apartment burst open, and Kara ran in. She was gasping for breath and looked to be in shock. "We've got a problem," she panted.

Zach grabbed her to steady her. "Kara, what is it? What's wrong?"

"Jay and Ray just got jumped on patrol. They're still in one piece, but they're all beat to heck." Kara took in a deep breath to compose herself. "The people of Caotico. They're turning on us. They're sick of getting killed, and they've decided that they're going to kill all of us in revenge."

By eleven o'clock in the morning, Brooke and Aubrey were sitting on the stairs waiting for someone to tell them where they were going. Jacob and Logan were still in their rooms, but the two older children had decided to try to eavesdrop on the various conversations happening around them.

Ray and Jay had been declared 'lucky' by AJ, with only a few bruises and, for Ray, a broken nose. Casey had a concussion, but she had somehow escaped without any broken bones. And for some reason, the adults were all terrified— enough that none of the kids were going to be allowed in the mansion until further notice.

"I don't get it," Brooke whispered. "This Cage lady was *in the mansion*, and they didn't need to send us away after that."

"I think her attacking Aunt Casey too freaked them out," Aubrey murmured in reply.

"Where do you think they're shipping us?"

"Does it matter? We're going to be alone either way."

Brooke bumped her shoulder against Aubrey's. "No, we won't. We'll all be together, and besides, Mom and Dad wouldn't send us somewhere they didn't trust."

"Whatever." Aubrey spun her bracelet around her wrist three times. "When did you recover your sense of optimism, anyway?"

"I'm a kid. Kids heal fast."

"Yeah, or you're faking it, so that Jacob and I don't feel bad."

Brooke gave a thin smile. "Don't know

why I'd do that."

Aubrey mirrored her smile. "Of course you don't."

The front door of the mansion opened, and two men in black military combat uniforms walked in. One had an assault rifle strapped to his side, while the other was unarmed.

"Huh," Brooke said quietly. "They look like a death squad, but at least they're an *attractive* death squad."

Aubrey rolled her eyes.

A third man walked in behind the first two. He was much older, with gray hair cut in a precise military style.

"Gabriel!" Brooke and Aubrey exclaimed simultaneously. The girls ran down the stairs and tackled the third man in a tight hug.

"Good god, you *cannot* be the Hamil girls," Gabriel Garrison laughed. "You are much too big to be them."

"I *am* nine," Brooke replied as she and Aubrey released him. "Ten in August."

"And I'll be nine on the twenty-ninth." Aubrey paused and looked down at the floor. "This Saturday."

Brooke reached out and took her sister's hand, squeezing it comfortingly. Garrison looked unsure of what to say, but he was saved by Cass, who joined them with Jacob. The boy hugged Garrison with the same enthusiasm his sisters had showed and said, "Hi, Uncle

Gabriel!"

Cass chuckled at the confused expression on Garrison's face. "I certainly didn't teach him that."

Garrison crouched down in front of Jacob. "Why don't we stick with just Gabriel, okay, buddy?"

"Okay, Just Gabriel."

Cass stifled a laugh behind her hand, and Garrison looked up at her. "As if there was ever any question that these are your children."

"Alright, kids, why don't you go finish getting whatever you need."

Once the trio was gone, Garrison hugged Cass. "You holding up okay, kid?"

"I'm managing."

Garrison gestured at the two men who were with him. "You remember Johnny Aller and my grandson David?"

"Of course."

David Garrison was only twenty and was in his first year of working with his grandfather. He was young, eager, and honest, and with his military-cut black hair and blue eyes, he looked almost exactly like Gabriel had looked at the same age.

Johnny Aller was a thirty-five-year-old member of the Security Legion and former member of the Alumni. He had begun working private security with Garrison five years prior, after breaking up with his boyfriend Rob

Munroe, and he seemed much happier now than he had been in decades. His light brown hair was kept longer than either Garrison's, but it made him look no less professional in his black uniform.

Johnny looked directly at Cass and signed something to her. He had been voiceless since birth and communicated solely in sign language, which everyone in the Heroics base understood. Everyone who had known him when he was younger, at least.

"I'm sorry, Johnny, I really never got the hang of reading sign," Cass admitted apologetically.

"He asked whether you knew any more about Alice Cage," David said.

"Oh, right. No, we don't have anything yet. We're working on it. We'll let you know if we find anything, though."

'*Good*,' Johnny signed.

"Why don't you two wait outside?" Garrison prompted. The two other men nodded and left, and Garrison raised an eyebrow at Cass. "You look like you want to ask me something."

"I don't know what you're talking about," Cass replied evasively.

"Cass, I've known you almost your whole life. You can't really fool me as easily as you think you can."

There was a pause, as Cass shifted her weight between her feet. "Did you know this whole time that Casey is my sister?"

Garrison looked stunned. He slowly took a seat on the bottom step. "How did you find out about that?" he asked in a whisper.

"Found her birth certificate. And Diana van der Aart's diary. But that's not an answer." She hesitated. "Actually, I guess it is."

"I knew," Garrison admitted. "Why do you think I didn't deliver her to him all those years ago? I knew what he would do to that girl."

"I can imagine, since he tried to strangle me to death."

"It would've been worse for her," Garrison said softly. "He hated Robin— Casey —much, *much* more than he ever hated you, Cass."

"Why?" Cass asked, her voice hoarse.

"Because he wasn't allowed to torture her." Garrison ran a hand over his face and sighed. "He wasn't allowed to hurt her, so he hated her. And if he had gotten his hands on Casey while the Heroics kids were fighting those controlled empowereds, he would've made sure that she felt every single bit of agony that he hadn't been able to inflict on her when she was a child. You know how much pain that would've been."

Cass shivered. "I do. But I don't get what any of that has to do with why you didn't say anything after John Wechsler was dead. It's been a decade, Garrison."

Garrison met her gaze solidly. "Nobody would want to know that, Cass. Nobody would *want* to be his child. As confusing as it can be to not know where you came from, not knowing is better than being a Wechsler. You know that, too."

"You're not supposed to be logical," Cass muttered as she took a seat next to him.

"Why, because I'm a dumb soldier boy?"

"Not much of a boy anymore," Cass retorted lightly.

"Don't I know it. The little kid I watched grow up has three kids of her own, and they're all smarter than me."

"They're all smarter than most people." Cass hesitated, then opened her mouth to speak again.

"Before you ask," Garrison said, "no, I don't know whether something your father did to you could've given your children powers. You've asked before."

"I know, but it's still bothering me."

Garrison put a hand on Cass's back comfortingly. "I can't help you. But don't worry so much. They're good kids, Cass. That's all that matters."

The front door opened, and AJ walked in. Garrison stood and walked over to him, holding out his hand. "Anthony. It's been too long."

AJ shook his hand. "Mr. Garrison."

"I told you that you can drop the 'Mr.'."

"I told you that you can call me 'AJ'."

"Good point." Garrison pointed at AJ's sling. "I hear that's courtesy of Alice Cage."

"Yeah, it was an anniversary present."

"She always was terrible at figuring out what to give people." Garrison clapped AJ on his good shoulder. "Glad you're in one piece, Hamil."

"Thanks, I think. Where are the kids?"

"Upstairs, finishing getting ready," Cass replied.

"Good." AJ lowered his voice. "You realize what Saturday is, right?"

Cass sighed and closed her eyes briefly. "I do, but I don't know what to do. I'd rather her hate me for a few weeks than have her get hurt, AJ."

"I feel the same way, but—"

"You're talking about Aubrey's birthday?"

AJ and Cass turned to Garrison, looking a bit surprised. "Uhm, yes," AJ replied.

"She mentioned it when she was talking to me. Not on purpose. She and Brooke were bragging about their ages, and she said that she was going to turn nine this weekend. She didn't even seem to have realized that she'd probably be with me until she said it out loud."

"I'm sick of Alice Cage ruining our lives," Cass growled. "I'm sick of her making us run and hide. I'm sick of her tormenting my children."

"Don't get caught up in anger, Cass. You know how badly that usually goes for you. Your temper won't help you keep anybody safe," Garrison warned. "It's Tuesday. You have some time. Maybe you'll be able to at least figure out whether the kids are at risk before the weekend." He checked his watch. "I'm going to go make sure everything's good with Johnny and David."

Once Garrison was gone, AJ scoffed. "Judging by how quickly Alice has been moving, I doubt it will even take the rest of the week. We'll either be free of her or dead by then."

Cass gave a weak laugh. "I remember when you were the uplifting one."

"I'm too pissed to be uplifting."

"It'll be okay, AJ." Cass kissed him quickly. "We'll be okay. W-We have to be."

"How can you—" He broke off when he saw that she was shaking, and he pulled her into a one-armed hug. "You're right," he murmured, gently stroking her hair. "We'll be okay."

Casey and Zach stepped into Casey's bar an hour after their daughter had been sent away with Garrison. "I hate this," Zach said quietly. "I feel so useless."

"We are useless," Casey replied. "All we're doing is sitting here and waiting for Alice Cage to get bored with her games and start picking us off." She went behind the bar counter and pulled out a bottle of scotch. As she poured a glass, she asked, "Want any?"

"It's noon, and you aren't supposed to be drinking."

"Do you want any or not?"

Zach sighed and sat on one of the barstools. "Whiskey?"

Casey smirked, took out a different bottle, and began to pour. "Now you know how I feel."

"Maybe not. I'm feeling more like this is strangely familiar."

She slid the glass of whiskey to him. "What do you mean?"

"You, me, this bar, glass of scotch, glass of whiskey. All that's missing is the oddly appropriate Cole Swindell song that was playing when you introduced yourself to me."

Casey stiffened. "You know the agreement. We met the day you became the liaison between Heroics and the Legion."

"We're the only ones here, Casey. We don't need to pretend that we didn't meet two weeks earlier, and far more intimately."

"Zach, please," Casey whispered.

"Okay, alright, whatever." Zach took a drink from his glass. "You want to keep pretending that we haven't been a thing for a hell of a lot longer than you've ever admitted to your sister, fine."

"It's still so weird to hear that. To hear

Cass referred to as my sister. I mean, sure, I've considered her my sister for years and I've called her such, but… actually having you say it and mean it? It's… It's weird."

"Understandably so." Zach swirled the whiskey around in his glass. "Have you read any more of your mother's diary?"

"Bits. Apparently she was engaged to a guy named Carsten Doherty. She cheated on him with John Wechsler, even though she did apparently love him. Doherty was killed in a car accident before I was born, and since Brooke had already figured out that John had cheated on her with my mom, nobody saw the point in pretending that I wasn't John's kid." Casey took a large gulp from her scotch. "From what I understand, my mother was pretty sure that John or Alice, or both, killed Doherty, but she stuck around. She was more loyal to the Vigilance Initiative than she was to the man she loved." Casey gave a scoffing laugh. "I guess that adds fuel to my theory that she was incapable of truly loving anyone."

"You aren't her, you know," Zach said softly.

"Some days, I'm not so sure."

"Case, I'm serious."

"So am I." Casey pulled an ice pack out of a freezer, wrapped it in a towel, and pressed it against her black eye.

Realizing that he was going to get nowhere in the argument, Zach asked, "How's the concussion?"

"Hurts like a bitch," she mumbled.

"That's what you get for using quality material in your bar. If you had a low-class establishment, this wouldn't have happened."

"I'd probably have a face full of splinters instead."

"Hm. Good point."

Casey lowered the ice pack and sighed. "We need to figure out what to do, moving forward. We need to figure out what to do about Cage."

"And we will. I have a Legion meeting to get to, so maybe there will be something new."

"What are the odds of that?"

"Hell, you people are *such* pessimists," Zach muttered.

"Pretty much," Casey said with a shrug. "At least I still have my sense of humor."

"I'll believe that when I see it."

Casey pulled a refrigerator magnet off of the freezer at her feet and stuck it to the back of his hand. "Good enough?"

Zach irritably pulled the magnet off of his hand and had to shake it off when it instead stuck to his fingers. "It never ceases to amuse you that I'm magnetic, does it?"

"Not really. Probably never will." Casey took Zach's empty glass from him and set it in the sink behind her. "Try not to get punched in the face at your meeting tonight."

"I won't." He smirked. "Magnetic

personality, remember?"

"It's your *body* that magnetic, not your *personality*, jackass." Casey paused. "I really just said that, didn't I?"

"Yes. Yes, you did."

"I walked straight into that. I'm ashamed."

"Don't be mad at yourself. We both know that you find me pretty damn attractive. No need to be ashamed of the truth."

Casey groaned. "I will never understand why I *ever* slept with you."

"I'm pretty sure I just established that it was—"

"Shut the hell up, Zach."

Zach leaned across the counter and kissed her quickly. "Yes, ma'am." He grinned and backed away when she swatted at him irritably. "I have a meeting to get to."

"Thank every god ever believed in."

He headed for the door, but before he left, her voice stopped him. "Zach?"

"Yeah?"

Casey hesitated. "Just… be careful, okay?"

Zach smiled slowly. "I will be. I promise." He gave her a mock salute and left the bar.

Kara and Justin crouched down at the edge of a rooftop in the southern district of Caotico City. They watched as a large group of teenagers, all carrying various blunt weapons, walked down the street below them. "What the *hell* is that?" Kara wondered.

"Not sure. Hope we don't have to fight them. I'm not even sure *I* could take that many people with baseball bats," Justin muttered.

"I would advise you to stay the hell away from them," a male voice said from behind them.

Justin and Kara turned and saw that they had been joined by Rob "Cryo" Munroe and Monica "Scarlett" Lin. "Hey," Kara greeted. "You guys know what that is?"

Monica nodded. "They've started hunting vigilantes. They decided that one of us is killing all of those random citizens, so they decided that they're going to kill us off, one by one, until the serial killer stops. Then the last person they killed will probably get branded a murderer."

"Idiots," Justin snarled. "Don't they understand that we're doing the best we can?"

"Their people are dying," Kara said quietly. "All they understand is fear."

"Yeah, well, now our people are dying," Rob growled, his voice low and bitter.

Kara and Justin exchanged a horrified glance. "What do you mean?" Justin demanded.

Monica took in a deep breath. "Last night, not long after that gang jumped Blackout and Clash? Another gang jumped Janek "Svetlo" van Houten. They beat him to death. He left behind a wife and a nine-year-old daughter."

"Hell," Kara breathed, covering her face with her hand.

Justin let out a stream of much more colorful curses and kicked a nearby vent. He moved as if he wanted to go down to the street, but Kara dragged him back into the spot he had been standing in.

"Don't let this get out of hand, Archer," she warned.

"It's *already* out of hand," he spat.

"He's not wrong," Rob said darkly.

"But she's right," Monica insisted. "If we start intentionally engaging in fights with civilians, we're going to end up being regarded as the problem by more than just a few small clusters of hateful killers. The whole city will be against us. We can't afford that."

Justin stuck his hands in his pockets, looking furious. "Well, how exactly are we supposed to continue doing our jobs if random people are murdering us now?"

"I-I don't know," Monica admitted. "But we have to try, don't we?"

"I'm not sure we do," Rob said. "You know how much I hate agreeing with Archer here, but we can't do our jobs if we're going to be risking getting stabbed in the back."

"We've always risked that," Kara said in a quiet voice.

"Maybe. But maybe we don't need to do

it anymore." Rob shook his head slowly. "If they don't want our help? We don't need to give it to them. I say we all stop helping the people of Caotico. And when the city gets overrun by criminals, then they can come crawling back to us."

Casey looked up as AJ walked into the bar. "Your wife kick you out?"

"She needs a bit. This is taking a lot out of her. She finally figured out how to have a stable family, and Alice walks in and tries to take it all away again."

"I know the feeling."

AJ sat down across the counter from her. "Talk to me, Casey."

Casey took in a long, slow breath. "I have a three-year-old daughter that I can't say 'I love you' to, a wonderful man would give me everything but I can't be as emotionally consistent with him as I want because the last person I actually said I loved blew herself up after admitting that she was a psychopath, my father tried to commit genocide after finding out how by torturing my little sister, and the only way I can think of handling any of these things is by getting wasted, which I can't do because of my job, so I continually get just to the edge of my limit, knowing full well that if I take one more drink I will be tipsy enough that I won't make myself stop, because that's *all I can do*."

"Oh," AJ said simply.

Casey gave a sharp laugh. "That's all you've got?"

AJ reached out and took her hands in his. "Case, I don't know what to say to you. I don't. I don't have some big motivational speech to get you through this. All I have is that you've got a whole hell of a lot more. You've got every single one of us. And we might be a bit scattered and broken right now, but *you've got us*, okay? You've got us."

Casey smiled slightly. "Seems like you do have a bit of a motivational speech in you."

"I guess I do."

"It could use some work," she joked.

"So could your face. Or is black in again?"

Casey shook her head, laughing. "Jackass. If you aren't nice to me, I'll tell the others how I *really* first found out that you and Cass were together, all those years ago."

AJ smiled. "And if you do that, *I'll* tell the others all about how you had already slept with Zach by the time he first became the liaison."

"You wouldn't," Casey said slowly.

"Don't test me," AJ replied with a grin.

"The fact that you are my actual brother-in-law disgusts me."

AJ gave her a friendly pat on the shoulder. "You started this, Case. Don't be foolish enough to think that I won't finish it."

Casey laughed, but it quickly faded out. "I really want a drink, AJ. And I know that's not a very good sign."

"You're right. It's not. And this will probably get worse before it gets better, and you will probably end up halfway through a thing of scotch before I even find out about it. But we'll get through it, Case. We'll get through all of this. You have to believe that, or there won't be anything for you on the other side of that bottle."

"This is insane, Raseri," Zach said as he left the Security Legion meeting with Wade "Raseri" Toracid. "Everyone in there is insane."

"They're afraid," Wade replied. "Roving packs of vigilante hunters scare everyone."

"I get that, but cutting down on patrols won't make the situation better. It'll only make it worse. Everything is going to get worse until we stop this serial killer, and doing our jobs *less* won't magically make that happen."

"Agreed. What do you think Heroics will do?"

Zach shrugged. "I'd imagine that they'll try to patrol even more, now that we're slacking off, but they can't do too much more than they're already doing. There just aren't enough of them."

"And they're probably busy enough with all of this Alice Cage nonsense."

"Oh, definitely. We really needed that

psycho around right now."

Wade shook his head slowly. "And I hear one of her people assaulted your wife this morning. Same minion who shot the Heroics medic."

"I— she's not my wife, but yeah." Zach's brow furrowed. "How did you hear about that?"

"It was in a pretty crowded bar, Kov. Word gets around."

"Right."

"Is she okay?"

"She's fine," Zach replied shortly. "She's tougher than she looks."

Wade gave a short laugh. "I'd certainly hope so. She doesn't look all that tough."

Zach looked uneasy. "No, I guess she doesn't." He checked his watch. "Speaking of... uh, the girlfriend, she's expecting me, so I should get home."

When Zach turned to leave, Wade sighed. "Dammit." He grabbed Zach by the back of the neck, kicked his legs out from under him, and forced him down onto his knees. As his grip on Zach's neck tightened, Wade pleasantly asked, "What made me so suspicious?"

For some reason, Zach couldn't move. He choked out, "Never told anybody girl who shot medic was girl who hit girlfriend. And you've... never been near the bar. Never should've seen girlfriend."

"I knew I was pushing too hard," Wade

commented. "Oh well. Sarah's been looking for a toy to play with."

"Who… are you?" Zach gasped.

"My name is Edward Caito. I'm a serial killer." The man tightened his grip on Zach a little more and then raised his hand and used Zach's own metal manipulation ability to rip a railing off of a nearby wall. He smiled slightly. "And thanks to you, I have another power in my very extensive collection." Caito pulled a piece of the railing into his hand and, with a quiet laugh, brought it down on the back of Zach's head.

15

AJ looked up and frowned when he saw Kate walking past the library of the Heroics mansion. "Kate?"

She backed up and entered the room, looking nervous. "What is it?"

"It's nine o'clock at night. You were cleared to go home hours ago. What are you still doing here?"

Kate shifted her weight back and forth between her feet. "I-I was just... I had some things I wanted to take care of, and... I... I was just... doing stuff."

AJ stood up and walked over to her, folding his arms across her chest. "Kate, you have to go home eventually. You need to stop hiding here. This is the kind of behavior that made you break down in the first place, remember?"

"I-I can't... go home."

"Why not?"

"I..." Kate swallowed, avoiding his gaze. "Niall kicked me out of the house," she whispered.

"*What?*"

"Niall kicked me out of the house," Kate repeated.

"I heard you the first time; I just didn't believe what I was hearing." AJ adjusted his tie. "This is insane. You aren't... He shouldn't have…"

"AJ, you and I both know that he had to," Kate murmured. "I attacked my own brother. And I can't even convince myself to live for my sons, so what's to say I won't attack them, too? I've been sort of… hiding… in my old room upstairs. I figured it wasn't a problem, since the kids were out of the house and you, Cass, Casey, and Alix aren't afraid to beat the crap out of me if I go over the edge again."

"I'm not sure hurting you is the productive course of action, especially since I'm worried about you hurting yourself." AJ ran a hand through his hair. "I just can't believe Niall would actually do it."

"Please don't be mad at him," Kate begged. "He's just doing what he needs to do to protect his children."

"I don't think I *am* mad at him, Kate. I just never thought he'd actually be able to choose between you or the boys. He loves all three of you far too much."

"That's exactly why he was able to do it, AJ," Kate said softly. "Because he knows that I'd want him to put the boys first."

AJ gave a small nod and hugged her. "If you need anything, kid, tell me. Please. And no matter what you feel like right now, understand something: You aren't a bad mother. Because if you were, you'd be a hell of a lot more bitter about this situation than you are. You're putting your sons first, too."

Kate took in a shaky breath that sounded close to a sob. "It hurts, AJ."

"That's okay. That's good. Because you're feeling something, Kate. And no matter how much it hurts, in the long run it'll be better than feeling nothing."

"Does it ever get better? All of this?"

"I don't know. But I know you're strong enough to find out. Fair?"

Her grip on him tightened. "Fair," she whispered.

The next morning saw a tense and subdued meeting of the Heroics team. Kate and Niall were sitting side-by-side, but they were both stiff and seemed uncomfortable. Alix was slumped down in her chair, looking exhausted. Jay and Ray both still clearly showed the multiple bruises from their assault the day prior. Justin and Kara, who had gotten into a heated argument the night before, refused to look at each other. AJ was quietly murmuring something in Italian to Cass, who had a worried expression on her face. Casey, in her seat at the head of the table, was staring down at her tablet but not actually reading anything on it.

"So," Kara said after several minutes, "is anybody going to start this thing, or...?"

"Y-Yeah," Casey stammered. "S-Sorry, it's just..."

"What's the matter?" Cass prompted.

"Zach didn't sleep here last night."

Justin snorted. "You didn't get laid? I'll file the police report right away."

"Shut up, Justin," Cass snapped. She turned her attention back to Casey. "What do you mean?"

"He usually…" Casey swallowed, looking scared. "Even if we don't… *sleep together*… we usually… sleep together."

"And you still think you aren't dating," Cass said lightly. She squeezed Casey's hand. "He's probably fine, Case. Maybe his Legion meeting ran long, and he didn't want to disturb you if you were already asleep."

"His Legion meeting was at one o'clock yesterday afternoon," Casey murmured. "How long could it have possibly run?"

Cass shot an anxious glance at AJ, but she repeated, "He's probably fine. After our meeting, we'll see if we can figure out where he is, okay?"

Casey nodded, but the worry on her face didn't fade. She straightened in her chair and cleared her throat. "Uh. Right. As we all have probably figured out, based on what happened to Jay and Ray, civilians in Caotico have decided to turn vigilante against us."

"They murdered a Legion hero yesterday," Justin said. "Put another three in the hospital, and a fourth this morning."

"The speed of all of this is terrifying." AJ fidgeted with his tie and adjusted the strap of his sling. "There's no way this should be happening this quickly."

"The fact of the matter is that it is, though," Kate replied. "So, what do we do about it?"

"We watch our backs," Ray said. "We aren't going to stop doing our jobs just because a portion of Caotico has decided to be stupid."

"Should we really be risking ourselves if they're going to turn on us every chance they get?" Justin asked, a bitter note in his voice.

Ray turned to him slowly. "Yes. That's what we do. Trust me, Justin, I know how angry these mobs are. I have the broken nose to prove it. But that doesn't mean that we stop protecting everyone else."

"Fine," Justin grumbled. "So, then, what do we do?"

"We should try to find Cage first, I think," Jay said. "We're more likely to get something done with the target we've beaten once than the unknown serial killer we've made no headway with for months."

"I think I might have something on that, actually." Kara leaned forward. "I've been thinking about the fact that Brooke recognized Alice as being a schoolteacher. So I did some digging. Alice was working in Caotico as Ada Shade. Before she came to Brooke's school, she was living in Riverdale, the city twenty-five minutes north of us. I looked into Riverdale from the time we thought Alice died to the time she showed up a schoolteacher, and I found something rather… well, horrifying, but interesting too. In the three years before Alice came back to Caotico, five children disappeared from Riverdale. None of them were ever seen again, and it was the first time anyone under eighteen had gone missing in Riverdale and not reappeared within six months, dead or alive." Kara swallowed. "The first child to disappear was named Whitney Finnegan."

"Whitney Fi—" Alix pinched the bridge of her nose and closed her eyes. "Oh, hell."

Kara gave a small nod. "Her age at the time and her general physical description would make her a pretty good match for Finn."

"I don't want to end up like the others."

Everyone turned to look at Kate. "What was that?" Kara asked.

"That's what Finn said to me. 'I don't want to end up like the others.' How much do you want to bet that at least some of those other kids were taken by Alice too, but Finn's the only one she left alive?"

"I'm going to see if I can talk to her." Alix stood up and headed for the door.

"Uh, no, you aren't," Cass said. "You don't even know where she is, and besides, she's working for Cage. She may be beyond helping, Al, and I don't want to risk losing you if I don't have to."

"We weren't beyond helping," Alix replied softly. "As for finding her? I'm sure it won't be too hard."

"Alix," Kara said as she stood, an uneasy expression on her face. "Maybe you shouldn't."

"I'll be fine."

Kara took a few steps towards her. "I'm not sure you will. Just sit down, and we'll talk about what to do."

"I know what to do."

"Do you?" Kara stepped forward again. "Or do you just *think* you do?"

Alix stiffened. "Kara, back the hell off. Right now."

"No."

"Dammit, Kara, I know what I'm doing," Alix snarled. Her eyes darkened, and she emphasized her words by punching the back of the chair that Niall was sitting in. Niall immediately fell onto the floor, as his chair disappeared out from under him in a swirl of shadows. The chair reappeared above Kara's head, but she seemed to be expecting it, as she caught it easily and set it back down on the floor.

The room was dead silent as the two women stared at each other, Kara looking sad and Alix looking horrified. Alix began to cough, so heavily that she doubled over and had to support herself by putting one hand on the table. She paused long enough to stare down at the blood that had coated the hand she was using to cover her mouth before she continued.

"Alix?" Cass whispered.

The coughing woman shook her head firmly and disappeared into shadows. As a bewildered Kate helped Niall to his feet, Kara returned his chair to him. "What the hell is going on?" he asked.

Kara sat back down in her own seat slowly, sighing. "There's something I need to tell you all about Alix."

Alix reappeared in an alley in the center of the city, close to where she had first met Finn. She spit out a mouthful of blood and cleared her throat. As she wiped her bloody hand off on her pants, she muttered, "I'm really gonna kill Alice." She glanced around the alley once, before sitting down on the ground and waiting.

Only ten minutes later, Finn's voice said, "Waiting for me?"

"I figured you'd find your way to me eventually," Alix replied, standing up. "Though you're much faster than I was expecting."

"I was in the area." Finn leaned against the wall of the alley. "What is it that you want, Thief?"

Alix put her hands in her pockets. "I wanted to tell you that you don't need to work for Alice Cage. You don't need to be her minion."

Finn's gaze was as unreadable as it had

ever been. "Yes, I do."

"No, you don't. Trust me, Finn, I know what it's like to feel like she has total control of your life. To feel like you can't do anything to escape. But believe me when I say that you don't need to feel that way. You can get out."

"You might know a lot about Alice Cage," Finn said softly. "However, you have absolutely no idea what she's done these past few years." She turned and started to walk away.

"Actually, I'm pretty sure I have a few ideas, Whitney."

Finn stopped dead in her tracks. She turned to face Alix slowly, tears in her brown eyes.

"How old were you? When Alice kidnapped you?"

After a long pause, Finn murmured, "Ten. Turned eleven later that year."

"Old enough to remember who you are."

"Old enough to remember what happened to all the other kids when they tried to turn their backs on her, too."

"How many were there?" Alix asked gently.

"Four from Riverdale. Two from one of the suburbs, uh, Deaton. All between eight and twelve." Finn paused. "All dead."

A shiver ran through Alix. "Finn, I'm sorry that you had to go through that. I really am, but you can walk away. She can't hurt you, if you trust us."

Finn seemed to shut down. Her expression went blank, and the emotion in her eyes vanished. "She can, though." She cocked her head to one side, studying Alix for a moment. "And she said you were sick. That you were dying. That's why she wanted the confrontation now."

"I figured as much. But our conversation isn't over."

"It is." Finn turned and began to walk away again. "There's no point in trying to save me, Thief. It's already too late."

Once the teen was gone, Alix tightened her hands into fists. "Oh, kid," she whispered. "If it wasn't too late for me and Cass, it's not too late for you." She bowed her head, sighed, and disappeared into shadows.

When Alix showed back up in the mansion, she found Cass sitting in the library. "Hey. Sorry about earlier, I—"

"Do you have a middle name?" Cass asked, her voice tightly controlled.

"I— What?"

"A middle name. Like how Brooke, Aubrey, and Jacob have the middle names Robin, Alexandra, and Carter. Do you have one?"

Alix frowned. "No. I'm the expendable clone of a psychopath. I'm lucky I have a *first* name, let alone a middle one. I guess if I needed one for something I could use 'Cage,' but—"

"*ALIX CAGE TOLVAJ!*"

"Oh, that's not good."

Cass was on her feet, looking furious. "What the hell is wrong with you? Why wouldn't you tell us that using your powers is killing you?"

Alix swallowed. "Because I've almost worked out how to make it stop."

"That's not a good enough reason, Al."

"What do you want me to say, Cass? That I'm scared? That I think Alice is here now because she knows something about whatever it is her serum did to me? That I'm sorry for prioritizing my job over my health?"

Cass folded her arms across her chest. "Those would all be good things, yeah."

"Too bad." Alix turned to walk out, but Cass grabbed her arm.

"Alix, please, talk to me. I need you to be okay."

"Why do you care?" Alix grumbled.

Cass looked stunned. "Why do I... Alix, you're my best friend. I love you. *That's* why I care."

Alix yanked her arm away from Cass's grip and rubbed her temples, as if she had a headache. "I'm sorry, Cass. I can't do this right now. I can't take the time to justify myself to you. I just can't."

"Maybe you should make the time," Cass

murmured. "Come on, Al. Talk to me."

"I can't," Alix whispered.

Cass slowly reached for Alix's arm again, but she didn't get a chance to get close. Alix's eyes went so dark they were almost black, and she quickly moved away from Cass's touch. As she moved, a sweeping whip of shadow appeared out of nowhere and hit Cass directly in the abdomen. Cass doubled over in pain and stumbled away from Alix.

"What the *hell*?" Cass asked through gritted teeth.

Alix's eyes were already back to their normal color. "I-I... I didn't... I'm sorry." She turned and ran out of the room, directly into Justin.

"What exactly do you think you're doing?" he demanded.

"I don't need to fight with you right now, Justin," Alix grumbled, pushing past him.

"Well, too bad, because you're going to have to put up with me." Justin followed her. "You know, Al, if something's wrong, you can tell me."

"Yeah." Alix laughed sharply. "Like you care."

"You know damn well that the only one allowed to screw with you is me. There's a reason for that."

"And what reason is that? The guilt from when you used to be a complete asshole towards me for something outside of my control?"

Justin's jaw twitched. "I was wrong, and I acknowledged it and apologized for it. I was a stupid kid. You know that."

"You're a stupid adult, too." Alix rounded on him, her eyes edging back towards black, and a grin on her face that was more sadistic than usual. "You want to know what your problem is, Oliver? You're afraid. You're afraid that you'll fail every person you care about, so you latch on to every opportunity to make up for whatever jerk moves you pull, because maybe you won't end up a deadbeat dad."

"Back off, Alix," Justin said in a low, dangerous voice.

"Oh, did I hit a nerve? What are you going to do? Punch me? Go ahead. Hit me. I dare you."

"No." Justin swallowed stiffly, forcing himself to stay calm. "This isn't you. And if you want a fight, you're going to have to pick it with someone else. I'm not that guy anymore." He took a few steps back, a sad look on his face. "You need help, Alix. I don't know what your problem is, but you need help. Because at the rate you're going... you'll end up a lot more like Alice Cage than you want to be." Shaking his head slowly, Justin turned and walked away.

Andrew Sullivan moved out of the way at the last second, as an arrow buried itself into a tree directly next to his head. He raised his hands in surrender. "Wrong Sullivan brother."

Kate lowered her bow slowly. "Sorry, Andrew. I was just practicing."

"I know." Andrew pulled the arrow out of the wood and carried it over to her. "Though you don't usually practice in the forest outside the walls of the mansion property."

"Yeah, I just…" Kate trailed off, staring down at her boots.

"Needed to get away?" he prompted sympathetically.

"Something like that." Kate took her arrow from him and stuck it back in her quiver. "What are you doing here?"

"Casey wanted to talk to me. I was walking down the path and heard the distinctive sound of weaponry."

"She probably wants to ask about Zach. He wasn't here last night, and she's worried— whether she'll explicitly say so or not."

"I haven't heard from him, but I'll tell her that in person." Andrew put his hands on Kate's shoulders. "How are *you*?"

"Tired. Exhausted. Worn out."

Her brother-in-law smiled slightly. "Okay, but that's every day for you."

"True." Kate hesitated. "Have you… Has Niall…"

"He told me what's going on."

"Oh. So you probably hate me right now."

Andrew's grip on her shoulders

tightened. "Nobody hates you, Kate. Not me, and especially not Niall. Do you really think we do?"

"I think somebody *should*."

"Why would you think that?"

"After everything I've done? Come on, Andrew."

Andrew gave her a sad smile. "Kate, I think you need to think long and hard about why you're so much harder on yourself than any of us are on you." He hugged her tightly. "Just think about it, okay?" He tapped his hands on her shoulders once and continued towards the mansion.

Zach groaned softly as he opened his eyes. His vision was still blurry and his head was pounding. At some point after being knocked unconscious he had been drugged, he somehow knew. Other than that, everything that had happened since he had talked to the man he knew as Wade Toracid was a hazy blur.

As his vision began to solidify, Zach realized that he was in some sort of wooden cage in the middle of a room that didn't seem to have any doors. There was another cage on the opposite side of the room, in which a blond-haired man was unconscious.

"What the hell?" Zach whispered.

"I figured you'd be waking up soon," a female voice said from behind him.

Zach looked back and found himself

facing a woman with dark brown hair. She was smiling coldly. "Where am I?" Zach demanded.

"That depends on how good you are at fighting."

"What do you mean?"

The woman pointed at the blond man in the other cage. "That's Tag. He's one of the serial killers."

"One of?"

"There are three. Tag, Edward Caito, and myself."

Zach swallowed. "I guess that explains why you were so hard to stop."

"Among other things," the woman replied cheerfully. "Anyway, the general point of this room is simple. There are two of you here. One of you gets to leave alive."

"That's absurd," Zach spat. "I'm not going to kill that man, even if he *is* a serial killer."

The woman shrugged. "Then you'll die, and he'll get to leave. It really doesn't matter to me at all."

"You'd sell one of your accomplices out for some sick game?"

"I'd kill Tag myself, but it's much more amusing to force you to do it for me." The woman patted the top of Zach's cage. "But that's tomorrow's fun. Enjoy tonight's sleep, Mr. Carter. Tomorrow night, you'll either be dead or a murderer."

16

When Kara opened her front door, it was almost one in the morning. Claire was asleep on the couch, with James sleeping on top of her. Kara gave a small smile and sat down on the arm of the couch near Claire's head, gently running her fingers through the other woman's hair.

Claire woke slowly from the contact and frowned up at her. "Hey," she mumbled. "What time is it?"

"12:47."

"I assume you don't mean it's the afternoon."

Kara chuckled softly. "No; it's morning."

"Funny definition of 'morning,' Hall."

"Shhh. You'll wake James."

Claire glanced down at her son, whose head was resting on her collarbone. "I doubt it," she whispered. "Kid could sleep through a bomb going off."

Kara smiled and interlaced her fingers with Claire's, bringing her arm up so she could briefly press her lips to the back of Claire's hand. "You know I love you, right?"

An alarmed look formed on Claire's face. "What's wrong?"

"Why does something have to be wrong?"

"Sudden declarations of love from your wife are always concerning when said wife is a superhero. I'm pretty sure it's a written rule."

"Everything's fine. I promise." Kara paused. "I guess I'm just worried. And when I worry, I worry that the people I care about don't know how much I care about them."

"We know." Claire rested her free hand on Kara's leg. "Trust me, Kara. We know. And I definitely know that you love me. I love you, too. Always will."

Kara squeezed Claire's hand and leaned against the back of the couch. "I can't exactly sleep in this position, so I'm going to go to bed."

"No fair. I wanted to go to bed three hours ago, but I have a four-year-old weight on my chest that I'd rather not wake up."

"I'm not going to help you. This way, I'll get the entire bed to myself."

"Bitch."

"Oh, absolutely." Kara laughed and carefully picked James up. "There, I saved you."

"Knew you were a superhero." Claire stood up stiffly. "Have fun. I'm going to bed."

"Abandoning me so quickly?"

"Yes," Claire deadpanned. She kissed Kara and headed for the bedroom.

James, his head resting on Kara's shoulder, stirred quietly. "Wha'sgoinon?"

"Nothing, baby. Go back to sleep."

"'Kay, Mom," he mumbled, already halfway there.

Kara stood there for another twenty minutes, just holding the sleeping boy and wondering whether she had as much time left with her family as she had always thought she would.

AJ walked into the control room carrying two mugs of coffee. He handed one to Cass and sat down in the chair next to hers. "How's everything going out there?"

"Hit and miss. Jay and Kara stopped a bank robbery at eight thirty. Ray and Justin have seen nothing. Kate and Alix almost got attacked by another one of those mobs at nine fifteen, but they're okay."

"Alix is in the field?"

Cass took a slow sip from her coffee. "I didn't want her to be, but she went out anyway. She's stubborn. Big surprise."

"Explains where Aubrey gets it," AJ joked.

His wife smiled slightly. "That it does." She glanced at him. "Alix is the one who suggested the name 'Jacob,' right?"

"Uh, yeah, why?"

Cass pointed at Diana van der Aart's diary, which was sitting next to a keyboard. "It's your middle name."

AJ almost choked on his coffee. "What?"

"Anthony Jacob Sadik. Alix got us to name our son after you."

"Aw, come on. Having one kid named

after a family member was enough."

"I know, right?"

AJ studied her for a moment. "Anything else interesting in that diary?"

Cass stared down at her coffee. "I'm not sure. I-I stopped reading when I got to my date of birth. I'm… not sure I want to know the truth of what they did to me, AJ."

"Understandable."

"Is it?"

"Of course. Curiosity is natural, but so is fear."

Cass pulled him towards her by his tie and kissed him lightly on the mouth. "Thank you."

"What for?"

"Everything."

AJ laughed softly. "I haven't done much, Cass."

"You're very wrong about that, AJ." Cass released him and turned towards the door when she saw Casey walk in. She was carrying a glass of scotch and looked like she hadn't slept.

"Casey," AJ greeted hesitantly.

"It's nine thirty in the morning," Cass said, her voice gentle. "Isn't it a little early for that?"

The other woman didn't seem to hear her. "Have you, uhm, have you heard from Zach?" Casey asked in a hoarse voice.

"No. I haven't. I would've let you know if

I had."

Casey downed her scotch terrifyingly fast. "Okay. Thanks."

Cass stood up slowly. "Case…"

"Don't need or want the lecture right now, Cass. I really, really don't."

"Actually, I'm pretty sure you *do* 'need' it," Cass retorted.

Casey got in her face, looking furious. "You have no idea what I need, so don't try to play that card on me, Cassidy. We haven't been sisters nearly long enough."

"No, but you look rather similar when you're both pissed off," AJ commented. He stood and pushed his way between them. "Alright, stop it, both of you. Turning on each other isn't going to help anything."

"It'll make me feel better," Casey snarled.

"It really won't, and you know that."

Alix appeared in the doorway and hesitated. "I… take it this is a bad time."

"Actually, it's a perfect time," AJ said quickly. "What do you need, Al?"

"Kate didn't handle that mob trying to kill us this morning very well. I was wondering if one of you could talk to her. She's practicing at her spot in the woods like she does, and she won't listen to a thing I say."

"Maybe because you're so good at tact," Casey said bitterly.

Alix didn't even glance at Casey, though

her jaw tensed to indicate that she had heard the jab. AJ closed his eyes briefly before saying, "Cass, why don't you go? I'll take over control, Alix can go back into the field, and Casey can go sleep off however much she drank last night."

"I'm fine," Casey snapped.

"Sure you are. Go upstairs before I knock you out myself. And don't think I won't do it."

Casey looked prepared to argue, but she turned on her heel and stomped out of the room. Alix watched her go and then murmured, "I thought she could always handle her alcohol pretty well."

Cass gave a scoffing laugh. "She can handle alcohol. She can't handle Zach being missing."

Alix raised an eyebrow. "She never heard from him?"

"No."

"You don't think he's…"

"We don't know. And to be honest, I'd rather think that he's just being stupid than think that he's dead." Cass's voice softened. "Especially because I'm not sure how Casey would take the latter."

"I'd imagine just about as well as you'd take me being dead," AJ replied quietly.

Cass shivered. "Don't make me think about that."

AJ hugged her briefly. "I'm sorry," he murmured. "Go talk to Kate. She could use some advice from someone who's been where she is."

"Where's that?"

A grim smile formed on AJ's face. "Smack in the middle of self-hatred."

Cass mirrored his smile. "Ah, yes. I'm quite familiar with that place." She kissed AJ on the cheek and headed for the door. "I'll go find her. I'll talk to you two later."

Kate took in a long, slow breath, her eyes focused on a specific knot on a tree a few yards in front of her. She waited until her heartbeat was steady, and she released the arrow in her hand.

Before it could strike the tree, the arrow was caught by Jay, who appeared in front of Kate in a blur. "Hey there," he greeted brightly.

"You're lucky you're fast, West."

"Eh. Arrows can't hurt that much, right?"

Kate snorted. "Keep telling yourself that." She pulled out another arrow and aimed again. "What do you want?"

"Kara was checking in with Ray, so I wanted to make sure you were okay."

"I'm fine." Kate released the arrow in her hand, and it missed the tree entirely, disappearing into a bush.

"Looks like it," Jay said dryly.

Kate prepared another arrow. "Shut up. How's Ray doing as leader man?"

"Good. He's a lot smarter than I thought

he was. But I think he'll feel better when he's back in the number two spot and you're back in charge. He likes giving orders, but he likes you more." Jay smiled slightly. "We *all* like you more."

Another arrow missed its mark. "I'm not going back in charge, Jay."

"What do you mean?"

"I mean I'm done. Ray can have the field leader post. I don't want it."

Jay was silent as Kate went to retrieve the two arrows that had gotten lost in the bushes. "You don't really mean that, Kate."

"I do. I can't handle it anymore, Jay. I can't do it." Kate wandered back to the spot she had been shooting from and examined the arrows in her hands. "Can I ask you something?"

"Well, yeah, sure."

"Why did you and Abigail get divorced?"

Jay seemed surprised. "There were a few reasons, which you know, but when it came down to it, twenty-one was too young for either of us to be married."

"I was barely eighteen," Kate whispered. "Wasn't I too young, too?"

"Not necessarily. You and Niall were— are —very good for each other. Maybe it was fast, maybe you were quite young, but you've been married for ten years. Eleven this November. Clearly something worked." Jay studied Kate for a long moment. "Kate, don't second-guess your entire life just because you have some problems."

"I can't help it. My head won't shut up about everything I've ever done wrong." Kate threw an arrow at a tree off to her right in a burst of frustration, and it buried itself in the dead center of the wood.

"That feeling never really goes away," Cass said quietly as she joined them.

"Thanks, Cass, that makes me feel so much better," Kate replied sarcastically.

"I'm serious. I still feel like that sometimes, and my life is significantly better than it was when those voices first started." Cass put her hands in her pockets. "But I've learned to ignore it, as best I can. Because I shouldn't let myself ruin my own life based on a few mistakes I may or may not have made. I'll never get anywhere if I do that."

"Some days I feel like I don't want to get anywhere. Some days I just want everything to stop."

"That's a bit of a different impulse," Cass said gently. "That's the impulse that made you want Justin to kill you."

Kate stared down at the ground, while Jay looked horrified. "Wait, you—"

"I think so," she murmured. "I don't know, I..." Kate took in a deep breath. "Yeah. Yeah, I guess that's what I wanted."

"And now?" Cass prompted.

Kate pulled back another arrow and

aimed it at the knot she had been aiming at before. "I'm not going to let myself die. But I'm not quite sure I want to let myself live, either."

"God, Kate," Jay whispered. "Why didn't you say…"

"It doesn't matter," Kate said stiffly. "None of it matters. I'm fine." She let her arrow loose and missed again.

Cass smiled sadly. "I'm sure you are."

Jay's wristband beeped. "I-I… Kara needs me back in the city."

"Go ahead, Jay," Cass said. "We're fine here."

"Are you sure?"

"Positive."

Jay nodded and rested a hand on Kate's shoulder. "You don't need to carry all of our weight, you know. You don't need to deal with your pain by yourself. We're a team for a reason. Talk to us." He squeezed her shoulder, gaze her a small smile, and sped off.

"He's right."

"Please, Cass. I can't talk about this for more than a few minutes at a time." Kate went to retrieve her arrow.

"You can barely talk about it at all. A few extra minutes won't change that."

"Everyone wants to talk to me. Niall tries to talk to me all the time. Ray and Kara check in with me every hour. AJ takes my blood pressure every time he can corner me, supposedly to check on me since my incident with Justin but really so that he can try to get me to talk to him. People want to talk to me, but I can't do it, Cass. Every time I open my mouth, I say something I regret. Or I end up feeling like even more of a failure than I already am. So why would I want to talk?"

"I—"

"If she doesn't want to talk, we could always fight."

Cass and Kate turned towards the new voice and found Finn leaning against the tree that Kate had thrown an arrow into. "Oh, good, just what I wanted," Kate muttered.

"Go back to Alice, kid," Cass said, a warning tone in her voice. "You can't beat both of us, and whatever it is you came here to do? It isn't something you're going to *want* to do, I promise you that."

Finn straightened off of the tree. "I'm sorry, Mrs. Hamil, but I have my orders." She started towards Cass. Kate, looking annoyed, stepped forward. In seconds, she was on the ground unconscious.

"*Kate!*" Cass exclaimed, stunned.

"That's pretty much how our last confrontation went," Finn said, staring at the downed vigilante. "I see she hasn't learned anything."

Cass stepped between Finn and Kate. "Maybe she hasn't. But I think you'll find that I'm a tougher fighter than I look."

"Indeed. Trained by Gabriel Garrison and

his assortment of security agents, yes?"

The confident look on Cass's face faltered briefly. "What would you know about Garrison?"

"Only that he worked for the Vigilance Initiative." Finn paused. "Alice is not a fan."

Cass scoffed. "Alice isn't a fan of much."

"No. I suppose not." Finn took a small step backwards. "If you want to fight me, Mrs. Hamil, so be it. It will not prevent me from completing my mission."

"I'm up for proving you wrong."

Cass threw the first punch, and it was instantly clear that her fight was going to go very differently than Kate's extremely brief one had. While Finn avoided the swing, it was much closer than anything Kate had pulled out. The two were relatively evenly matched for about two minutes, until Finn struck a blow directly on the spot where Alix had accidentally hit Cass the day before. Cass stumbled backwards with a quiet yelp of pain.

"You're never going to beat me in a fist fight, Mrs. Hamil," Finn said matter-of-factly. "My power is enhanced reflexes. I can block every move you make."

"Maybe," Cass replied through gritted teeth. "But maybe you're holding back."

"I don't understand."

"You put Kate on the ground pretty easily. She's not a bad fighter. Better at long-distance, sure, but she's not a bad fighter. You shouldn't be having this much trouble with a forty-two-year-old mother of three who hasn't been in a real fight in a very long time."

"I... don't want to hurt you."

"Why?"

Finn hesitated, looking troubled, but before she could respond, Alice's voice said, "Because she's been instructed not to."

Cass looked behind Finn and saw that, at some point, Alice had appeared, along with a forty-something man with sandy brown hair. "Oh, how nice of you to show up, Alice," Cass said with forced pleasantry. "If you don't mind standing there while I shoot you?" She pulled her gun out from behind her back, but Finn disarmed her with ease.

"I figured you might be a tad upset with me over what happened with Anthony," Alice said. "That's why I wanted Finn to confront you first."

Cass laughed loudly. "A tad upset? You shot the man I love in front of our daughter. I'm well beyond 'a tad upset'. I'm closer to 'homicidal rage'."

Alice shrugged. "He lived, didn't he? What's the difference?"

"You psychotic *bitch*, you—"

"Be quiet," the sandy-haired man snapped. "The only reason you're still alive is because Alice insists on it. *I* voted for killing you right here."

"You're never going to let that go, are

you, Edward?"

"Not really; no."

"Who the hell are you?" Cass asked, sounding almost tired.

"Edward Caito. Serial killer."

"Most serial killers don't advertise themselves as such."

Caito shrugged. "You'll be dead soon anyway. Where's the harm?"

Alice looked at Finn. "Take Tess here to the car. Then come back for Oliver."

"And just in case you can't handle it," Caito said snidely. He held out a hand, and Kate's metal bow reformed into solid handcuffs. Caito smirked at Cass. "Neat power, huh? I duplicated it from a Legion hero. I think you're acquainted."

Cass stared at Caito, so stunned that she didn't even try to resist when the handcuffs were forced onto her wrists. "What did you do to him?" she asked quietly.

"Well..." Caito checked his watch. "I presume he's probably dead by now."

Cass gave a quiet laugh and shook her head slowly. "Then you're as good as dead yourself."

"That's fine with me. You people are heroes; you'll make my death quick."

Alice grinned. "The question you need to ask yourself, Tess, is whether I will grant you the same favor."

17

At eleven A.M. exactly, Zach's cage collapsed open, each side falling away and the roof dropping on top of him. Zach gave a quiet grunt of pain as he pushed the thick wooden bars off of himself and stiffly stood up. The hours of confinement had made it difficult for his legs to support his weight, so he used the piece of cage to lean on as he surveyed the room. Tag's cage had also opened, but the other man had not reacted. He was still lying on the floor of his cell, now with a piece of wood on top of him.

High up in the ceiling of the room they were in was a speaker, through which came Sarah's voice. "Wake the hell up, Tag. I haven't got all day." When he didn't respond, the floors of both cages lit with electricity.

Zach stumbled off of the platform at the same time as Tag woke with a yelp. "Sorry, Kov," Sarah said, without a hint of apology. "Didn't have time to set it up so that I could shock one of you at a time."

"What in all hell is going on?" Tag demanded, sounding groggy. "I was about to go on a hunt with Sarah, and then…"

"Oh, yeah, I knocked you out. Kept you down until I was ready for you. Didn't want you using your power to escape. Mostly everything in here is wood or stone, so I wasn't worried about Kov, but your power was a little more troublesome."

Tag stared up at the speaker. "Why am I here, Sarah?"

"You and Kov are going to have a little fight. Whoever survives gets to leave. Admittedly, this fight won't be quite as much fun, since you're both kind of out of it, but I'll take what I can get."

"This is insane," Zach said hoarsely. "This is completely insane."

"Yeah," Tag agreed. He held out his palm, and small spheres of golden light formed inside it. "But I've killed a lot of people. Hell if I'm going to stop now, especially if it'll save my life."

Zach sighed softly. "Alright, then. If that's how you want to handle this, fine. I'm not going to argue with someone like you." He held out a hand, and the metal in the speaker in the ceiling ripped out and formed into a sphere that hovered above his palm. "Don't think I'll go quietly just because I'm a hero."

Tag laughed. "Maybe not quietly, but you'll damn well go quickly, vigilante man. I've been waiting for a chance to beat the crap out of one of you."

Zach's hands tightened into fists, and all metal still in the room began to vibrate, trying to break free to get to him. "You're welcome to try."

"Kate, can you hear me? Kate!"

Cass's voice slowly broke through the fog in Kate's head, and she opened her eyes carefully. "Ow," she muttered.

"How are you feeling?" Cass asked. She was sitting in a chair directly across from Kate, her wrists tied to the arms by thick leather straps.

"Like I really need to stop trying to fight Finn." Kate looked down, seeing that she too was tied to a chair, with leather bindings around her wrists and ankles. "What did I miss?"

"Well, it seems that we've been kidnapped by Alice, Finn, and the serial killer that we've been trying to find. Apparently, we don't need to try to look for people because they inevitably find us. Oh, and if you feel funny, it's because you were only out for a short time after Finn hit you, so they drugged you with something."

Kate stared at Cass for a long moment. "Wonderful. We have quite the track record these past few weeks, don't we?"

Cass glanced down at the bindings on her wrists. "I don't know; I think we're doing pretty well," she said dryly.

"Any idea where we are?" Kate asked as she shook her head to clear some of the fog.

"None. They put a bag over my head."

"Why didn't they drug you, too?" Kate grumbled.

"Who knows?" Cass scoffed. "Although given the number of chemicals that I've had put into me, it probably wouldn't have worked anyway. Most painkillers don't do anything anymore. *That* is tons of fun, let me tell you."

"I'd imagine." Kate fidgeted in her chair, turning her wrist so that her palm was facing upwards. She then attempted to pull out of the leather strap. Instantly, an electric current ran through the metal chair. "*Son of a bitch*," Kate spat, putting her arm back flat on the chair immediately.

"Sorry; I forgot to warn you about that."

"Electrified chairs? Come on! Who does that?!"

Cass raised an eyebrow. "Probably the same kind of woman who murders her own clones for fun."

"Good point."

As if on cue, the door to the room they were in opened, and Alice walked in. "Sounds like somebody tried to escape," she said, in her best scolding teacher voice.

"It was less an escape attempt and more me moving slightly," Kate complained.

"Yeah; it's a little sensitive. It was set up by someone a little more sadistic than I am."

Cass scoffed loudly. "I wasn't sure that was possible."

"I'm not *sadistic*, Tess. I just don't particularly care if my enemies die in horrifically painful ways."

Kate and Cass exchanged an almost bored look. "I thought you were smart, Alice," Kate said. "I'm starting to doubt myself."

"Funny. Won't save you from a terrible death, though." Alice folded her arms across her chest. "See, I'm looking to find a way to kill a large number of empowered people at once. And I think Tess knows how I can do it."

"I do?" Cass asked, confused.

"I believe so." Alice hit a button on a device on her wrist, and the wall opposite the door lifted up, revealing a large black safe. The only form of input to unlock it was a small hole a few feet off of the floor.

Cass went pale. "Oh, god. The blood locks. I completely forgot about them."

Alice sneered at her. "How could you have possibly forgotten them?"

"I-I thought they were all destroyed when Stephanie blew up that warehouse."

Kate took one look at the expression on Cass's face and knew that it was bad, but she had to ask anyway. "What's a blood lock?"

"A type of safe designed by John Wechsler," Alice replied. "It can only be open by a blood sample from the person who locked it. He never produced them other than the few that he used himself. Never said why."

"Maybe cutting your arm open whenever you need your passport wasn't something that was going to appeal to a lot of people," Kate said sarcastically.

"A possibility." Alice shrugged. "It didn't matter. I was always more interested in what was in *this* safe. His *special* safe. He kept it separate from the others. I have a feeling that I know what's in it. Do you, Tess?"

Cass was now so pale that she looked about ready to pass out. "You can't, Alice. Not even you are that insane."

Alice just smiled. "Tell me whether it will work, Tess. Tell me whether it's in that safe, and tell me whether I can open it."

"That's why you took Casey's blood," Cass realized, ignoring Alice's requests. "You're going to take mine too, and you're going to try to isolate every bit of DNA that was given to us from our father to see if that will work on the blood lock."

"*Our* father?"

"Hush, Kate." Cass was staring intently at Alice. "But you know that if it doesn't work, the safe will incinerate everything inside of it."

"You know some of John's inventions better than I do. You know whether I can get this safe open. You're going to tell me, and *you're going to tell me whether the device will work*."

Cass shook her head slowly. "Go to hell, Alice."

Alice's smile didn't waver. "Do you know why I brought Kate Oliver here? I was going to have Finn kill her or seriously maim her back

239

in that forest. But then I realized that it was so much smarter to bring her along. Because I've come to learn something about your family, Tess. The best way to get any of you to do something isn't to point a gun at you. It's to point a gun at someone else." Alice took out a revolver and emptied it of bullets. She put one bullet back into the cylinder, spun it, and snapped it back into place. Then she pressed it against Kate's right shoulder. "I have plenty of bullets, and I have plenty of time. We'll do this one joint at a time until you tell me what I want to know."

"Kate, I'm sorry, but I can't," Cass said quietly.

"It's okay." Kate swallowed. "I understand."

Alice pulled the trigger, and the gun simply clicked. No bullet.

"Is the device John built in that safe, Tess?"

"Go to hell."

Click.

"Will the device work?"

"My answer hasn't changed."

Click.

"Can your blood open the lock?"

"Why don't you go ahead and try it?"

Click.

"How do I open the safe, Tess?"

"I suggest a blowtorch."

Click.

Kate took in a deep breath and closed her eyes, surprised at how badly she was shaking. Cass's defiant expression hadn't changed, but there was fear in her eyes. They both knew that Alice had gone through five of the six chambers in her revolver. Unless she hadn't actually loaded the gun, the next time she pulled the trigger would be a guaranteed bullet in Kate's shoulder.

"Explain the device to me, Tess."

"I…" Cass fidgeted in her chair, taking a moment to look at Kate. Then she sighed and lowered her voice. "My father found a small… addition to a person's DNA that is only there if they have powers. He found a way to target and kill based on that abnormality."

Kate was staring at her, horrified. "Cass…"

"But it… it was a quick and painless death, and he didn't think that was terrible enough for the vigilantes, so he put it away and stuck with his other plans. The device was his backup. He just died before he could use it."

Alice lowered her gun. "Is it in this safe?"

"… Last I saw it."

"Will combining your blood and that of Robin be enough to open it?"

Cass sighed. "I legitimately do not know."

Alice smirked. "That wasn't that hard,

was it? I told you. The biggest weakness of you Hamils is your protective instinct." She pulled a knife and a small vial out of her pocket and cut an unnecessarily large gash into Cass's forearm. After collecting some of Cass's blood in the vial, Alice said, "I'm going to go examine this, along with Robin's sample. You wouldn't mind waiting around here, would you?" With a cackle of a laugh, Alice turned and walked out of the room.

"You okay?" Cass asked Kate through gritted teeth.

"Yeah, though you shouldn't have done that."

"Couldn't help it."

"I know," Kate said softly. She looked at the cut on Cass's arm, which was slowly dripping blood onto the floor. "How about you? Are you okay?"

"I've had worse." Cass paused. "And better."

"Try not to think about it. I've heard that helps."

Cass gave a humorless smile. "Has that ever helped you?"

"Not a once, but I figured it was a nice sentiment." Kate hesitated. "Your father built a genocide device, and you never thought that was important to mention?"

Cass was silent for a long moment, staring down at her own blood. "I honestly thought that it had been destroyed. I didn't want to think about… about how close he almost came to killing all of you." She swallowed, and her eyes began to water. In a whisper, she said, "Kate, if Alice uses that device, it won't just kill you and the rest of my friends. It'll kill my kids. It… It might even kill me."

"What are you talking about? You don't have powers."

"Not… exactly," Cass replied carefully.

"I don't understand."

"You know how Alice and my father learned how to give people powers? And you know how they tested their experiments on me all the time?" Cass's hands were in tight fists, and she was trembling. "I read Stephanie's diary. They tested the power serums on me, too. And they gave me a power. Something to do with intelligence."

Kate's brow furrowed. "But… I mean, you're sure as hell smarter than me, but you're not—"

"Because my father and Alice… *toyed* with my brain. Mostly to see whether the powers had affected it, but also so that I wouldn't be able to access that power. Because they couldn't afford to have me be smarter than them, for risk of me starting to fight back." There was a moment of silence as Cass struggled to keep her voice steady. "The power is still in my head, but I can't access it. They severed the connection, somehow. But it's still in my blood, so I was able to pass it on to my children."

"Oh my god, Cass. I don't… I don't even know what to… what did AJ say?"

"Haven't told him yet."

"How could you have not told him?"

"I'm not sure how to tell him that whatever downsides our children inevitably have thanks to their powers are because of me."

"Nothing that your father did to you is your fault, Cass. None of it."

Cass gave a weak laugh.

"What's funny?"

"Nothing, it's just… an hour ago I was trying to make you feel better about yourself. Now here I am, just as much of a mess, if not more so, than you've ever been."

Kate grinned. "Consider it returning the favor."

"Might not have another chance, so that's fair."

"No. We'll get out."

"You have a plan?"

"Not exactly, but I suddenly no longer want to die, which is pretty good motivation to figure something out."

Cass smiled. "Nice to have you back, Kate."

"I don't know how long it'll last," the younger woman admitted.

"I'll take what I can get."

Zach dropped to his hands and knees, panting as blood pooled under him from a split lip and a deep gash in his side. He could tell that a few of his ribs were bruised at the very least, more likely fractured, and he could feel more blood dripping down the side of his face from an injury to his temple.

Tag was leaning against the wall several feet away from him, also winded and wounded. His nose was broken, as was one of his knees, and his left arm was hanging limply at his side. The collar of his t-shirt was soaked red from a gash to the side of his throat.

"I'll give you credit, Kov," Tag said, the arrogance in his voice weaker, but still clearly present. "You lasted a lot longer than I thought you would."

"Enough, Tag," Zach said. "We don't need to keep doing this. If we worked together for five minutes, we could both get out of here alive."

"I don't *want* us both to get out of here alive," Tag growled. "I tried to be in the Legion when I was a teenager. All of you turned on me because of some stupid shoplifting. It wasn't like anybody was getting hurt. I was kicked out over nothing. When Caito found me, I knew that I was going to get to do something important, like I've always been meant to. Now that I'm allowed to kill heroes? My true purpose in life is going to be able to be fulfilled."

Zach tightened his fist, mentally finding a small shard of metal on the floor a few feet from Tag. "Is that really how you want to be remembered?"

"Let me think." Tag held out his hand, forming several small golden spheres. "Hell yes, it is."

"Okay," Zach said softly. He lifted one hand off of the floor.

The shard of metal jumped off of the floor, sped towards Tag, and hit him in the heart with the same force as a bullet. Tag had enough time to look shocked before he dropped to the floor.

Zach lowered his hand slowly. "I'm sorry," he murmured, before collapsing sideways, unconscious.

18

Niall entered the control room at eleven thirty, the exact time that his shift began. He hesitated, surprised, when he saw AJ sitting in the chair. "I thought Cass was on before me."

"She is. She was." AJ stood. "She went to talk to Kate."

"Oh." Niall shifted his weight awkwardly. "Is she… Is Kate okay?"

"She's been better, but not all of it is because of what happened between you two."

"I love her, AJ. I always will. I just can't…" Niall looked down at the floor.

"You can't risk the chance of her going off the deep end enough to hurt Ciaran and Rick," AJ finished softly.

"Does that make me a horrible person?"

"No."

They just stood there in silence until Niall rubbed the back of his neck and said, "I guess I should take a seat, huh."

"Yeah. I guess somebody has to." AJ headed for the door, pausing briefly to pat Niall on the shoulder. "Everything will be okay, Niall. You'll see. Just give it time."

"Somehow that doesn't make me feel better," Niall joked weakly.

AJ gave him a small smile. "It'll have to do for now."

Once out of the control room, AJ noticed that the lights were on in Casey's workroom. He headed over there and found her bent over what looked like a box of multicolored wire. Her glasses were pushed up into her hair, and yet another glass of scotch was on the table next to an assortment of screwdrivers.

"I told you to get some sleep."

"I can't sleep," Casey muttered. "I'm trying to fix the GPS system for the sunglasses."

"I thought that couldn't be fixed. I thought you had to build an entirely new system before we'd get that ability back."

Casey picked up a screwdriver and stuck it into the mess of wires. "Yeah, well, maybe I'm just stupid."

AJ took a few cautious steps towards her. "Casey, I think you need to take a break."

She slammed the screwdriver down on the table so hard that it dented the metal. "I am *fine*, AJ!" she snarled. "Back the hell off and go do your own job!"

"I am doing my own job," he replied calmly. "Team medic, remember? It's my job to make sure you all stay healthy. And what you're doing right now clearly isn't healthy."

Casey dropped the box onto the table next to the screwdriver and rested her head in her hands. She took in a slow, shaky sigh. "AJ, what if Zach's…"

"We don't know that," AJ said quickly.

"That's the *point*! God, I don't want to be crying over a guy, but I… I don't… I can't… I lo…" Casey shook her head slowly. "I don't know what to do."

AJ closed the distance between them and pulled her into a hug. "We'll figure it out. I promise you, Casey. We'll figure it out."

Casey gripped him tightly, burying her face in his shirt. "I can't lose him, AJ. Not before… I just can't."

"I know," AJ murmured. He kissed her on the top of the head. "Trust me. I know."

They stayed there for a minute until Alix appeared in the room. Casey pulled away from AJ and growled, "What do you want, Tolvaj?"

"I-I… Ray sent me to find Kate, because she hadn't checked in for a while. When I got to her practice spot, her quiver was there and some of her arrows were there, but she wasn't. There was also some blood. And it looked like somebody had been dragged towards the road."

Casey and AJ exchanged a startled glance. "Oh, god," Casey muttered. "Do you think Kate did something?"

"I'm not sure. I feel like she would've gone more *self*-destructive at this point." Alix turned to AJ. "Have you talked to Cass since she went to see Kate?"

AJ fidgeted with his tie, pale and worried. "No. I don't think she came back here. I assumed they were still together."

"What are we supposed to do?"

Casey, looking exhausted, picked up her glass of scotch. "At this point? Hope for a goddamn miracle."

Alix leaned against Casey's worktable, staring down at her hands. "I think I know where I can find one."

Justin clapped a hand on Ray's shoulder and he stepped up onto the edge of the roof next to him. "How you holding up, brother?"

"I'm alright. I'll be better when Kate takes her job back."

"Will you?"

Ray gave Justin a sideways look. "What do you mean?"

"You like being in charge. Don't you?"

"I don't... hate it. But Kate's my sister, and she's the field leader. I don't want something that would hurt her."

Justin smiled thinly. "Want to know a secret, Ray? I'm not sure she'd be hurt."

Jay and Kara joined them. "The mayor is going to hold a press conference in front of city hall," Jay reported. "He wants to tell people to calm down so that there's not another killing."

"Does he really think that will work?" Justin asked, scoffing.

"I think we had better damn well hope it does," Kara replied darkly.

"Why does this keep happening to us?"

Cass snorted. "What do you mean 'us'? It's always *me*."

Kate gave a sharp laugh. "This is true. Maybe one day you won't be the team member who ends up tied to a chair."

"I can hope, but we all know it's not going to happen." Cass sighed softly. "I'm sorry, Kate."

"What for?"

"Alice wanted me. You shouldn't even be here." There was a pause as Cass bit her lip, moving her arm slightly in a vain attempt to stop the steady— if slow —drip of blood.

"You aren't allowed to blame yourself for Alice Cage being a terrible person." Kate bowed her head. "Plus, this is probably the universe getting back at me for killing my siblings and being the worst wife and mother in the world."

"Do me a favor. If I'm not allowed to blame myself for Alice, you aren't allowed to blame yourself for deaths that you didn't cause." Cass laughed sarcastically. "As for being the worst mother in the world? Why don't you ask Casey and Alix how they feel about their mothers? And you're not a bad wife either, Kate. You're sick. That is not your fault."

"It's not easy for me to get that through my head, Cass."

"I know, sweetie. That's okay. You'll

figure it out."

Kate gave a thin smile. "Funny how it's easiest for me to talk to you when I'm about to be executed."

Cass mirrored her smile. "Yeah, it's weird how quickly this kind of situation can make you open up. Y'know, the first time I told AJ that I thought I was in love with him was after my father had held a knife to his throat. And Casey is just about to crack and admit all of her feelings for Zach with him missing. And there was that time Justin didn't tell us he was engaged until some bad guy beat the crap out of him. Nobody on this team is very good at admitting things unless something bad is happening."

"You must admit a *lot*."

"Very funny, smartass."

The door opened, and Alice walked back into the room along with Finn. Alice was holding a small vial, different from the one used to collect Cass's blood, but still filled with a red blood-like fluid.

"I hope you used this time to say your goodbyes to one another, because I was able to synthesize something that should be close enough to John Wechsler's DNA to work on this damn machine," Alice said brightly.

"Can I ask something first, Alice?"

Alice grinned widely. "Why, of course you can, Tess."

"What's the point? Why do you want to

kill empowered people anyway? You're a brilliant scientist who could be making billions and instead you're scrounging around the remnants of your college secret society hoping to commit genocide against a group that has done absolutely nothing to you."

"The point?" Alice laughed loudly. "Tess, there isn't a *point*. I didn't have a reason to hate empowered people when I helped found the Vigilance Initiative. All I wanted was an excuse to perform science however I wanted, and at the end of the day I wanted an excuse to kill people. Now that everyone else in the VI is dead, well, my motivation is a bit different. I hated every single one of those self-righteous fools, but I am the only one who had a right to kill them. Technically, I killed the Sadiks because I sent one of my clones to kill them, but I didn't get to kill any of the others. That is *all* the fault of empowered lunatics like you. So, to honor my original motivation, I am going to kill everyone with powers and then I'll kill the two of you."

Cass snorted. "Great plan, but Kate and I should both have the thing in our blood that your little weapon targets, so… we'll already be dead."

"That is a *good point*. I really should do something awful to at least one of you first." Alice turned to Finn, still grinning. "Finn, execute Targeter for me."

"Whoa, wait, wait a minute." Kate glared

at the woman tied across from her. "Thanks a lot, Cass."

"My sarcasm may have gone too far," Cass said flatly.

"*You think?*"

Finn took her gun off of her belt. She studied Kate briefly, the same strange look in her eyes. Then the rested the gun against the side of Alice's head.

"People of Caotico, we *must* calm down!" Mayor Salvatore Hannover leaned against his podium, gripping it tightly as he surveyed the crowd of people in front of him. "We are reasonable human beings, and I *know* that we are smart enough not to turn on each other like this! The vigilantes in this town have been protecting and serving us for *years*, and it is not right to treat them this way just because one person has decided to make things so difficult! I—"

"You are *so right*, Mr. Mayor," Caito said as he exited the crowd and walked up to the man.

"I'm sorry. Who are you?" Hannover asked, confused.

"My name is Wade Toracid. I'm the Legion hero 'Raseri.' I've been working to find the killer working in this city."

"Oh. Well. Thank you, Mr. Toracid."

Caito got closer to the mayor, smiling. "I would just like to apologize to you and the people of this city for not catching this awful person sooner." His smile turned to a cold grin. "The thing is, we aren't really happy with the way you mortal jackasses have been treating us, so we've been… slacking."

Hannover's grip tightened further on his podium as the crowd began to murmur angrily. "Mr. Toracid, I doubt you speak for every member of the Legion, and you certainly don't speak for Heroics, so I would appreciate it if you just let me finish what I was saying."

"No… I don't think so." Caito turned to look at the news camera next to him. "Hey, watch this!"

And he threw a sphere of light through the mayor's chest.

19

"What in the hell do you think you're doing, girl?" Alice demanded as the cold metal of Finn's gun pressed into her scalp.

"What I should've done after any of the six times you executed a child in front of me," Finn said in a cold, calm voice.

"Apparently, I should've executed you, too," Alice snarled. "You fool. You can't kill me. You don't have the guts."

"I don't have to."

Alice laughed. "Then what's the plan? I won't let you just walk out of here with these two. And you won't be able to do this by yourself."

Finn grinned and repeated, "I don't have to."

The door to the room opened again, and AJ and Casey walked in. "I was hoping to get a gun so that I could return the favor of a bullet, Alice, but then I remembered that I'm not a jackass."

"Well, well, Anthony, look who got a sense of humor," Alice said sarcastically. She glared at Finn. "What have you done?"

"Alix contacted me," Finn said in a quiet voice. "She told me that I had one last chance to make the right choice. And she was right. So I did."

"You're a fool. And I'm going to make

sure that you die a horrific death."

"I really don't think you can scare me at the moment," Finn replied. "I am the one with the gun."

"Nice attitude," Casey said to Finn as she headed for Kate. "Still doesn't make up for you bashing my face into a table."

"... Yeah," Finn said sheepishly. "Right."

"Make friends later," Alice snarled. "I knew I needed to stop using children and creations as my minions."

"Well, Alice, it is my life's ambition to make sure that you never get the opportunity to use *anyone* as a minion *ever again*," Alix said as she walked into the room. She looked at AJ, who was examining the gash in Cass's arm. "I just talked to Niall. It's a good thing you talked him into staying at the base, because apparently a lunatic from the Security Legion just executed the mayor on live television."

"Wait, *what*?" AJ stared at her. "What the hell is going on?"

"Oh, crap," Casey murmured. "The last prison escapee."

Alice smirked. "Yeah, you all seem to have forgotten about him. Edward Caito? Power duplication? Your friendly neighborhood serial killer? Even if you do prevent me from killing all of you, you won't be able to stop the city from despising everyone with powers now that Edward has killed the mayor."

"You manipulative bitch." Casey gave a soft, humorless laugh. "You played us. Coming into our home and shooting AJ and not just getting blood from me and Cass by killing us... It was part of the plan. Distract us from trying to stop a serial killer in order to make sure his job was finished."

"You always were the smart one, Robin." Alice folded her arms across her chest. "Now, are we going to do anything, or are you going to let me open this safe? I'm getting bored." She glanced around the room. "Although, this is a mighty interesting party we have here. My clone. The son of Giada and Austin. The daughter of Brooke and John. The daughter of Diana and John. Look at you all. The next generation of the Vigilance Initiative. Not that you're anything to be proud of."

As AJ removed the bindings from Cass's wrists, she said, "You're pride isn't exactly something that we want."

"The Vigilance Initiative may be our inheritance, but it's not our destiny," AJ said coldly. "We aren't them. We aren't you."

"Are you sure about that?" Alice's gaze turned to focus on Alix. "I understand someone has been having some difficulties."

"What the hell would you know about them?" Alix asked angrily.

Alice smirked. "Well, clone, I know that the reason for those difficulties is because you're turning into me."

Justin, Ray, Jay, and Kara turned towards city hall as they began to hear screams. "What the hell is Hannover saying to those people?" Justin wondered.

"I don't think that's a reaction to a speech, Archer," Ray said slowly.

Niall's voice crackled into their ears. *"Guys, you have to get to that press conference right now."*

"What's going on, Control?" Ray asked.

"Somebody just executed the mayor."

"I'm sorry, *what?*" Ray looked at his companions. "Clash, Pilot, go. You're fastest."

As the two hurried off, Niall said, *"I just told Thief. She's... busy. I'll update you on that later. A guy who claimed he was from the Legion walked up to Hannover and killed him. That's all I know about that. But there are already two separate groups forming mobs in the northern district, and it looks like a crowd is forming around the police station in the center of the city. It doesn't look good. Be careful."*

"Aren't we always?" Justin joked as he adjusted how his quiver was sitting on his back.

"Right. Sure. Whatever."

"Still no word on Targeter?" Justin asked, the slight tremor in his voice betraying his anxiousness.

"... No. Thief's on it."

"She'd better be doing a good job of it. Or have you not noticed that she's not exactly right in the head at the moment?"

"Not the time, Archer," Ray said quietly. "Come on. Let's check on the gathering at the police station."

"I'm not turning into you," Alix growled, her hands tightened into fists.

"Oh, but you are," Alice replied, false sweetness in her voice. "At least, your personality is. See, the serum that you stole instead of doing anything to save me from a burning building? Its original purpose wasn't to fix your aging rate. Why would I want to fix that? No. What I wanted was to copy my personality more accurately into my clones, since I had successfully duplicated everything else. But the only way that I could do it was with a serum that would readjust your age rate and also would essentially make you allergic to your powers, even though those powers are what allow the personality to overtake yours. I didn't see the point in using something that would probably make you drop dead in the middle of a mission for me, so I never gave you the serum. Fortunately for me, you ended up doing it yourself. And now it's so bad that you can barely keep it together long enough to have a conversation. I can tell because of the way your eyes are darkening right now."

Alix's eyes had indeed darkened in color.

She was trembling slightly and looked paler than normal. "You're lying."

"Am I? Why don't we work out some sort of deal, Alix? If you let me use the weapon that should be in that safe, you'll get a quick and painless death. Wouldn't you prefer that over what you're getting?"

"Shut the hell up," Cass said quietly. She was standing next to AJ, a furious look on her face. "Shut the hell up, Alice."

"Why? I'm not doing anything wrong. I'm simply giving this stupid creature the most logical—"

Alice never got a chance to finish her sentence, because at that moment Alix used her powers to take Finn's gun, aimed it at Alice, and shot her twice in the chest.

"*Alix*!" Cass yelled, stunned.

Alice stumbled back a few steps, genuinely surprised. She touched one of her wounds and stared down at the blood that coated her fingers. After a moment, she looked up at Alix. Before she could say anything, Alix shot her again, this time in the head.

As Alice's body fell to the floor, the room went dead silent. Alix was shaking so badly that she dropped the gun. Several seconds of silence later, AJ whispered, "Al, what did you do?"

The woman's eyes hadn't darkened at all. "What I should've done a long time ago," she murmured.

"W-We should go," Casey said slowly. She looked a mixture of shocked and terrified. "We should get out of here."

Cass's voice was oddly calm. "Finn, can you lead Kate out of this building? I have a feeling she'll be needed outside. And if you're really planning on starting over, you'll probably be needed, too."

"O-Of course," Finn stammered.

"What d-do you want me to d-do?" Kate asked.

"Get to Casey's bar. Get your backup bow. And hope that the mayor's execution doesn't cause all-out war."

Justin and Ray slid down a ladder on the side of a building into an alley near the police station. They glanced around the corner and then promptly ducked back into hiding when they saw the huge, furious crowd of people that had surrounded the doors.

"This looks bad, Blackout," Justin said. "This looks really, really bad."

"Well," Ray said carefully, "the cops in this city aren't useless. They'll figure this out. We have to trust them."

"I'm not sure the cops will be able to stop this," Kara said as she and Jay joined them. She had a deep gash in her temple that Jay was trying to attend to as they walked.

"What the hell happened to you?" Ray demanded.

"The mob by city hall saw us and tried to kill us. A piece of glass hit Pilot in the face." Jay moved Kara's face to one side to get a better look at the cut. "You're going to need stitches."

"I'm shocked," Kara replied dryly.

"You'd better be more careful there, Pilot," Jay said with a grin as he let her go. "Your wife'll divorce you if you lose your good looks."

"Oh, you're *so* funny."

"Not the time, guys," Ray said sharply.

Kara felt her wedding ring through her glove, unable to anxiously spin it beneath the material. "Are you sure? Imminent fights bring out the snark in all of us."

"*Everything* brings out the snark in us," Jay pointed out.

"True."

"I'm leading children," Ray said, shaking his head slowly. "You're all children. I'm shocked Targeter didn't have a nervous breakdown sooner."

"Now who's not choosing their time wisely?" Justin muttered.

Before Ray could reply, a person in the crowd threw a trashcan through the front window of the police station. Immediately, a fight broke out between the mob and the police officers trying to maintain order.

"Oh, not good," Ray mumbled. "Pilot, Clash, try to break that up. Archer and I will try to get into the station to find out what the cops are planning on doing about all of this."

"Do try not to get arrested," Kara replied.

"Thanks for the vote of confidence, Pilot."

Alix leaned against the wall silently, not looking at Cass, AJ, or Casey. The three were standing in a loose triangle, each glancing over at her every few seconds. "What should we do?" Casey asked in a whisper.

"Nothing," AJ replied stiffly.

"AJ, she…" Casey shifted uncomfortably. "She *murdered* Alice."

"And any one of us would've done the same thing if the gun had been in our hands," AJ murmured.

"You don't know that."

"We do," Cass said softly. "I've done it."

"You didn't *murder* our father, Cass," Casey hissed.

"I wanted to. I considered it a few times when I was younger. I can't exactly fault Alix for having the guts to actually do it to her own demons."

Casey took in a slow breath. "I get that, but guys, this is bad. This is really, really bad."

"You know I can hear you all, right?" Alix finally asked in a low voice.

They turned to face her. She was still leaning against the wall, but she was now staring at them with eyes that were beginning to darken in color. Small spheres of shadow began to appear around the room.

"Al," Cass said in a calm, quiet voice. "You need to calm down."

"I don't need a lecture, Cass," Alix growled. Her voice was different, higher, as if it was trying to crack but she wasn't letting it.

"Actually, I know that." Cass glanced at AJ, who looked worried but nodded. She cautiously walked over to Alix. "What you *need* is to calm down."

"Shut up."

"No." Cass stopped only a foot away from Alix, easily stepping out of the way of a sharp blade of shadow that swung at her. She smiled slightly and watched as Alix's eyes darkened even more, so that they were black. "You need to calm down. Even if you need to vent first. Go ahead. I can take it."

Alix studied her for a brief moment, her entire body trembling. Then she punched Cass in the face.

"*Alix, stop!*" Casey screamed as the younger woman dragged Cass to the ground and began to hit her repeatedly. She went to break up the fight, but AJ grabbed her arm.

"Don't," he murmured.

"Your wife is getting the crap beaten out of her and you're just going to let it happen?" Casey asked incredulously.

"Cass knows what she's doing," AJ said

stiffly.

"Does Cass *ever* know what she's doing?"

AJ winced as Cass took a particularly nasty blow to the jaw. "I hope so."

After another few seconds, Alix paused, her fist raised above Cass's face. She was breathing heavily, her eye color now flickering between the darker black and her normal metallic gray.

"Are you done?" Cass asked, her voice surprisingly calm despite the blood covering her face. Alix punched her once more, and Cass then grabbed the other woman by the wrists. "That's enough, Alix," she said gently. "That's enough."

Alix took in a shaky breath that was almost a whimper. "Th-There's an injector in the right pocket of my vest. Take it out, and use it on me."

"Why?"

"*Please*, Cass," Alix whispered. "Please."

Cass kept her grip on Alix's dominant wrist but released her other arm. She reached into Alix's pocket and pulled out an injector full of a clear fluid. There was a pause as Cass studied the liquid, then she pressed the injector against the side of Alix's neck and pushed the button.

Alix's body went rigid, and her eyes immediately settled on their normal lighter gray. She started to fall sideways, but Cass caught her before she could slam into the floor. As Cass gently lowered Alix to the ground, AJ and Casey hurried over to her.

"You're going to give me a heart attack if you don't start coming up with better plans, Cassidy," AJ said.

"Sometimes you just need to hurt somebody," Cass murmured. "It's not healthy, AJ, but it's something Alix and I can both understand. Sometimes you need to hurt someone to understand that you've hurt someone." She gently brushed Alix's hair off of her forehead. "She just needed to hurt someone, and I've taken beatings before. I could take another one for her."

AJ kissed the side of Cass's head. "You're too good for your own good."

"Don't remind me," Cass said dryly.

"If you hadn't just been beaten to hell, I would smack you in the back of the head," Casey grumbled as she paced back and forth.

"I'm fine, Casey. I swear."

"And Alix?"

"I should be okay," Alix whispered. She opened her eyes slowly and blinked a few times.

"What did you have me inject you with?" Cass asked.

Alix looked up at her and paused, taking in a long, slow breath. "The formula that takes away my powers."

20

"Get the hell out of my precinct," Chief Olivia Dearden spat as Ray and Justin made their way over to her through a crowd of overwhelmed and confused police officers.

"Chief, hear us out. We only want to help," Ray said.

Dearden folded her arms across her chest. "Look, I know you two are Heroics. I know the mayor was killed by someone from the Security Legion. But nobody in the mobs outside is paying attention to what uniforms you guys are wearing, and frankly, they don't care. They're pissed at *all* of you. So unless you want to get strung up for something you didn't do, go home."

"That's not what we do, Chief," Justin replied. "We help people even if they hate us. That's our job."

"Well *my* job is making sure that people don't get killed. That includes people like your team." Dearden sighed. "It also includes anyone from the Legion that *didn't* kill the mayor, so if you want to *help*, tell your counterparts to get the hell off the streets. I don't need another hero getting murdered by an unidentifiable mob. Got it?"

Ray glanced at Justin, who nodded. "You've got it, Chief. We'll do the best we can."

"Is this really the best that we can do against people who don't even have powers?" Jay demanded as he slammed into a brick wall.

Kara pulled a pipe away from a middle-aged woman who was screaming at her. "Apparently so!"

"That's depressing." Jay paused, running a hand through his hair. "I'm getting tired, Pilot."

"So much for your endurance."

"You know that only makes it so that I can move fast for an extended period of time without giving myself a heart attack. It doesn't make it any easier for me to fight for a long time. You're getting tired too."

Kara gave a breathless laugh. "Don't know what you're talking about. My lungs always hurt like this."

"You have a four-year-old. You should definitely be able to run around a lot longer than this."

"Oh, shut up."

Ray's voice buzzed in their ears. "*The Chief of Police wants all heroes to clear off the street.*"

"Are we going to obey that order?" Kara asked as she pulled two men off of a downed police officer.

"*I'm up for a vote. Does anybody want to go home?*"

"To hell with that," Jay said. "These people might be out for our blood, but they're going to end up getting themselves killed. It's our job to make sure that doesn't happen."

"*Okay. Control, what's the most recent report on where the biggest mobs are?*"

Niall's voice joined Ray's. "*Police station, center of the city, Faustin Street, and Cambridge Avenue.*"

"*Four places, four members of Heroics.*" Ray gave a short laugh. "*The convenience is probably a bad sign.*"

"Where do you want us to go, Blackout?" Kara asked.

"*Archer will handle the station. Pilot, see if you can fix the city center. Clash, Cambridge Avenue. I'll take Faustin Street.*"

"Oh, fun, I get the place that put a piece of glass through my face." Kara sighed. "Does nobody have any sense of superstition?"

"Don't be so boring, Pilot," Jay said with a grin. "It'll be fun."

Kara kicked away a teenage boy who was trying to take the cap off of a nearby fire hydrant. "Your definition of fun needs some work, Clash."

Ray left Justin at the police station and started running along the rooftops towards Faustin Street. As he went, he keyed a speed dial into his communications system.

"*Ray?*"

"Are you working today?"

Olivia Sampson gave a small relieved

sigh as she heard his voice. *"No. Chief Dearden just sent out an emergency call for any available officers to come in, though."*

Ray swallowed. "Are you going to answer it?"

"It's my job, same as yours, honey."

"I know. Where's Isaac?"

"At Nina's, next door. She's going to watch him while I head in. It's bad, isn't it? Dearden wouldn't have called us all if it wasn't."

"I-I'm not sure we're all going to make it out of this," Ray admitted softly. "Civilians are ripping this city apart. After what they did to Svetlo from the Legion... I think it's pretty clear that they have no problem ripping *us* apart, too. And I'm pretty sure that's what they want."

"Oh, infierno. *This is insane."*

"I know. Just... be careful out here, okay? If anything happens to me..."

"Isaac's not losing us, Ray. He's not."

Ray gave a small, tired sigh. "I certainly hope you're right."

Cass and AJ helped Alix to her feet carefully. "Are you okay?" AJ asked in a soft voice.

"I don't know," Alix admitted.

"Can we worry about this when we aren't in Alice's freaking base of operations? The woman may be lying in her own blood, but that

271

doesn't make this any better of a place to be," Casey said.

Alix paused. "She has a point."

"One thing first." Cass looked over at the safe that was still in the room. "AJ, can I ask you for a bit of a ridiculous favor?"

"What is it?"

"I need some of your blood."

AJ sighed. "Needy."

"Oh, shut up. Casey, do you have your knife?"

"Of course."

"Can I borrow it?"

Casey hesitated. "Sure." She pulled her knife out of her boot and held it out to Cass, who took it and pulled AJ over to the safe.

"Uh, can somebody tell me why this is happening *before* you stab me?" AJ asked nervously.

"I can't risk my or Casey's blood being enough to trigger this thing opening. And Alix's is almost identical to Alice's, and who knows if my father programmed hers in. You're the only one here whose blood will destroy what's in this box."

"This is going to be fun," AJ said dryly.

"Grow up." Cass sliced the palm of his hand open in one quick motion.

"*Ow!* You know there are better places to cut than the palm, you jerk. Do you know how many nerve endings are there?"

"You're the medical guy, not me," Cass

272

muttered as she pushed his bleeding hand against the hole in the side of the safe.

"You're smarter than that," AJ snarked back.

Casey rolled her eyes. "Can you stop flirting and get on with whatever the hell it is you're doing?"

As if in reply, a loud sound, like a flash fire, came from the inside of the safe. Then a small red square appeared above the hole.

"This safe only opens if the blood of the person who closed it goes into this hole," Cass replied. "If you put the wrong blood into it, everything inside is incinerated. Now, I'm not positive that the weapon Alice was looking for is in here. But it isn't worth the risk."

"Damn. Just a minute or so too late."

Everyone turned in time to see a dark-haired woman pick up the gun Alix had used to kill Alice. She chambered a round and added, "I suppose it's alright in the end. Mass extinction is a bit boring."

"Who the hell are you?" Cass demanded.

"Sarah Ajam. I was an acquaintance of Alice Cage." The woman's eyes barely flickered over to Alice's body. "Which one of you killed her?"

"Me," Alix replied, her voice hoarse.

"Nice job," Sarah said appreciatively. "Honestly, I came here to kill her myself, but it's nice that you took care of it for me, clone."

"Go to hell," Casey growled, grabbing

Alix before the younger woman could move towards Sarah.

"Don't try it, clone. You might as well have just cut off one of your feet. You couldn't fight me if you tried."

Alix frowned. "How would you know—"

"Cameras. Lots of cameras. I'm fond of cameras. They let me know a lot." Sarah grinned. "They even let me watch Zach Carter die."

Casey took in a sharp breath. "What are you talking about?"

"Zach Carter. I watched him die." Sarah smirked slightly. "Oh, I'm sorry. Does that upset you?"

"You're lying," Casey said stiffly.

"Am I? Why don't you ask Wechsler over there whether the local serial killer has Carter's power?"

Casey hesitated before turning to face her sister. "C-Cass?"

The other woman was avoiding eye contact. "Case…"

"Cass," Casey repeated in a growl. "Tell me."

"Y-Yeah," Cass stammered. "There was a guy who was with Alice and Finn when they took us. And he, uh, he had Zach's power. Said he duplicated it from a Legion hero."

"That's right. And do you really expect us to leave alive someone we stole a power from?" Sarah scoffed. "I thought you were the smart one."

Casey, still holding Alix back, began to tremble. "You're lying," she repeated in a hoarse whisper.

"You know I'm not," Sarah said. She raised an eyebrow. "Oh, I'm sorry, that's right. You're going to have to go home and tell your daughter that her father's dead, aren't you? Well, at least, you would if you were going to be going home. I have no intention of killing you, but I doubt you'll survive what's waiting for you outside."

"And what would that be?" AJ demanded.

Sarah gave a slow grin. "The city is on fire. And all of you little heroes are going to pay for her." She aimed to gun at the group to keep them away as she backed out of the room.

Once she was gone, Casey released Alix and wandered over towards a nearby wall. "Case," Cass said softly. "It's going to be okay."

Casey paced next to the wall for a moment before spinning on her heel and punching the bricks so hard that something in her hand made an audible crack.

"*Case!*" AJ hurried over as Casey gave a scream of pain and dropped onto her knees. He knelt in front of her, lifted up her arm, and looked at her bleeding hand. "Oh, Casey. What did you do?"

"She's lying," Casey murmured, no longer even registering the pain. "She has to be lying."

"Maybe she is," AJ said in a gentle voice. "Right now, let's worry about fixing your hand, okay? We should get out of here and look at your hand, and we should get Cass and Alix checked out too."

Casey didn't seem to even hear him. "I can't lose him, AJ," she whispered. "I can't lose Zach."

AJ hugged her tightly. "I know, Case. I know you can't. We just need to believe that you haven't."

The sound of dozens of people shouting was the first thing Zach became aware of as he regained consciousness. After a moment of confusion, he realized that he was lying in the middle of an alley. His head was pounding, and he was covered in dried blood. He could tell that he was in bad shape, but he couldn't tell where he was. Zach carefully pushed himself to his feet, wincing as pain rushed through his cracked ribs. He stumbled to the entrance of the alley and looked out at the city street.

People were running all over the place. A few buildings were on fire, and others were being looted. Two small groups were in a brawl in the middle of the street, and all of the cars around them had been abandoned.

"What the hell happened?" Zach murmured, stunned.

"*Hey!*" a voice yelled from the opposite sidewalk. A woman carrying a baseball bat was glaring at him. "It's a Legion vigilante!"

The street went silent instantly. Even the people engaged in the brawl fell silent and turned to stare at him.

Zach swallowed. "Uhm. I-I don't know what's going on here, but..."

A different woman laughed sarcastically. "What's going on? What's going on is that one of your *buddies* killed the mayor. None of you stopped the killings that have been going on. Nobody from your little club has done *anything* to help us. So we're taking matters into our own hands."

The woman with the baseball bat tapped it against the palm of her hand. "You look like you've already taken a beating today. That's fair. But what has been happening to us isn't. And we don't really care who ends up paying for it."

Zach took a few steps backwards, holding up his hands. "I-I don't want any trouble."

A man who had been in the brawl scoffed. "Neither did any of us. Trouble just happened by."

Several people began to advance on Zach, but before they could get near him, a Mustang drove down the sidewalk and came to a screeching stop between them. The window rolled down, and Kaita squinted at Zach out of it. "Come with me if you want to live," she said urgently. She then smirked. "Always did want to say that."

"Kaita, please tell me what is going on," Zach begged as she drove away from the mob of people that had just been out for his blood.

"Long story short? Guy claims to be from Legion. Guy kills mayor on live television. Already angry public flips the hell out and starts crowding the streets. Jackasses take it as an opportunity to beat the crap out of people and light buildings on fire." Kaita glanced at him. "And where the hell have you been? Casey's worried sick, and you look like someone ran your face into a cinder block."

"Guy who claims to be from Legion? Probably is actually in the Legion." Zach leaned his seat back a bit. "The serial killer is Raseri."

"Seriously?"

"Seriously."

"Jackass."

Zach chuckled weakly. "I knew I could count on you to put things into perspective." He shifted his weight and winced. "He kidnapped me, and a friend of his basically put me in a cage match. It's a long story."

"Well, you'll need to go to the hospital, but I'm not going to risk taking you there right now. So for the time being, we are going to the bar and we are going to stay there. You are *not* going to be out on the street fighting, do you understand me?" Kaita sighed. "Casey would kill me if I let you out of my sight. She's had me looking for you all day."

"She's really been that worried? I wasn't gone all that long."

Kaita laughed. "Zach, that woman is so in love with you it isn't even funny anymore. Trust me. She's a wreck."

"Is it awful to be a tiny bit proud of myself for that?"

"Yes, and if you didn't look like you'd been kicked repeatedly, I'd hit you for it."

"Sorry. Rough week."

"Yeah," Kaita said gently. "Yeah, it has been."

Zach paused. "You should drop me off at the bar and then leave, Kaita."

"What? Why?"

"You don't have powers. These people don't want you. You can get out without risk of getting hurt."

Kaita gave a thin smile. "Zach, my mother was a hero. She died for this city. I don't give a damn what powers I don't have. I'm not going anywhere. Your people and Casey's people are my people, too. So shut the hell up, because I'm not leaving you to sit alone in your blood and hope that nobody decides to come looking for you. You're worth more than that. Got it?"

"Got it," Zach replied. "Thank you."

"No need to thank me, Zach."

"Yes." Zach stared up at the roof of the

car, a weak smile on his face. "There is."

"*Are you sure you're okay?*" Niall's voice asked in Kate's ear as she ran towards Cambridge Avenue.

"I'm sure," Kate replied. "Has Finn met Blackout on Faustin Street yet?"

"*She's almost there. You're positive you trust her?*"

"No, but I trust that she's trying. I really do believe that she doesn't want to be the bad guy, Control. I think this is a good opportunity for her to prove that." Kate paused awkwardly. "Of course, that's also for Blackout to decide now, which is why I sent her to him."

"*It's going to be alright.*"

"You don't know that, but thank you for saying it." Kate climbed to the top of a nearby roof. "Where on Cambridge *is* Clash, exactly?"

"*Tracking says about a hundred yards north of you.*"

Kate headed in the direction Niall indicated. "I have a bad feeling about this, Control. Everything is just a bit too quiet."

"*Maybe you got the easy assignment.*"

"We both know that's not how this ever goes for us."

"*Breathe, Targeter.*"

"I am breathing," Kate muttered. "I just have a bad feeling that I'm going to stop." She got to Jay's location and saw him in the middle of a crowd of people, running through and around them to tire them out. She was about to jump down to help when the metal door off of a nearby air vent leaped off and wrapped around her arms, legs, and mouth.

"Targeter? Is everything okay?"

Kate was unable to respond to Niall's question. She could only stand there, motionless, as Edward Caito joined her at the edge of the roof.

"You're a very interesting woman, Targeter," he said softly. "You keep coming back to the fight, no matter how many times people put you on the bench. It's impressive, truly. It's also aggravating as hell. Because, you see, you should've broken by now. You should be *shattered*. I didn't escape prison to watch a hero come back, over and over again, no matter how many times they should've put a bullet in their brain." Caito rested a friendly hand on her shoulder. "But I'm fair. I'll accept your victory if you can survive one last tragedy. You see, I've been watching this fight for a while. I know exactly how it's going to end, because your comrade doesn't see the danger he's in. I think you do, which is why you came here to step in. But I'm not going to let you. You don't get to be the hero, Targeter. That's your penance for leading a bunch of worthless vigilantes. You get to watch them all die."

Kate, her whole body trembling, watched as Jay's speed began to wind down. He came to a stop in the middle of the crowd, gasping for breath. The crowd around him seemed to realize at the same time that he was unable to use his powers, because they all simultaneously formed a circle around him. A man stepped forward.

"Looks like you're out of juice."

"Doesn't change my fighting ability," Jay panted.

The man snorted. "Right. Sure it doesn't."

Jay took a deep breath and looked around at the enraged people surrounding him. He seemed to have realized he was in trouble. "Look, the only reason Heroics is even out here is to help you. To make sure you don't hurt each other. To try to keep as many buildings from burning to the ground as possible. We aren't the enemy."

"Unfortunately for you," another man said from the crowd, "today isn't the sort of day where any of us would believe you."

"Hey—"

The first man who had spoken punched Jay in the face. Instantly, the mob followed suit until Jay was on the ground, and Kate could no longer see him amongst the other people.

Kate made a whimpering noise, and Caito patted her on the shoulder again. "If it makes you feel better, that would've happened whether you had been here or not." He smirked. "Sure was fun to watch though, wasn't it?"

There was a muffled noise from Kate, who looked furious and close to tears.

"No need to curse, dear. And don't be so pessimistic. Maybe he's not even dead!" Caito glanced down at the mob, which was still beating Jay. "He probably is, though. Or he wants to be." Caito shrugged. "Oh, well. That's enough entertainment for me." He turned and walked away.

After a minute, the metal bindings on Kate fell off. She dropped to her knees on the edge of the roof and watched as the crowd surrounding Jay quickly dispersed. The vigilante weakly tried to push himself up, but he collapsed back onto the ground immediately.

He didn't move again.

21

Once they were back on the Caotico City streets, Cass, AJ, Casey, and Alix were able to see just how bad those streets were.

"This is not good, guys," Alix murmured.

"New slogan for our team right there," AJ muttered.

"There is *fire*, AJ."

"Even better." AJ put his arm around Casey's shoulders. The woman was just staring blankly at the ground. "Come on. Let's try to just get to the bar. Al, get rid of your jacket. It's not safe to be a hero right now."

"I'm not one anymore, anyway," Alix said softly as she removed her navy blue vest.

Cass kissed her on the side of the head. "Shut up. I'll have more to add to that when I'm not bloody and exhausted. But for now, just shut up."

Kara cursed under her breath as she noticed that Central City Bank was on fire. "Why is it always the banks?" she mumbled. "Why does nothing bad ever happen to a jewelry store or a sporting goods store or *any store* in this city?" She headed towards the building to clear it, but a man ran up to her to intercept her.

"Miss," he said, panting, "are you a vigilante?"

"Depends on why you want to know," Kara replied, her head wound and her exhaustion overpowering her normal attitude.

"We got everybody out of the bank, but I think people are on the third floor of the office building next to it, and we can't get in there," the man said, not even reacting to her snappy response.

"Alright. Nobody who isn't rescue crews or a hero crew follows me, got it?"

The man nodded. "Yes ma'am."

Kara took in a deep breath and ran into the building next to the bank. She started up the stairs, but she had barely made it two steps when a loud banging noise came from the bank. Milliseconds later, the wall separating the two buildings exploded, and the office complex collapsed.

Ray slammed into the ground courtesy of a well-timed pipe to the ribcage by a man who looked twelve different kinds of angry. "Where are you people *getting* these pipes?" Ray grumbled irritably. "Did somebody loot a hardware store?"

The man swung at him again, but the pipe was grabbed at the last second by Finn. She wrenched the pipe from the man's hand and gave him one quick jab in the stomach. As the man stumbled backwards, wheezing, Finn held out a hand to Ray. "Actually, I saw three looted hardware stores on the way over here."

"Was that a joke, Finn?" Ray asked incredulously as he allowed the teen to help him to his feet.

"No," she replied flatly, giving him a blank look.

"Oh. Well then. Alright." Ray cleared his throat. "Control already filled me in on what's going on with you, so try not to screw up." He glanced down, noticing that Finn's hands were shaking. "You scared?"

"I-I'm not sure what I am," she admitted. "The woman I was afraid of for a significant portion of my life is dead, and she died pretty easily. I can't help but wonder how many people would be alive or uninjured if I had killed her myself years ago instead of being a coward and letting her control me."

Ray gave a thin smile. "Not killing someone isn't something to be ashamed of, Finn. You don't need to feel bad about that."

"Easier said than done."

"Yeah," he said quietly. "Yeah, I'm sure it is."

A cop pulled Justin away from a small cluster of people that were trying to take his bow from him. "You okay, Archer?" the officer asked.

"At the moment," Justin replied, adjusting his sunglasses as he looked at her. "Thanks."

"No problem."

Another cop clapped him on the shoulder. "You're helping us. We can help you." He shook his head slowly. "I've never seen anything like this. Not even during that whole controlled empowereds mess."

"That was contained," Justin said. "Mostly one street. Mostly just people like me. This is beyond that. This is anger that built up over a long time and finally exploded. There's not much we can do to stop it."

"We lose a cop and there's no replacing them," the female officer said. "We arrest or otherwise take down one of these guys? This is a freaking city. Eight more people will take their place."

"Well, I guess we'll have to just keep hitting people until there aren't eight more left then, huh?" Justin replied, false optimism in his voice.

The male officer laughed. "We'll certainly try."

Kate knelt down next to Jay's body and rested a hand on his chest. "Dammit, Jay," she whispered. She gently closed his eyes and kissed him on the forehead, then she tapped a button on her glasses. "C-Control?"

Niall seemed to realize instantly that something was wrong. *"Targeter? What is it? Are you okay?"*

"N-Not exactly."

"What is it?"

"Jay."

There was a long pause. *"What are you saying, Targeter?"*

Her voice cracked. "He's gone, Control."

Niall hesitated for another long moment. *"Oh, god, Kate. Are you okay?"*

"No," Kate whispered.

"Are you injured?"

"Not yet."

He sighed softly. *"What do you want to do?"*

Kate stared down at Jay. "I want to put an end to this mess. And maybe kill the guy who started this."

She could practically hear a grim smile form on Niall's face. *"Alright, Targeter. Be careful, okay? Please."*

"Always. Can you... Can you see if someone can..."

"I'll send someone for Jay. My brother's in the area."

"Thank you."

"Absolutely. It'll be okay, Targeter."

Kate smiled humorlessly. "No; it won't. But thanks for saying it."

"I don't have my keys with me," Casey said quietly as she, AJ, Cass, and Alix walked up to the door of her bar. This section of the city didn't seem to have had any issues yet, but they wanted to get off of the street before it did.

"That might not be a problem," AJ replied. "Kaita's car is in the alley."

Casey raised her head quickly, an alarmed look in her eyes. "What? She shouldn't be here, not right now."

"Let's find out." Cass banged on the door of the bar.

After a moment, the eyehole of the door slid open. Kaita's brown and blue eyes squinted at them through it. "Oh, thank hell," she murmured almost immediately. She opened the door. "I was hoping one of you would show up. All the phone lines are dead, including cell towers, and I accidentally left my communication glasses at home."

"Hell of a day for that," AJ joked lightly as he led Casey into the bar.

"Seems par for the course for one of us," Cass said, gently pushing Alix through the door as well.

Before they got too far into the bar, Kaita grabbed Casey by the shoulders. "Case, there's something you should know…"

"Zach's dead, isn't he?" Casey whispered.

Kaita frowned. "What? He's—"

"Not dead yet," Zach finished. He was sitting at one of the tables, holding an ice pack to his face. "The bastards sure as hell tried their best, though."

"You son of a bitch," Casey said hoarsely.

Zach grinned. "That's not very nice. You love my mother."

Casey walked towards him, and he stood up. She moved as if she was going to hit him, but AJ sharply said, "Casey! Hand!"

She stopped her swing an inch from his shoulder and slowly lowered her hand. She gave a choked sob and hugged Zach, starting to cry.

Zach, bewildered, hugged her back, ignoring the pain in his ribs. He looked at AJ, who was using a damp towel to clean blood off of Cass's face. "What was that about her hand?"

"She broke it punching a brick wall."

"Why would..." Zach carefully pulled away from Casey, resting his hands on her shoulders. "Next time you want a punching bag, I recommend not choosing a brick wall," he said lightly. He lifted Casey's chin so that she was looking at him. "Why did you punch a wall, Casey?"

She swallowed, wiping tears off of her cheeks with the back of her good hand. "I guess I just got frustrated."

"You never seemed the type to start punching walls, no matter how frustrated you were."

"Yeah, well, there's a first time for everything," Casey mumbled.

Zach smiled slowly. "Casey, why did you punch a wall?"

She stared at him for a long moment. "B-Because a criminal told me you were dead, and

I believed her." Casey took in a shaky breath. "Hell, Zach, I believed her."

"That's okay." Zach gently kissed her on the cheek. "I'm okay."

Casey pulled his head down so that she could rest her forehead against his. "You'd better be," she whispered. "I love you too much to lose you."

Zach gave a bright laugh. "What was that?"

She leaned back, and he could see that she was flushed pink. "Shut up, Zach. Let me enjoy the moment before your ego ruins it."

He kissed her lightly, grinning. "Yes, ma'am."

Kate got to the center of the city in time to see what was left of Central City Bank crumble to the ground. "Holy hell," she muttered.

She headed towards the remains of the bank and the buildings on either side of it, but before she got there, a woman who had burns down one of her arms stopped her. "You're one of the Heroics people, right?"

"Yeah," Kate said. "Do you need something, ma'am? Can I help you?"

"I'll live. I can get to the hospital. But one of your people ran into the Kingston Office Complex right before it collapsed. I didn't see them come out."

Kate swallowed with difficulty, her

mouth suddenly dry. "Thank you." She sprinted towards the rubble of what had once been the office complex. As she clambered through the piles of concrete, brick, metal, and drywall, Kate was horrified to see how much destruction was around her. She had no idea how the destruction had occurred, but whatever it was had been bad. There were rumors that a group of people had started bombing buildings randomly, but Kate had no idea how to know if it was true or whether she was at risk of getting blown up herself. All she knew was that if the woman outside had been telling the truth, one of her people was inside. She wasn't going to leave until she was sure whether or not it was the case.

As she came upon the remains of a staircase, Kate's breath caught in her throat. A woman was lying on the floor, her blonde hair darkened by soot and her maroon and orange uniform torn and bloodied.

"*Kara!*" Kate skidded to the ground next to the unconscious vigilante. She took Kara's face in her hands and brushed away some dirt. "Kara, please," Kate begged. "Please wake up. I can't lose another sibling. Not today. Kara, *please.*"

There was a long pause before Kara slowly opened her eyes. "Kate?" she mumbled. "Wh-What h-happened?"

"Building collapse. But it doesn't matter." Kate kissed Kara's forehead before resting her own against it. "It doesn't matter. It's okay."

"Kate?" Kara said in a thin voice.

"What, honey?"

"Kate, I…" Kara trailed off, sounding confused and disoriented.

"Kara, what is it? What's wrong?" Kate asked, pulling back to look her sister in the eye.

The younger woman swallowed, pain and fear on her face. "I can't move."

22

Paramedic Wyatt Jones climbed into the wreckage around Central City Bank. He and his partner Mara Mitchell had been doing this for hours, but they weren't going to stop until they either passed out or there was no one left for them to help. As he turned a corner, Wyatt saw a brunette vigilante kneeling next to someone who was lying motionless on the ground. He started towards them, but Mara grabbed his arm.

"What are you doing?" she asked in a sharp whisper.

"Helping them."

"Wyatt, they're vigilantes."

There was a pause as Wyatt just stared at her. "So?"

"So they caused all of this and you want to take the time to help them?"

"They didn't cause this, Mara," Wyatt said softly. "Haven't you been paying attention? This is all non-empowered people, no matter who killed the mayor. And besides. These people risk their lives every day to save ours. I'm not leaving one of them injured in a pile of rubble. If you don't like that, you don't have to follow me."

As Wyatt headed towards the vigilantes, Mara sighed. "Too bad I always will," she muttered before following him.

Wyatt approached the pair cautiously, his hands raised in front of him. The brunette vigilante, whom he recognized as Targeter from Heroics, didn't seem to hear him until he was much closer, and when she did she aimed her crossbow at him shakily. "It's okay," Wyatt said gently. "I just want to help." He could see that the person on the ground was a blonde vigilante with blood coming from her mouth. "Let me help your friend."

The reminder of the woman on the floor seemed to get through to Targeter, who lowered the crossbow, stood, and stepped back into the shadows. "Please," she whispered in a tired voice.

He was on his knees next to the blonde in an instant, and when he got closer, he realized that it was the one who went by 'Pilot'. "Hey there," Wyatt said softly. "I'm going to try to help, okay?"

Pilot nodded slightly. "There are probably better people to help, though," she croaked.

"Right now, let's just worry about you," Wyatt said. "What's your name?"

"Kara."

He had been expecting her to give him her hero name, but he wasn't going to bring it up. "You'll be okay, Kara. I'm going to do everything I can to make sure of that." Wyatt heard Mara stop behind him, and he said, "I see you decided to come along."

"I'm not letting you do something stupid by yourself. How is she?"

"Could be better. Could be worse," he muttered.

Targeter shifted uneasily. "Can you help her or not?"

"She needs to go to a hospital," Wyatt said. "I can stop some of this bleeding, but she likely has internal injuries."

"And I can't move," Kara murmured.

Wyatt stared down at her. "Then you probably have some damage to your spine as well." He looked up at Kate. "There's not much more I can do for her here, if you want her to live."

"Can I go with you?" Targeter asked, a shred of desperation in her voice.

Kara looked at her teammate quickly. "No. You need to go help the others."

"They're fine."

"No, they aren't. You said you couldn't lose another. Who did we lose?"

Targeter hesitated. "I-I don't know what you—"

"I'm not going with them until you tell me," Kara said in as firm a voice as she capable of. *"Who did we lose, Kate?"*

Targeter— Kate —stepped out of the shadows, removed her sunglasses, and crouched down next to Kara. "Jay," she whispered.

Kara closed her eyes and turned her

head away. "How many of us are even left?" she asked quietly.

"I don't know, Kara. I haven't seen anyone else. I've been having trouble getting in touch with the base since I notified Control of Jay's death. I think signals are getting out of whack." Kate swallowed. "It might just be us. I can't know for sure."

"You have to go find them. Please, Kate. I'll be fine with these guys. Please."

Kate nodded stiffly. "Okay."

"Wyatt, go get a stretcher," Mara said. "I'll stay here."

"Are you sure?" Wyatt asked warily.

"I'm sure. Trust me."

When Wyatt was gone, Mara gestured at a deep gash on Kate's arm. "Before you go, you should let me take a look at that. Stitch it up. It'll save you pain and trouble in the long run."

Kate nodded, looking exhausted. She sat down heavily on a cement block and allowed Mara to carefully pull back her sleeve. As she did so, Mara took a good look at the two vigilantes. They were both young, younger than she would've expected. Kara was definitely the younger of the two, in her early twenties, but Kate was likely under thirty as well.

"How old are you?" Mara asked softly as she cleaned the gash.

"Twenty-eight," Kate replied.

"But... weren't you in that battle, like eleven years ago? Heroics was there, and I can see their logo on your vests. How young were you then?"

Kate smiled humorlessly. "I was sixteen. Kara was thirteen. And yeah, we were in that fight."

Mara paused in what she was doing, stunned. "You were just kids."

"Yeah. We were just kids. Some days, it feels like we still are."

There was an awkward silence before Mara began to stitch up the wound on Kate's arm. "Who was Jay?" she asked gently.

"Our brother," Kara replied.

"I didn't realize you were sisters."

"Not by blood," Kate said. "The Heroics team, we grew up together. We're as close to siblings as people who aren't can get." As Kara made a quiet noise of pain, Kate reached down and grabbed the younger woman's gloved hand. After a brief moment, Kate looked at Mara. "We didn't do this, ma'am. You can blame us if you want. But we didn't cause this. We don't cause the violence. We've lost too many family members to it already."

"Why not just stop doing it all?"

Kate gave a soft laugh, and even Kara chuckled quietly. "This is all we know." Kate shrugged helplessly. "It's in our blood. It's how we grew up. It's what we are." She gave a long, slow sigh. "I'll be a vigilante until the day I die, ma'am. And unfortunately, in this line of work, that's going to be a lot sooner for me than it is for most people."

Wyatt returned, carrying a stretcher. "The military is here. They're starting to take control of the city."

"Good. We need somebody to." Kate brushed Kara's hair off of her forehead. "I'm going to go find the others, okay?"

"P-Please do," Kara said.

"Take care of her," Kate said to Wyatt and Mara. "Please. Take care of her."

"You have our word," Wyatt promised.

Kate hesitated, staring down at her sister for a long moment. Then she stood and headed out of the rubble.

Caito looked up at the sky and watched at three military helicopters flew past. "They got here sooner than I expected." He turned quickly, waving his hand to deflect a bullet as it was fired at him by Sarah. "I also expected more from you, Sarah," he said in a low voice. "Between Finn's enhanced reflexes and Kov's metal manipulation, did you really think you were going to be able to shoot me?"

Sarah shrugged and holstered her gun. "It was worth a try."

"Care to explain yourself? I thought you shared my vision? Or at least Alice Cage's. Why would you want to kill me when I did so much to turn the city against people with powers?"

"I don't know, Caito. Maybe you just annoy me."

"I should've known to kill you instead of Tag. He might've been stupid, but at least he would've supported this plan."

Sarah gave a thin smile. "You can't kill me, Caito. I'm much, much too good for that."

"I've stolen powers from fifteen different vigilantes. You have no powers. *You* can't kill *me*."

The woman yawned. "Yes, yes, fifteen different vigilantes. Except you can only hold four at a time, so you only have your four most recent. Enhanced reflexes from Finn, metal manipulation from Kov, volatile constructs from Tag, and enhanced endurance from that one guy you murdered a few weeks ago, uh, Newt. Not a very impressive move set if you ask me."

Caito's hand tightened into a fist. "I've been keeping pretty calm and controlled these past few months, Sarah. I won't hold back if you start a fight with me."

"I'm aware. I'm also aware that Tag's power, if used correctly, might cause problems if I try to fight you directly. And I can't just shoot you, because of Kov's power. I might be in some trouble if I fight you."

"It won't be a fight. It'll be a murder."

"That's what I was thinking." Sarah pulled a knife out of her boot and threw it at Caito. He smirked and waved his hand to deflect it, but nothing happened. His surprise prevented him from reacting quickly enough to use his enhanced reflexes, and the knife buried in his chest.

"Wh-What?" Caito stammered, staring down at the hilt sticking out from his body.

Sarah smiled. "You want to know how I survive without powers, jackass? I use my brain. And if I know I'm confronting someone with metal manipulation powers? I use ceramic knives."`

Caito dropped to the ground. Sarah walked over to him and pulled the knife out of his chest. She then kicked him hard in the face so that he was unconscious while he took his last breaths. As Sarah cleaned her knife off on Caito's shirt, she said, "Anti-climactic, I know. But honestly? You didn't deserve anything better."

Ray pushed himself to his feet, watching as the last person on the street ran away. He swayed slightly, his head pounding, but Finn put a hand on his shoulder to steady him. "The military is here," she said quietly. She paused. "If you... If you want to hand me over to them, I wouldn't argue."

For a moment, Ray just stared at her. She had a black eye and was leaning to one side slightly, as if she was favoring one of her ribs. She also still looked ashamed of herself. "I'm not going to do that, Finn. You have a lot of things to answer for. But you need to have a chance in order to do that, now don't you?"

She seemed surprised but nodded. "I-I... Yes, sir."

"Don't 'sir' me. It's weird." Ray patted her on the shoulder. "Come on, Finn. Let's go find everyone else." Before they could walk away, he saw the flash of a phone call in the corner of his glasses. "Hold on a second." He tapped a button on the frames. "Hello?"

"*Still alive, then?*"

Ray gave an exhausted, yet relieved, laugh. "Still alive, sweetheart."

"*Good. I am too. I'm going to pack up here and then go save our neighbor from our terror of a child.*"

"Great. I need to make sure that the others are okay. I'll call you with updates when I can."

"*You had better. I'll hunt you down if you don't. I can do that. I'm a cop.*"

Ray grinned. "I trust you." He paused, taking a moment breathe as his head started to hurt again. "Via?"

"*Yeah?*"

"I love you."

"*I love you too. Go find your family, then get back to your other one.*"

He chuckled. "It sounds bad when you say it like that."

"*It's true though. Stay safe.*"

"You too. Bye."

"Bye."

Ray hit the button that closed the connection and realized that Finn's hand was still on his shoulder, keeping him from toppling over. "Thanks for waiting. I had to take that."

"I understand," Finn said softly. "It's important."

"It is."

"It's strange. I remember the importance of family, but I don't remember what it's like to have one."

"Well, Finnegan, you should still have one. Maybe when the dust has settled a bit, you should try to find them."

"I'm not sure what they would say to me. I'm not exactly the same person I was when I left."

"That's okay." Ray patted Finn's hand and turned towards Casey's bar. "I have a feeling that, in the end, that won't make much of a difference to them."

Zach looked up as Justin walked into Casey's bar. The younger vigilante looked around briefly before saying, "Kate's not here?"

"No," Zach replied. "She, Kara, and Jay are the only ones who haven't checked in yet. We still can't get back in touch with Niall to see if he's heard from them, either."

Justin, looking worried and holding his

right hand in the air as if trying to stop the blood that was dripping from it, bit his lip. "D-Do you think they're okay?"

"I'm not sure, Justin. Why don't you go see Cass? She was bandaging Casey's hand. She can do yours, too."

Justin nodded and headed over to Cass and Casey. When he was gone, Zach walked over to AJ. "I have some bad news."

AJ sighed. "What is it?"

"Casey told me she loves me."

There was a long pause as AJ just stared at him. "I don't understand how that's…"

Zach grinned. "I take cash or credit."

After another pause, AJ laughed. "Trust you to remember that through all of this."

"I don't make a lot of money."

AJ put an arm around Zach's shoulders, lowering his voice and grinning. "You mean to tell me that Casey Cabot isn't a good enough reward for you?"

"I repeat: I do not make a lot of money."

"Oh, fine. It's all Cass's money anyway."

As AJ moved to pull out his wallet, the door opened again, and Kate stumbled in. She looked around the room, noting Alix at a table with Ray, Zach with AJ, Cass and Casey bandaging Justin's hand, and Kaita trying to convince Finn to take an ice pack for her eye.

"Good," she said hoarsely. "Everyone's here."

Ray slowly stood up. "Uhm. No, Kate,

everyone isn't. Jay and Kara aren't yet."

Kate sat down at a table a distance away from the others. "Kara's with some paramedics," she said. "She couldn't... couldn't move. She might have spinal damage."

Once this news slowly sank in around the room, Cass asked, "And Jay?"

For a moment, Kate just stared down at the table she was seated at. Then she murmured, "He's dead."

"You're wrong," Justin said immediately.

"I'm not wrong, Justin," Kate replied.

"But how do you know? We haven't heard from Niall in—"

"I watched him die," she snapped. She pushed herself up from the table, headed for the entrance to Casey's apartment, and slammed the door shut behind her.

The room was even more silent than it had been after the news of Kara. It was only broken when Justin whispered, "No."

"This is what they wanted," Finn murmured as Kaita finally managed to press an icepack against her black eye. "To destroy you all, whether by their hands or by riling up the public into doing it for them."

Alix gave a dry, humorless laugh. "Leave it to Alice Cage to have a plan come together even after she's dead."

23

The military regained control of Caotico within only a few hours, at which point Niall arrived at Casey's bar. "I had Andrew retrieve Jay's body," he said in a low voice. "He's at the mansion."

"Where the hell was the rest of the Legion during this mess?" Ray growled.

"Chuva forbid them from getting involved," Niall replied, sounding furious. "Andrew, Rob Munroe, Redwood, and Scarlett ignored him, but they were busy in the western district taking care of a city block that some idiot had set on fire."

"Remind me to kill Chuva the next time I see him," Zach snarled.

"Zach," Casey warned quietly.

"I already didn't like the guy, Case. He certainly doesn't win any points for being a coward."

"The roads are starting to clear up a bit," Niall said. "We can go to the hospital now, if anybody needs it."

"We should go there anyway to make sure Kara's okay. Kate said that she's there." AJ glanced around the room. "Plus I'm pretty sure several people here need to be checked out by doctors more qualified than me. Particularly the hands of Casey and Justin, Cass's head, everything on Zach—"

"Thanks man."

"—no problem, and Finn's ribs."

"I-I'm fine," Finn stammered.

"I'd rather somebody give you some x-rays to make sure. If something's wrong and we don't get it fixed, you could get pretty badly hurt."

Finn blinked, looking almost confused. "O-Okay."

"Where is Kate?" Niall asked.

"Upstairs. She told us about Kara and Jay and then stormed off."

Niall closed his eyes briefly. "You guys start for the hospital. I'll go talk to Kate."

"Can you handle that?" AJ asked, his eyes narrowed.

"Yeah," Niall murmured. "I can." He turned and headed for Casey's apartment.

Kate was sitting in Casey's desk chair, staring at the ceiling, when Niall walked in. "Hey," he said softly. "The others are headed to the hospital. You want to go?"

"This was my fault, Niall," she whispered.

"You know damn well that it wasn't. You weren't in charge. You weren't even involved in the fight that got Jay killed."

"I might've been if I hadn't gotten myself kidnapped."

"Stop." Niall rested his hands on Kate's shoulders. "You'll never get anywhere if you lock yourself in a cycle of 'what ifs' and 'might'ves'. Let's just go make sure everyone is okay. Alright?"

He gently pulled her to her feet, and she asked, "Where are the boys?"

"With Erica. Andrew had her take their kids, Ciaran, and Rick to Erica's mom's house in the suburbs, once we realized that this might be going downhill."

Kate nodded, but she paused as Niall headed for the door. "I love you, you know."

Niall turned back to face her. "I love you, too."

"But I'm still not... safe." Kate cleared her throat. "And until I am, us loving each other is not enough."

Niall gave a grim smile, his blue eyes watery. "I know."

Zach had a concussion and several fractured ribs, and his injuries were serious enough that he had been admitted for observation. The sheer number of hospitals spread throughout the city prevented the one he was in from being too crowded, but it was still hectic. He had been sitting in his bed for about an hour when Casey walked in, her hand in a cast.

"I hope you aren't planning on taking back that 'I love you'," he joked quietly as she sat down on the edge of his bed. "I'm still enjoying the moment, and I'd like it if you

308

wouldn't ruin it for me."

"I'm not going to take it back," Casey replied. "Although I'm still not sure why you want me so bad."

Zach rested a hand on her knee. "When are you going to get it through your thick skull that I'm in love with you?"

"It might take a few more years," Casey said lightly, giving him a weak grin.

"I can handle that. Can you?"

"Absolutely."

Zach grinned. "Good." He pulled Casey's hand up to his lips and kissed it. "So, why did it take you a whole hour to come visit me, Cabot?"

"I was getting you a gift." Casey pressed a button on the white band around her wrist. A minute later, Johnny Aller appeared in the doorway with Logan at his side.

"Thank you, Johnny," Casey said. The man smiled, nodded, and walked away.

"Daddy!" Logan yelled. She ran forward and almost jumped onto Zach, but she was stopped at the last moment by Casey.

"Easy, baby," Casey said gently. "Your dad's a little banged up. You need to be gentle, okay?"

"Okay." Logan carefully got onto the bed next to Casey. "Are you okay, Daddy?"

"I'm a lot better now," Zach replied with a wide grin. "You're much better company than your mom."

The girl giggled. "I am?"

"Definitely. I hope you behaved for Garrison."

"*I* did. But he said that he was going to handcuff Brooke, Aubrey, and Jacob together and put them in a maze until they stopped arguing."

Zach high-fived Logan and grinned at Casey over the girl's head. "I told you we had the better kid."

"I'm sure she'll catch up eventually," Casey replied dryly.

"Pessimist."

"I think I'm a realist, actually. She's *your* child. She's doomed."

"Oh, you think you're much better?" Zach challenged.

"I *know* I am."

Zach scoffed, but before he could reply, Alix stepped into the room. She was staring at the floor and rubbing her hands together. "Casey, could I... could I talk to you for a minute?" she asked quietly.

Casey paused. "Yeah, sure." She kissed Logan on the top of the head and followed Alix out of the room.

In a small waiting room that happened to be empty, Casey watched Alix pace back and forth. "You said you wanted to talk," she pointed out, after a few minutes.

Alix stopped and faced her, looking

nervous. "I just wanted to…" She swallowed. "Casey, I'm so sorry."

"Cass is the one who deserves your apology."

"I'm going there next," Alix said, her voice soft. "But you deserve one too. I was… I was a complete jackass to you. And the things I said to you about your father… I was wrong. And I'm sorry."

"If the things you said about Wechsler were true, I'm not sure you *were* wrong," Casey replied. "Pretty much everything you said I have in common with him were things that were true about me."

"Everything I said was true about him, but I should've said more. Because you have a lot in common with John Wechsler, Casey, but you're nothing like him. You use your genius to protect the people you care about. The people you *love*. You're a good person, Casey. That means that you can't be anything like your father."

Casey swallowed, her throat tight. "Do you remember when I said that we were done until you found Alix Tolvaj again?"

"Yes," Alix whispered.

Casey gave a slow smile. "It's nice to see you again."

When Kate and Niall walked into the hallway where Kara's hospital room was, they found Ray, Justin, and Claire sitting in chairs.

Claire stood and walked over to them. Her eyes with red as if she had been crying, but she smiled weakly. "Good. You're here. I was getting worried."

"How is she?" Niall asked.

"S-She, uhm." Claire fidgeted with her wedding ring. "The doctors said that she's going to be okay, except for, uhm…" She cleared her throat. "There was a piece of metal that went into her back and hit her spinal cord."

"Oh, hell," Niall whispered.

Claire cleared her throat again, her eyes starting to water. "They said that she has no feeling at all in her left leg. It's completely paralyzed." She took in a deep breath, her hands trembling. "It's, uhm, it's better than initially thought, because when she first came in sh-she was in shock and could barely m-move at all. S-So it's not as bad as… as it could've…" She broke off, bowing her head as she started to cry.

Kate hesitated for a brief moment before pulling Claire into a tight hug. "Shh," she said gently. "It's okay." Her voice cracked as Claire gave a soft sob. "It's all going to be okay."

Alix walked into Cass's hospital room, where she was being held for concussion observation. She was lying in her bed watching Jacob, who was curled up asleep next to her. Alix smiled slightly and asked, "Where are AJ and the girls?"

"Getting food," Cass replied. "They dragged Finn along, too."

"Good. I really do think that we can help her."

"So do I." Cass brushed Jacob's hair off of his forehead. "Jacob just wanted to sleep. Garrison said he wasn't resting at all after he left the mansion." She smiled slightly. "He's still calling him 'Uncle Gabriel,' though, so we know he's okay."

"He's definitely your child."

"Yeah, there's really no denying that. Of course, since I remember having him, I'm glad that people aren't second-guessing it." After a brief pause, Cass gestured at one of the chairs in her room. "You can sit if you want, Al."

"I'd rather stand."

"You've been standing for hours."

Alix gave a soft laugh. "You don't need to mother me, Cass."

"I'm not mothering you. I'm big-sistering you."

"What's the difference?"

"I'm not old enough to be your mother."

Alix snorted. "I'm twenty-six. You're forty-two. It's technically possible."

"Oh, shut up, Alix."

They were silent for a long moment, just watching Jacob sleep. Then Alix said, "I'm sorry, Cass. For everything."

"You don't need to apologize to me."

"Yes I do. For hell's sake, Cass, I punched you in the face. A *lot*."

"I know. You needed to."

"That's bullshit and you know it."

"Language," Cass said mildly. She gently ran her fingers through Jacob's hair. "Alix, you wanted to be able to grow and age like the human being you are. You might not have handled everything as well as I would've wanted, but I can't fault you for that. And the fact that Alice screwed with you yet again isn't something I'm going to hold against you. Trust me, I am not exactly pleased that you decided to beat the hell out of me, but you had Alice's personality and you weren't right in the head. I can't be mad at you. Although I might make you pay for it by making you babysit the kids."

Alix laughed. "Whatever you say."

Kate sat down next to Justin and pointed at his right hand, which was in a cast. "How is that?"

"Terrible. Some jackass stomped on it." Justin stared down at the cast for a long moment. "It's not good, Kate. But I think... I think it's an opportunity for me. Because I won't be able to hold a bow for a long time, and..." He trailed off.

"You're quitting," Kate realized in a quiet voice.

"No, I'm retiring."

"That's still quitting."

Justin smiled tightly. "Maybe. But Kate, when Dick Lance broke my hand all those years ago, my abilities took a blow. And now that it got damaged again, I'm never going to have enough faith in my powers to keep doing what we do. I'd still be able to use them, but with my dominant hand taking as much damage as it has, I can't rely on them. I don't want to end up pinned down and either hesitating too long because I'm worried about my powers not working or trying to do something and failing. I don't want to join the ranks of dead superheroes, at least not any time soon. I want to watch my daughter grow up, Kate. Not make my wife a widow just because I was too proud to admit that I have to stop."

Kate swallowed. "Wh-What will you do if you aren't with us?"

"I'm not leaving town, if that's what you're worried about." Justin grinned. "It turns out that me actually going to WI to actually work instead of simply collecting a paycheck has paid off. Cass offered to promote me. She said that I've proven my abilities enough that nobody will find it too odd. And I'm sure Casey will agree."

"Why would it matter to Casey?"

Justin smirked. "Cass told me that she's going to force Casey to accept fifty percent ownership of WI. She said that it was only fair, especially since, as the older sibling, Casey should've inherited the whole thing anyway."

"I hope to hell I'm there for that conversation, because it's going to be hilarious."

"I hope so, too."

Kate reached out and took Justin's good hand in hers. "I'm proud of you, little brother."

"For what?"

"For not ending up as big of an asshole as I thought you'd turn out to be when you were fifteen."

Justin laughed. "In fairness, I'm still an asshole."

"Yeah, you are. But you're one that I don't want to kill, and that matters."

"I love you too, sis."

Finn played with the tab of her soda can, trying to avoid acknowledging the fact that Brooke was staring at her across the hospital cafeteria table. Aubrey frowned at her sister. "Why are you being weird?" she asked.

"She's the one who locked me and Dad in that closet after Dad was shot," Brooke replied.

"Oh." Aubrey looked at Finn. "Is that true?"

"Uh, yeah."

"You're working for us now?" Brooke asked.

"Well, I'm doing whatever your parents and the rest of Heroics tell me to do, if that's what you mean."

Brooke studied her for a long moment before giving one short nod. "Okay." She went back to her sandwich.

Finn blinked. "Okay? That's it?"

"We're big on forgiving people in Heroics," Brooke said.

Aubrey shrugged. "Our grandfather was a mass murderer. Our mom used to work for him. I don't think we're allowed to judge."

"You're a bit young to have to know something like that about your grandfather," Finn said gently.

"Mom didn't want to tell us," Brooke said. "We found out anyway because… well, people talk."

Aubrey gave a small nod and whispered, "People talk."

Before Finn could ask any more questions, AJ sat down at the table between his daughters. "I hope they aren't driving you crazy, Finn."

"I don't mind."

"Good." AJ laughed softly. "Because it probably won't get much easier for you, if you keep working with us."

"I'd like to, but before I do, I have something I need to do first."

"What's that?"

Finn fidgeted with her soda can for a moment. "I-I'd want to know if my parents are still around."

AJ smiled gently. "I think that would be a really good idea, kid."

Alix gave a long sigh as she sat down next to Kate. "I have something to give you. And you have to make a decision on how you want to use it."

Kate raised an eyebrow. "That's ominous."

"It's meant to be." Alix pulled an injector full of clear liquid out of her pocket and handed it to Kate. "That removes people's powers. When Kara found me unconscious in an alley, I started carrying two of them around in case of emergency. Cass used the first one on me. That's the second."

"Why are you giving it to me?"

Alix stood up and walked away. "That's for you to decide, Kate. That's for you to decide."

"Ow," Kara groaned quietly.

Claire, seated in a chair next to her bed, gave a soft laugh. "Trust me, you have no idea how nice it is to hear you say that."

"You like when I'm in pain, Tyson?"

"I like it a lot better than when you couldn't feel anything." Claire lifted Kara's hand and kissed the back of her palm. "You scared the hell out of me, Hall. Way more than you did when you let Kelvin beat you half to death just to protect me while keeping your powers a secret."

"Yeah, well, you have terrible taste in love interests."

"That is true." Claire interlocked her fingers with Kara's. "How are you feeling?"

"I'm sort of in immense pain, but the morphine is starting to kick in." Kara took in a deep breath through gritted teeth. "Where's James?"

"With my parents. He's worried about you, but I didn't want him to be here until I had a better idea of what was going on."

"I-I want to see him." Kara swallowed. "When that building came down on me, I... didn't think I'd see either of you again. I really need to see him."

Claire leaned forward, kissing Kara on the forehead. "The drugs are going to knock you out pretty soon, honey. But I promise you, next chance I get, I'll bring him. Okay?"

Kara was already starting to lose consciousness, but she was able to murmur, "Okay."

"Good." Claire sat back in her chair, watching her wife drift back to sleep. "Good."

Clarice looked up as Kate walked into her cell. A surprised expression formed on her face. "I was expecting it to be Hamil. I never thought she'd allow you to come."

"She's preoccupied." Kate leaned against the cell door. "You said that if I came here, you'd explain why you'd want to kill other empowereds. I'm here. Talk."

For a moment, Clarice just stared at her. Then she said, "Wechsler abducted Dick and me once. And he explained to us— with proof —that Stephanie had been a part of his little gang. Then he told us all about how we kids had been intended to be sort of anti-vigilantes. That we were meant to protect normal people from the violence perpetuated by people with powers. It made sense to us. We had always felt that Stephanie had been manipulating us, and now we knew why. We also hated ourselves, and our powers, and Wechsler gave us an explanation for everything that we had been feeling. But we knew that none of you or the other Alumni would believe us, so Dick and I simply tricked the Alumni into thinking they were doing the right thing. Into believing that you all had been turned. Is that a good enough answer for you?"

"It is."

Clarice gave a thin smile. "Hamil isn't going to have me transferred to the general population, is she?"

"She is. She gave her word."

"She's a fool then. I've learned a lot over these past few years, but that won't make me unwilling to use my powers to escape the moment I'm able to."

"We know. But I'm not going to give you that chance."

Clarice chuckled softly. "You going to kill me, Targeter?"

"I considered it. That's why Cass was so adamant that I not come see you. She was afraid that I would." Kate walked over to Clarice and held out her hand. "But I'm not going to do that."

Clarice, looking confused, accepted Kate's hand. Kate pulled her to her feet. "What game are you playing, Targeter?"

"I'm not playing a game. I'm giving you an opportunity to leave this hole." Kate stabbed Clarice in the side of the neck with the injector and pressed the button. "Most moral or ethical call? Maybe not. But I'm not in a very good mood, and it's either this or a knife. I think I chose the high road."

Clarice pulled away from Kate, staring at her with a confused look on her face. "What the hell did you just do to me?"

"I removed your powers, permanently." Kate turned and headed for the door. "You wanted the freedom, Clarice. Use it."

AJ walked into Cass's room and sat down in a chair. He gave a soft smile at Jacob. "Kid's tired."

"I'm glad they weren't here during all of this," Cass murmured. "Where are the girls?"

"Tormenting Alix and Finn last I checked."

Cass raised an eyebrow. "Brooke is okay

with Finn?"

"Seems to be. I think she's understanding that Finn wants to try. And since Brooke is a hundred times more mature than either of us, she's accepting that."

"That's good. I was worried that she'd be upset, or that she'd upset Finn and ruin the progress she's already made."

"Nah. I think Finn's still in shock that we haven't killed her."

"Reminds me of some people I know." Cass was silent for a long moment. "Do you know if anybody ever saw that woman again? The one who told Casey that Zach was dead?"

AJ shook his head. "Zach said that her name was Sarah and that she was one of the serial killers, but nobody has seen her."

"I have a feeling we'll be seeing her again," Cass muttered.

"I'd imagine so. We have a habit of people coming back to try to kill us again."

"We really need to work on that habit." Cass rested her head against the wall behind her bed. "This one was bad, AJ. Jay's dead, Kate's a mess, Kara may never walk fully walk again, Alix has no powers, Justin's hand injury means that he will probably have to retire… We're a fractured mess."

"We'll survive," AJ said, getting to his feet. He walked over to Cass and kissed her gently. "We will."

"You're annoyingly confident, Hamil."

"You're annoyingly self-sacrificing, Hamil."

"Fair enough."

AJ sat down on Cass's bed and gently ran his hand over his son's head. "We might need to put Heroics on pause for a little bit while we get everything sorted out."

"Since the civilians are still incredibly pissed off and the general public is blaming us for everything under the sun, that's probably a good idea regardless. The military is going to be poking around for a while, anyway."

"Lovely," Cass muttered. "Will we even be useful anymore?"

"Even if we can't be as useful in the future as we used to be, Heroics will always exist as long as we keep fighting. Even if it's just two vigilantes and a small handful of base operators. None of us are going to give up. That's what we do."

Cass smiled slightly. "You're right. It is what we do."

"And we aren't going to stop because of a bunch of murderers." AJ took Cass's hand in his and squeezed it. "If we did, that's when Heroics would truly die. And it's never going to if we have anything to say about it."

EPILOGUE

Sarah sat down at a desk across from a black-haired man in a military uniform. "Everything went mostly according to plan, sir," she reported.

The man gave her a steady look. "Did it, Captain?"

The woman fidgeted in her seat uncomfortably. "Uh, I-I... I thought it did, sir."

"Well, your instincts are correct." The man stood and faced the window behind him. "Captain Amirmoez, what was your task in Caotico City?"

"To pit Alice Cage and Edward Caito against each other, sir, making them destroy each other." Sarah paused. "Though I ended up killing Caito myself."

"Naturally. I'm impressed you managed to put up with the man as long as you did."

Sarah fidgeted once more. "Colonel Reznik—"

"Ah! Captain, your observational skills have suffered in your months away."

"What?" Sarah studied the man briefly before realization struck her. "My apologies. You're a general."

"That's right. Promoted due to my actions to quell the utter chaos in Caotico City."

Sarah smiled slightly. "Chaos caused by

you, of course."

Reznik pretended to be offended. "Chaos caused by Alice Cage and Edward Caito, Captain Amirmoez."

"Right. My mistake, sir."

The newly-appointed general sat back down. "I'm right where I need to be for the rest of my plans to move forward. All thanks to your efforts."

Sarah laughed softly. "Is this where you shoot me in the head and dump my body in the nearest landfill?"

"Not at all." Reznik slid a major's rank insignia across his desk to Sarah. "This is where I ask you to continue being my right hand."

Sarah picked up the piece of metal and examined it. "What would be in it for me?" she asked casually.

"An awful lot of power." Reznik smirked. "And the chance to bring a lot of agony to a lot of empowered people."

A grin slowly formed on Sarah's face. "The second one sounds promising. When do we start?"

"Immediately. My plans will take a while to reap the proper benefits, but those benefits will be huge, Major Amirmoez." Reznik leaned back in his chair. "Nation-altering huge."

FAMILY TREES

CABOT / CARTER

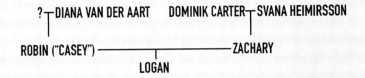

? ⊤ DIANA VAN DER AART   DOMINIK CARTER ⊤ SVANA HEIMIRSSON

ROBIN ("CASEY") ——————————————— ZACHARY
                        LOGAN

OLIVER / REESE

JUSTIN OLIVER ⊤ ERIN REESE
RILEY

SAMPSON / ABASCAL

RAY SAMPSON ⊤ OLIVIA ABASCAL
ISAAC

SULLIVAN / OLIVER

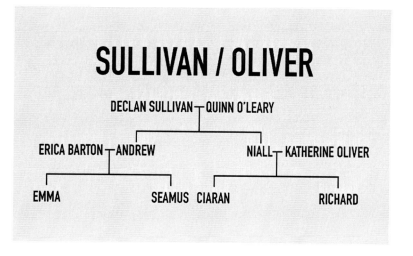

DECLAN SULLIVAN ⊤ QUINN O'LEARY

ERICA BARTON ⊤ ANDREW   NIALL ⊤ KATHERINE OLIVER

EMMA   SEAMUS CIARAN   RICHARD

TYSON / HALL

KELVIN JONES ⊤ CLAIRE TYSON — KARA HALL
JAMES

WECHSLER / HAMIL

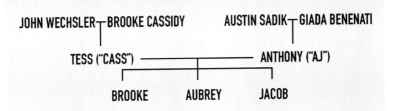

JOHN WECHSLER ⊤ BROOKE CASSIDY   AUSTIN SADIK ⊤ GIADA BENENATI

TESS ("CASS") ——————————— ANTHONY ("AJ")

BROOKE   AUBREY   JACOB

ABOUT THE AUTHOR

Alex Kost lives in New Jersey with her parents and their dog. If you want to fangirl over *Star Wars* with her, or ask anything about something she actually wrote, you can find her at alexkost.tumblr.com